HIGHLAND HOME

BRIDES OF THE HIGHLANDS
BOOK 2

KIRSTEN OSBOURNE

ARE YOU SIGNED UP FOR DRAGONBLADE'S BLOG?

You'll get the latest news and information on exclusive giveaways, exclusive excerpts, coming releases, sales, free books, cover reveals and more.

Check out our complete list of authors, too!

No spam, no junk. That's a promise!

Sign Up Here

www.dragonbladepublishing.com

Dearest Reader;

Thank you for your support of a small press. At Dragonblade Publishing, we strive to bring you the highest quality Historical Romance from some of the best authors in the business. Without your support, there is no 'us', so we sincerely hope you adore these stories and find some new favorite authors along the way.

Happy Reading!

CEO, Dragonblade Publishing

Additional Dragonblade Books by Author Kirsten Osbourne

Brides of the Highlands Series
Highland Heart (Book 1)
Highland Home (Book 2)

CHAPTER ONE

AILIS MCAFEE GLIDED through the grand hall of the castle. She brushed her delicate fingers against the vibrant blossoms that decorated the space, carefully selecting a symphony of hues for her sister Fiona's upcoming wedding. The sweet scent of daisy and heather wafted through the air, filling the room with a promise of joyous days to come. As she weaved her way through the bustling preparations, Ailis couldn't help but harbor a sense of excitement and anticipation, eager to witness her sister's happiness bloom like the flowers she held.

"Think ye these marigolds too bold?" Ailis asked, contrasting the fiery blooms with daisies and bluebells on the table. They had two days left before the wedding, so they expected many guests. Now it was the right time to study how the hall would look with the blossoms.

"Bold is what our Fiona deserves," Moira replied, eyes twinkling. "Ye ken she ne'er shied from making a statement."

"True," Ailis conceded, giggling as she added marigolds to the arrangement. "Remember her sneaking into kitchens or leading ye on wild chases?"

"Twas ye who always found us," Moira countered, tying ribbons around bouquets. "Like when I climbed the tallest oak."

Ailis smiled at the memory. The sisters shared a knowing glance during the preparations, acknowledging the weight of Fiona's upcoming union.

"I'm glad she and Alisdair will be staying here at the keep

with us. I was worried for a bit that she would decide to move to McClain lands," Moira continued.

"I would have missed her every day," Ailis replied. "But 'tis her path to walk."

"I'm glad that for now, her path will stay here with us," Moira whispered.

"As am I," Ailis affirmed, patting her sister's shoulder. "I canna imagine life without our sister."

AILIS PLACED THE last foxglove in the woven basket, her ears catching hushed tones from behind the grand oak doors. Fiona and Laird Duncan McAfee were discussing the wedding's seating arrangements.

"Father, we cannot have the McClains beside the McAfees," Fiona insisted. "Eventually we'll all get along, I hope, but for now…"

"But we must show unity," their father replied.

Approaching unnoticed, Ailis suggested, "We alternate the seats of our clan with those of the McClains."

Duncan nodded. "Fiona, see it done as Ailis advises."

As preparations unfolded, Ailis noticed Lachlan McClain at the periphery of the celebration. She approached him, filled with curiosity.

"Good day, Lachlan," she began. "Does the merriment not tempt ye to join in?"

"The care with which ye all prepare for the wedding fascinates me." He smiled. "It tells me yer dedicated to family and tradition. I like to see that it's not only Clan McClain who feels that way."

Ailis replied, "The union of Fiona and Alisdair marks more than a marriage—it is the intertwining of two clans' destinies. This alliance will benefit both clans."

Lachlan smiled. "Perhaps ye'll share with me some of the traditions of yer clan."

"Aye, of course. I've grown up with our traditions, and I realize many are shared by all the Highlands. But there are a few that are just true of Clan McAfee. We invite all the villagers to the keep when the harvest is in, and we hold a feast. There is dancing and we all eat our favorite foods. There is laughter late into the night."

He grinned. "That sounds like fun to me."

"Aye, tis a great deal of fun. I hope ye and yer brothers will still be around for the feast this year."

"Well, we know Alisdair will be around because he will be laird of yer clan, but I hope Brodie and I find a way to stay as well. At least for now."

Or forever.

"We truly are a large family. Everyone is welcome to give their opinions to the laird. Me father never turns anyone away. It doesn't matter how small the problem is. He is willing to help."

"That's a sign of a good leader," Lachlan enthused.

"It is. I hope yer brother will be just as good of a leader."

"I dinna think ye have to worry about that, lass."

"I love the stories that we hear about the clan from the elders. Every story will last forever in me heart. And I love the fires of Beltane," she gushed. "It means that the long winter is over, and summer is coming. I count down the days leading up to it every year."

He nodded. "I enjoy Beltane as well. It means I'll soon be able to swim in the loch behind the keep of the McClain lairds, which was one of my favorite things to do as a boy, and I still look back on it fondly."

Lachlan listened as she described the annual Lughnasadh games and the tradition of handfasting beneath the ancient Rowan tree to unite two souls. "It sounds as if most of our customs are the same as yers, as we observe all the Highland festivals."

"But perhaps our most cherished pastime is the ceilidh," Ailis continued, her eyes lighting up with pride as she spoke of the beloved Highland custom. "It is a gathering where we come together to share stories, dance to lively tunes, and strengthen the bonds between our kin and neighbors."

"We do the same," Lachlan replied, nodding as he listened intently, clearly captivated more by Ailis's voice than anything. Each clan had its traditions. How the McAfees celebrated fascinated him.

"As much as I cherish the traditions of me own clan, I am drawn to the warmth and spirit of yers," Lachlan confessed. "And I love to hear ye talk about anything."

Ailis smiled warmly, her eyes reflecting the flickering light of the hearth. "Our traditions are a testament to the enduring spirit of our people, a thread that weaves through generations and binds us together in times of joy and sorrow."

Ailis traced the McAfee crest on one of the tapestries that hung from the wall in the great hall. Lachlan listened, captivated by her explanation of how each knot represented family strength and unity.

"Each thread binds not only the cloth but also our clans," Ailis continued.

Lachlan compared the artistry to the McClain clan's symbols etched on sword hilts and mantles. "We still have much to learn of the McAfees."

Ailis smiled. "I'm glad ye want to learn about us."

"I'm always happy to learn, especially about our allied clans."

LATER, FIONA APPROACHED with an urgent request for Ailis.

Fiona pointed out a puckered section along the bodice of her wedding gown. "It looks odd, and I'm afraid it will cast a shadow upon the entire day." She shook her head. "I know I'm being picky, but it is the only time I will be a bride."

"I'll ensure every line falls perfectly into place. Ye need not worry," Ailis reassured her sister.

As Ailis worked, Fiona relaxed, her trust in Ailis's talents becoming her solace. "Thank ye," she said, gratitude warming the cool Highland air.

"Think nothing of it," Ailis replied, focused on the task. "The wedding is all about yer happiness."

Ailis finished adjusting Fiona's wedding gown and glanced around the grand hall filled with activity. Servants placed beeswax candles on tables, their flames prepared to flicker into the night. Colorful tapestries depicting McAfee valor and McClain strength decorated the walls, representing the upcoming union.

The collaboration between the two clans filled Ailis with pride and hope for the future. She thought they'd done an admirable job of highlighting both clans.

"Lachlan," she acknowledged as he approached. Suppressing her emotions, she responded gratefully to his compliment on her decorating skills.

When Lachlan offered to help arrange the feast, Ailis hesitated, torn between propriety and desire. Eventually, she accepted his offer, acknowledging it would reflect their lands' abundance and people's spirit.

"Let us make merry in the labor, for the joy of the task is in the sharing of it." Lachlan grinned. He didn't add that he simply enjoyed being around Ailis, whether they worked together or just talked to one another.

In the McAfee keep's kitchens, rosemary and thyme scents intertwined. Ailis examined parchment scrolls filled with generational recipes while Lachlan stood beside her, emanating confidence.

"Here's the McAfee roast," Ailis began, tracing the recipe. "The secret lies in the marinade. It's a recipe handed down to me from me great-grandmother."

Lachlan studied it closely. "A fine choice. We McClains prefer different foods for our festivities, but this sounds delicious as well." He didn't mention the foods they ate at the McClain celebrations, for how could he explain that women had come back in time to marry into the McClain clan? It would make no sense to most people.

"Let's combine both for this feast," Ailis suggested, envisioning tables full of dishes symbolizing unity. And her clan would try new recipes at the same time the McClain clan did.

"That won't be possible." Caitlin McClain approached them from behind. "Our recipes are secrets that dinnae leave McClain land, but if ye come to us, ye may taste them. The cooks in our clan are very concerned about the recipes being copied by others."

Ailis nodded, deferring to Lachlan's mother. "I understand that each clan has its secrets." She wanted to ask more questions, but it didn't seem right. "Clan McClain seems different from others. We've all heard the rumors about the seven sons in every generation. Is that why the seventh son is always the one to inherit?"

Caitlin smiled. "I'm afraid the secrets of Clan McClain must remain exactly that. Secrets. But ye are welcome to visit again any time."

Ailis looked at the older woman for a moment before nodding. "I see. I willna ask any more questions."

"Tis probably for the best," Caitlin replied kindly. "I would have to keep telling you that I canna tell you anything."

Ailis giggled. "I suppose I've been put me in me place then."

"Never. I like ye, Ailis, but I love me family. All secrets are not equal. Some of the McClain secrets could mean bad portents coming to our clan. I could never be the cause of that."

"I understand. I... will you tell me a bit about Lachlan's childhood?"

Caitlin smiled. "He's me second son, and he's always been very close to his father. Even when he was a small boy, he wanted a wooden sword so he could be a great warrior like his father and uncles."

"And ye have seven sons like the rumors say?"

"Aye, I do. And yes, the youngest will become laird when it is time. Many of the rumors ye've heard about us are true, but not all. I promise, the McClains are good people."

Ailis studied the older woman's face, deeming her trustworthy. "Thank ye for answering me question, Lady McClain."

"Please, call me Caitlin."

A short while later, Caitlin left to check how things were coming in the great hall, Lachlan and Ailis continued working together.

Their conversation flowed effortlessly between shared duties and personal experiences. Ailis recalled her first failed attempt at baking honey bannocks as Lachlan shared a similar story about porridge.

Chuckling together, they bonded over their shared expectations and vulnerabilities. "I can cook now, but not back then. It has become a joke in me family how terrible I was," Ailis added. "Now I even make me own tinctures for use when I'm healing others."

As they worked on the menu, each dish chosen represented the land that shaped them. It didn't matter to Ailis that they didn't use McClain recipes as long as they used recipes that represented the Highlands.

Ailis studied the parchment-strewn table, resting her hands momentarily. The air was filled with warmth and the subtle scent of crushed thyme. Despite her fatigue, being with Lachlan kept her spirits high.

She spotted Fiona and Alisdair across the great hall, whispering intimately. Fiona's eyes met Ailis's, exchanging a smile of sisterly affection, yet leaving Ailis yearning for a deeper connection like theirs.

Turning to Lachlan, she wondered if perhaps he would be the man who she would connect with. She hoped so.

"Ye seem close to both of yer sisters," he observed.

"True," Ailis agreed, her mind wandering, "but I wonder if there will come a day when I'll find a man who understands me like they understand each other."

Their conversation halted as Moira burst into the hall announcing the arrival of more McClain visitors. Ailis and Lachlan exchanged silent agreement—this talk could wait.

Lachlan offered his arm. "Come now, we must greet me clansmen ourselves."

"Lead the way," Ailis replied. She took his arm, noting the muscles that bulged. He would be a good man for her, and she felt that her father would approve of him.

As the celebration around the newcomers quieted, duty pulled Ailis from Lachlan. She turned to him, eyes filled with shared understanding and a hint of regret for their separation.

"Ailis," Lachlan began, his tone reflecting mutual respect, "might we reconvene tomorrow to continue our preparations?"

"Aye, Lachlan," she replied, a tangle of emotions weaving through her as she watched him disappear into the crowd.

Determined, Ailis focused on the tasks that awaited—the backdrop of her sister's nuptials. Each fold of cloth and carefully placed bloom echoed the depth of Fiona's love and the strength of the McAfee clan's unity.

AILIS ESCAPED THE celebration preparations and found solace in the solitude of the hills outside the castle. The Highland air whispered against her cheeks as she contemplated her clan's expectations, with her heart yearning for freedom. Lachlan's disarming smile and mischievous eyes image lingered in her mind. She wondered if the possibility of affection existed between their duties to their clans.

The Highlands reflected her inner turmoil as a solitary falcon soared above, symbolizing the heights one could reach should destiny permit. As the sun painted the sky gold and crimson, Ailis returned to the keep, contemplating the vast and untamed future before her. Fiona's wedding would be a testament to unity and peace. And mayhap there would be time to dance with Lachlan. She wanted to feel his arms around her once again. They'd shared many dances, but she'd not been certain of her feelings for him back then. She was now, and the idea of his arms around her gave her something to look forward to.

In the quiet recesses of her heart, Ailis dared to dream of love—fierce and unyielding like the Highlands themselves. With each step, she hoped that tomorrow might bring her and Lachlan together once more.

⫷ ❖ ⫸

CHAPTER TWO

Ailis regarded the weathered target ahead, ignoring the din of pre-wedding festivities. Lachlan joined her with a roguish smile.

"Ye think ye can best me, lass?" he teased, his eyes gleaming playfully.

"Perhaps I do." Ailis chuckled. "A McAfee never backs down from a challenge."

Their friendly rivalry charged the air as they faced off in knife-throwing, which Ailis had never lost a contest in. Why, she'd even beaten all competitors at the Highland Games where she and her sisters had met the McClain brothers. Determination surged within Ailis as she grasped the hilt. With graceful strength, she threw, striking true at the target's heart.

The onlookers gasped. Lachlan seemed impressed. "Ye wield a knife as if born to it," he conceded warmly. "I thought how well ye threw may have been a fluke for the Highland Games, and yet, it seems constant."

She smiled. "I never would have competed if I hadn't been certain of my abilities."

The crowd dispersed, leaving them alone. A quiet turmoil grew within Ailis as she recognized her feelings for Lachlan deepening beyond mere jest. He was charming and witty, but their clans' union depended on political alliances, not emotions. Despite this knowledge, she was tempted by Lachlan's gaze to forget such weighty responsibilities.

Lachlan approached Ailis. "I have heard ye are a great story-teller. Would ye share a story of a heroine who triumphs against the odds?"

Ailis's pulse quickened as she considered his request. "I'll try." Her calm voice hid her inner turmoil. "But remember, not all tales end as we hope."

"Let's hope this one does," Lachlan replied, handing back her knife. Their hands brushed for a moment.

Ailis felt a shiver run through her at the touch of Lachlan's hand, a sensation that lingered even after he withdrew. She took a deep breath to compose herself before she began her tale, her voice carrying a melodic cadence that drew the attention of all who were near.

"In a land filled with mist and shadows, there lived a young woman named Marta," Ailis began, her eyes filled with the fire of storytelling. "She was no ordinary maiden but possessed a spirit as fierce as the wildest storm and a heart as pure as the mountain springs."

As she wove her story, Ailis painted vivid pictures with her words, transporting her rapt listener to a world of daring adventures and impossible challenges. The tale unfolded like a living painting, with Marta at its center as she faced adversaries both mortal and magical. "Each encounter tested her courage and strength, shaping her into a formidable heroine."

From the dark depths of treacherous caves to the towering heights of enchanted castles, every scene was filled with palpable danger and thrilling action, pulling Lachlan deeper into the fantastical realm that Ailis had created with her masterful storytelling. Every word dripped with magic and wonder, leaving Lachlan mesmerized.

Lachlan listened intently, his gaze never leaving Ailis. Her voice rose and fell like a melody, filling the air with the essence of bravery and love entwined in the words of her tale.

"Marta's path was fraught with dangers and betrayals," Ailis continued, her eyes flickering with emotion. "But through it all, she remained steadfast, guided by her unwavering belief in doing what was right, even when the odds were stacked against her."

As she spun her tale, Ailis couldn't help but notice the way Lachlan's expression softened with each turn of events in Marta's journey. It was as if he saw himself reflected in the heroism and sacrifices of the fictional heroine.

"And so, as Marta stood at the precipice of darkness, facing her greatest challenge yet," Ailis concluded, her voice tinged with a hint of longing, "she found that it was not the battles she won that defined her, but the love she dared to embrace."

Ailis gazed at Lachlan, her heart laid bare in the depths of her emerald eyes. The connection between them was palpable, a silent understanding passing between their shared gaze. For a fleeting moment, time seemed to stand still. The world around them faded away as they existed in their own bubble of unspoken emotions.

Lachlan broke the silence, his voice soft yet filled with a depth of emotion. "Yer tale is one of courage and sacrifice, Ailis." His eyes searched hers. "It speaks of a love that transcends boundaries and defies all odds."

A rush of conflicting emotions stirred within Ailis—desire warring with duty, passion clashing with reason. She understood that her feelings for Lachlan went beyond mere admiration. They had blossomed into something deeper, something she couldn't easily dismiss.

As they stood there, she gazed upon his lips. For a moment, she wondered what it would feel like to be kissed by a warrior such as the man before her, but she knew better than to find out. Instead, she turned back toward the keep. "We must return. The pre-wedding ceilidh is starting soon."

Lachlan nodded, but he appeared as reluctant as she felt.

AILIS STOOD POISED on the edge of the dance floor. In the midst of the pre-wedding celebration, Lachlan McClain extended his hand for a dance.

Ailis obliged, taking his hand as they stepped onto the dance floor. Their movements became an unspoken conversation.

"Ye dance well," Lachlan observed quietly.

"As do ye. I wouldn't have expected a warrior to be as comfortable as ye seem to be on the dance floor."

"The battlefield and ballroom are similar," he replied, eyes shining with humor. "Both require strategy and anticipating yer partner's moves."

Ailis giggled. "I think I ken. I hope ye're not trying to win on the dance floor."

"Always," he answered.

"Are ye trying to win against me or others on the dance floor?" she asked, grinning up at him. She certainly understood being competitive, as she was extremely competitive by nature, but not as she danced. Nay, dancing was a time to enjoy herself and the partner she was dancing with.

"Oh, the others, of course. Dancing with ye means I've already won the best prize of all," Lachlan whispered.

"Yer words flatter me." Ailis blushed slightly.

"Are ye excited about the wedding?" he asked, guiding her through the dance's final steps.

Ailis nodded. "I'm glad Fiona has found happiness and an alliance that pleases me father. And that they are one and the same. I canna imagine marrying just for an alliance when there is love out there, just waiting for us to find it."

As the music ceased in the great hall, Ailis and Lachlan caught their breaths, the lingering connection between them undeniable.

"Thank ye for the dance, Lachlan," Ailis said. She hoped there would be many more opportunities. Shaking her head, she scanned the room to make sure everyone was taken care of. She couldn't lose herself in the man beside her and neglect her duties.

"And thank ye, Ailis," he replied, letting go of her hand.

Ailis left the great hall for a moment, needing to just be with no one watching. The feelings for Lachlan the dance had stirred within her had surprised her more than she cared to admit.

In the quiet corridor, Ailis caught her breath, feeling the cool air on her flushed cheeks. The stone walls seemed to whisper ancient secrets.

Lachlan broke the silence. "Ailis, yer movements were like a loch's waters dancing under moonlight."

She turned and met his gaze. "Ye flatter me again. Perhaps ye were meant to be a courtier and not a warrior."

"I think not." His smile faded into contemplation. "In another life, we could explore this grace without our duties weighing us down."

His words resonated with Ailis. "I wonder what paths we would choose if not bound by our clans' legacies."

A moment of shared vulnerability held them together before the sounds of the celebration interrupted their reverie. Ailis stepped back. "We must return," she whispered reluctantly. "Me father will be looking for me, and he will not be happy to find me alone with a man. He likes ye, but he doesn't like any man enough to let him be alone with his daughters."

Lachlan nodded, though his eyes mirrored her reluctance to return. "Aye." He offered his arm, and she accepted it gracefully.

As they rejoined the great hall, each fleeting glance and touch heightened their anticipation for their next encounter. Through the clamor of festivities, their stolen moment lingered—a silent promise of something both desired and feared.

DURING THE PRE-WEDDING revelry, Ailis escaped to the moonlit gardens, leaving Lachlan among his kin. Moonbeams illuminated her path, and an archway of roses became her refuge.

Sensing her absence, Lachlan found her beneath the blossoming arch, moonlight weaving silver into her dark hair.

"Ye've left the festivities," he observed.

"And ye've noticed me absence," she countered, her soft tone betraying her inner unrest. What she would give to be able to live her life without worrying about the clan. But that was something that would never be.

"I often feel adrift in expectations," Ailis confided. "Like a pawn on a chessboard."

"Ye're not alone," he assured her, closing the distance between them. His breath made her shiver.

"Being near ye feels like teetering on a cliff's edge," she murmured. "Exhilarating but treacherous."

"At least I'm not alone." He reached out to stroke her cheek with the back of his hand. "Facing the unknown together will bring courage."

"I wish I were free to do so," she answered sadly.

"I ken. We must not meet alone again, then." He carefully studied her face to see if it was what she wanted.

She nodded. "If I see ye alone, I will return to where I was. I hope ye'll do the same for me."

"I shall," he murmured, but he knew he'd seek her out whenever possible. He was drawn to her in a way he never had with another woman.

Ailis allowed herself one last glance back, letting distance grow while dreaming of what could be between them.

She returned to the festivities, where Moira was watching for her. "Where did ye go?"

"I was in the courtyard. I needed some time alone without all the noise," Ailis answered, not willing to admit the full truth.

Moira's expression told Ailis that she didn't believe her, but Moira said nothing.

"I think we should move the two clan tartans closer on the wall," Ailis suggested, not wanting to continue to deceive her sister.

Moira nodded. "They are too far apart to indicate two clans joining together. It won't be a complete merge of the two, but many will see it that way."

"We'll see to it after everyone has retired for the night."

AS THE CELEBRATION continued, Ailis found herself with Lachlan yet again. Shadows danced across their faces in the torch-lit grand hall, reflecting her uncertainty. They stood apart, but the space between them hummed with unspoken words.

"Ye seem troubled, Ailis," Lachlan remarked, gently breaking the silence.

Ailis hesitated for a moment. "Just thinking about the wedding tomorrow."

"I'm certain me brother and yer sister will be very happy together," he said.

"I hope so. They went through a lot to get to the point where Father would allow them to marry," she replied.

He nodded. "I'll be staying on for a while as Alisdair learns more about yer clan."

Ailis worried her heart would betray her feelings for him, so she nodded. "We enjoy having ye here," she replied formally. She wondered if her heart could take seeing him so often, unable to truly express her feelings.

Lachlan watched her for a moment before finally walking away. He'd hoped she would express happiness at the thought of him staying longer, but she'd disappointed him.

Much later, Ailis stood watching Lachlan as he moved through the crowd.

"Ye are contemplative this eve," observed Lachlan, his presence commanding and comforting.

"Merely gathering me thoughts," she replied evenly. "Fiona looks so happy."

"As does Alisdair. I'm pleased they've found one another. The alliance is exactly what Clan McClain needed." He didn't say it, but they both knew the McAfees needed the alliance a great deal more than the McClains.

"And Clan McAfee," Ailis added. "I worry the unrest we've seen will not end with this wedding, though I hope it does."

"We cannot know unless we ask those who are leading the unrest, and they seem to be hiding their actions from our view."

"Like cowards."

"Aye," he grumbled. "They are very cowardly. Merely thinking to kidnap a woman makes them cowards. And they carried it out."

"Do ye believe Fiona's kidnapping is connected to the men who keep attacking in unmarked plaids?"

He nodded. "I believe so, as do me brothers. But there is no proof. We cannot accuse without proof and still have peace."

ON THE TERRACE, Ailis and Lachlan stood, unaware of the cloaked figure watching them from the shadows. He coldly whispered to himself, "Marriage between the McAfee sisters and the McClain men cannae be permitted."

The figure knew their union would jeopardize his ambitions of uniting all the Highlands under one ruler—him. Control over the clans was essential, and he'd do whatever was necessary to fulfill his goal. They'd already thwarted his plans when Fiona married Alisdair. The same could not be allowed for the remaining sisters.

"Love can be a powerful weapon when wielded correctly," he mused.

He observed the couple with a sinister smile. He would wait for the perfect moment to strike, sowing doubt and discord among them. For now, he must have patience.

He watched as Lachlan uttered something that made Ailis howl.

They didn't know it yet, but the man in the shadows plotted against them—against them falling in love, and against the world as they knew it.

CHAPTER THREE

L AIRD ARRAN SINCLAIR stood before the hearth of the Sinclair keep, his coal-black eyes fixed on the shadow emerging from the tapestry-draped doorway—a figure covered in a cloak.

"Arran Sinclair," the man beneath the hood insisted. "The union between yer clan and the McAfees is vital. A marriage must be arranged quickly. We seek Ailis's hand now that ye have failed to secure a union between one of yer sons and the eldest lass."

Arran's shoulders tensed, his tartan sash tightening across his chest. With a slow nod, he answered, "Me sons are prepared to court the sisters honorably and diligently, but the girls seem to care naught for them."

"Courting them with honor may not have the results we're looking for. We cannot allow the McAfees to make their alliance with the McClains stronger than it already is. It is vital to our plan that we become allies with all we can and separate those whom we canna make alliances with."

Arran nodded. "Aye. Me sons and I will make certain they dinna marry."

"That may be harder than ye think. The girl is becoming fond of Lachlan McClain. I dinnae want to have to choose another laird to be me second-in-command," the man warned. The cloaked figure studied him silently before receding into the shadows.

Arran began to plan, knowing that this alliance was more than just affection—it was a play for power. If he did what he should, he would be second in command to the shadow man. Together they would rule over all the Highlands. He must make certain it happened that way, but without his sons knowing he was obeying another. They must never catch his weakness.

As silence enveloped the room, Laird Sinclair allowed himself a moment of solitude to weigh his options. Within the cold walls of his ancestral home, duty and desire waged war in his heart. No stranger to sacrifice, he was ready to pay the price for the sake of the entire Sinclair clan—and power. What man didn't want power?

THE OAK DOOR creaked open as Arran Sinclair emerged, observing his sons training with sword and shield. The clang of steel filled the air.

"Enough," he commanded. Callum and Ian halted their sparring.

"Father," Ian panted, "what news?"

"The McAfee lass, Ailis," Arran announced, "Her heart seems inclined toward Lachlan McClain."

Ian's expression tightened, but Callum remained silent.

"We must succeed now where we've failed before. Time is short," Arran warned. "Ailis must choose to marry a Sinclair or our legacy will crumble. Ye must win her over, Ian. Or if ye cannot, we must find a suitable Sinclair who will do as we tell him and win her hand."

Determination flared in Ian's eyes, the same that had carried the Sinclair line for generations. "Consider it done," he replied. "Ailis McAfee will forget McClain ever caught her eye. I will court her."

Arran regarded his sons, seeing their unwavering resolve. "Go now, prepare," he instructed. "Tomorrow brings a new day and the future of our clan. If one of ye cannae catch her eye, we will have to find another Sinclair man who will follow our orders and marry her."

As his sons left, Laird Sinclair reflected on the sacrifices made for ambition. Their cost was etched into his face and woven into his clan's history.

Duty, above all else, would guide their hands, even as it constricted their hearts.

A WEEK LATER, Ailis stood behind Fiona, her fingers skillfully braiding her sister's long hair and twisting it in a knot behind her head. "Ye look more beautiful than ever," she murmured.

Fiona met her gaze in the mirror. "Thank ye. Tis difficult to find the balance between wife and lady of the clan at times, but I am trying to make it work."

"We are always here to help ye," Ailis assured her, patting Fiona's shoulder. "Moira and I would do anything."

Fiona nodded, grateful for Ailis's support. "I ken ye would. Yer the best sisters anyone could ask for."

Ailis observed her sister, then turned toward the window, pondering the growing presence of Lachlan in her life. She recalled his lingering gaze, the warmth of his touch during a dance, and their laughter in moments of joy.

Her heart raced yet her doubts lingered. Their history was just a collection of fleeting moments. Could something enduring emerge?

She recalled his eyes, stormy and mischievous, his voice smooth as whisky when he spoke her name. The attraction was palpable, pulling her closer with each encounter.

But duty whispered caution. As the middle McAfee daughter, she was supposed to nurture and protect others. Was it wise to be drawn to Lachlan?

She glanced back at Fiona's hopeful face and recognized her

own yearning—to follow her heart despite uncertainty.

And as they descended the staircase together, Ailis held fast to the belief that, just perhaps, courage and grace could also guide her through the labyrinth of her own heart.

AILIS STEPPED OUTSIDE into the misty morning, her skirts brushing against the damp courtyard stones. The weight of her father's decision hung heavily on her mind. He had consented to Ian Sinclair's courtship, but only if Ailis agreed as well. It was a duty she reluctantly considered for her family's sake.

When Ian touched her arm, she felt nothing. But she knew her father didn't want her to turn Ian down, despite the fact that they all believed the Sinclairs were behind the men who kept attacking the McAfees. Her father believed in keeping enemies close, and Ian represented his father and his clan.

"Ye seem burdened," Ian observed, confidently striding toward her. His hair gleamed in the sunlight, barely concealing the calculating glint in his eyes.

"Good morning, Ian," Ailis responded emotionlessly. "Shall we begin our walk?"

As they strolled away from the keep, Ailis spotted Kevin McClain, Lachlan's guard, trailing discreetly behind them—a silent testament to Lachlan's jealousy. If Lachlan truly cared for her, why not come forward himself?

"Does it bother ye, having a McClain follow us?" Ian inquired, noting her glance over her shoulder. He all but spat the word McClain.

"Nay," Ailis lied smoothly. "I just wonder why Lachlan would send a man to follow me instead of following me himself."

The path meandered through the woods, leaves rustling with secrets above them. Ailis sensed Ian's calculated charm, but she lingered on Lachlan—his sparkling blue eyes filled with mischief and warm laughter. His caresses spoke volumes more than words.

"Is there something amiss?" Ian asked, sensing her distraction.

"Nothing that need concern ye," Ailis replied tersely, eyeing Kevin in the clearing ahead. Annoyance flitted across her face at Lachlan's refusal to pursue her while denying others the chance.

"Very well," Ian conceded, wearing a discontented expression.

Ailis could not force herself to care about Ian's moods. He was a difficult man to be around on the best of days, and she had no desire to have any sort of relationship with him.

Ailis and Ian walked the wooded path, a natural cathedral of pine and oak above them. He plucked a wildflower from the underbrush and offered it to her.

"For ye, fair Ailis," he offered, his voice lilting but cool.

She accepted the bluebell with a laugh that hid her inner turmoil. "Ye honor me," she replied, struggling with sincerity. He had done something kind. It would not be right to throw the flower in his face as she would like to do.

As they resumed walking, Ian boasted about his army's might while she lingered on Lachlan, absent yet present in her mind. Ailis glanced at Kevin, their stoic guard, wondering if he shared her weariness over Ian's pomp compared to Lachlan's quiet strength.

"Indeed, ye speak of great responsibility." She shifted her gaze to the canopy above—the interlaced branches symbolizing the tension between personal desires and political responsibilities. "I ken ye didn't expect to be yer father's heir. It must have been hard for ye when Malcolm was killed for kidnapping me sister."

"He did what he did of his own accord," Ian replied, using the same words his father had once used.

"Of course," Ailis muttered, not looking at him as they continued their walk.

The glade shimmered before them, a secluded sanctuary within the murmuring woods. Ailis spotted a deer grazing. The sight awakened an ancestral instinct inside her.

Without hesitation, Ailis pulled her knife from its scabbard on her belt and threw it with practiced ease. Silently, the blade found its target. The deer fell lifeless in a heartbeat.

"Most impressive," Ian murmured, his voice carrying a hint of surprise. "I wasn't aware of yer skills with a knife."

"Then ye weren't present at the Highland Games," Ailis replied swiftly. "Only Malcolm was there from yer clan. Why is that?"

At Ian's shrug, she went to the deer.

"I still think yer skill amazing. Women aren't taught to fight with knives."

"Any lass would do the same," Ailis said evenly, adrenaline still pumping through her.

"I suppose." He stepped forward to claim the catch but stopped short. "Regrettably, I'm too sore from training to help carry it back."

"Too sore?" Ailis scoffed. This man claimed to want to court her and be her husband, and he wouldn't help her carry a deer? He brought shame to all Highlanders with his refusal.

"I've been honing me skills for many hours," Ian retorted. "Greatness requires sacrifice."

"Aye. I've practiced many hours to learn to throw me knife." Ailis gave him a cool, amused glance and bent down to lift the deer. Her sense of duty compelled her onward. She hoisted the carcass and remarked wryly, "Good thing I dinnae share such grandeur. *Me* shoulders can handle this burden."

"Allow me, milady," Kevin, the McClain guard, said firmly as he took the game from Ailis. His eyes met with Ian's in a silent challenge.

Ailis hid her amusement and maintained a neutral expression, playing her part in clan politics. "Thank ye, Kevin. Ye are a good man to help me."

Walking through the woods, Ailis matched Kevin's confident stride. The rustle of fallen leaves whispered beneath their footsteps as Ian trailed behind. Kevin smiled at her. "Yer throw was perfect, as always. Ye and yer sisters are accomplished warriors."

"Me father raised us to be strong." She knew Ian was listening, but at that moment she didn't care. He wasn't even willing to help with the deer.

In the clearing, they hoisted the deer onto a sturdy branch and its blood seeped into the soil. Ailis turned toward Ian, his tall figure emerging from the shadows. She made a show of thanking Kevin for his help. "Thank ye for bringing the deer back for me. It would have worn me out to do it, but I would have."

Kevin nodded, his eyes sparkling with laughter as he knew what she was doing. "I will always help if I am able."

"Thank ye for the company." Ailis gazed at Lachlan. He stood, watching them intently.

A sweet smile bloomed on her lips, meant for Lachlan. She wanted to call to him that he needn't send his men following her, but she didn't want Ian to know how much it bothered her.

Ian bowed slightly, but Ailis barely noticed. Turning, she approached the keep as Lachlan's watchful eyes followed her every step.

As soon as she crossed the threshold, he appeared at her side. "Ye shouldna walk with Ian again," Lachlan warned.

"Is that a request or a command?" Ailis asked, meeting his gaze squarely.

"Consider it… a heartfelt entreaty," he replied. Their mutual attraction was undeniable yet tangled in clan loyalty and politics.

Ailis held herself with dignity. "Yer concern is noted." She continued through the keep with determination.

She was inside the building when Lachlan caught up with her again. Ailis faced him, her eyes burning with determination. "I am beholden to no man's command on whom I may walk with," she declared, standing firmly as an equal.

"Ye put yerself at risk," Lachlan countered, leaning forward. "What if Ian's intentions are less than honorable?"

"We understand his intentions are less than honorable. But if ye want to help me, next time, ye may follow along or join us," Ailis replied. "It is not for ye to dictate me choices. I am well capable of discerning one's intentions and protecting meself. He saw me skill with a knife in the woods. He would be a fool to try to hurt me."

"Is it yer pride then, Ailis? Is it too much to ask that ye consider how this might affect our clans?" Lachlan asked.

"Consideration does not require obedience," she stated. "Me actions are taken with both clan and heart in mind, yet I must also listen to me heart and me own mind."

The silence between them was heavy with unspoken truths. Lachlan's glare remained unwavering, but Ailis stood firm.

"Ye are as stubborn as the winter frost," he lamented, torn between admiration and frustration.

"Perhaps," Ailis acknowledged with a hint of a smile. "But 'tis a necessary trait for one in me position."

Gracefully, she turned away, sensing Lachlan's intense gaze. As she reached her bedchamber, his voice echoed through the corridor. "Ye have not heard the last of this matter, Ailis!"

"Nor have ye," she murmured. The matter was far from over. Behind her chamber door, she finally caught her breath.

Ailis settled into the quiet sanctuary of her room, the soft glow of the hearth casting a warm light over the chamber. She moved with practiced grace, deftly undoing the clasps of her cloak as she let it fall to the floor in a whisper of fabric.

The encounter with Lachlan lingered in her thoughts, his intense gaze stuck in her mind. She couldn't deny the tug of attraction between them, even in the middle of the complex web of duty and expectations that bound them to their respective clans.

As she combed through her hair, each stroke a soothing rhythm against the tangles, Ailis couldn't shake the image of Lachlan's earnest expression. His concern for her safety was evident, underscoring the genuine affection that simmered beneath their cautious interactions.

But thoughts of Ian also intruded upon her reflections, his polished facade masking darker intentions that sent a shiver down her spine. Ailis knew she treaded on dangerous ground, navigating a path strewn with thorns of duty and desire. The memory of her walk with Ian lingered like a bitter aftertaste, his smooth words veiling a sharp edge that made her question him.

With a sigh, Ailis settled into the plush chair by the hearth, the flames casting flickering shadows across the room. She reached for a small wooden box on the side table, its polished surface cool to the touch. Opening it, she revealed an assortment of trinkets—tokens of moments shared with her sisters, reminders of love and laughter in a world fraught with tension.

She fingered a delicate silver pendant, a gift from Moira on her last birthday. Ailis held it up to the firelight, watching as the metal gleamed and sparkled, illuminating the chamber.

How she wished she knew all the answers to the questions Lachlan brought to mind. And how she wished she knew how to tell Ian to go away without upsetting their precarious clan dynamics. There had to be a way to know the right thing to do.

◆———————✦———————◆

CHAPTER FOUR

A ILIS SAT ON a stone bench in the walled garden, taking in the scent of heather and thyme. Moira and Fiona joined her, their presence comforting.

"I do not like Ian Sinclair," Ailis whispered. "The very sight of him unsettles me. Yet, I fear that if I dinnae give him a chance to court me, then I will let Father down."

"Never mind him," Moira replied. "Lachlan McClain is the one who captures yer heart."

"But he doesn't court me," Ailis argued. "He sends his guards to follow me yet remains distant. If he truly had feelings for me, he would have approached Father about courting me." She shook her head. "He needs to show how he feels or I will find another."

Fiona leaned forward. "Perhaps he has his reasons," she suggested. "A woman can never ken what is happening in a man's mind. Their thoughts are foreign to us."

Eventually, they parted ways.

In the grand hall, Fiona's soiree commenced. The torchlight cast dancing shadows as musicians played inviting melodies. Throughout the night, Ailis stole glances at Lachlan McClain. Each time their eyes met, a jolt surged through her.

Despite her outward grace, Ailis's heart wrestled with her inner turmoil. She observed Lachlan joining the dance. She knew she could easily join him, but she wanted him to invite her. Why hadn't he spoken to her father?

While goblets clinked and people whispered, their unspoken

connection intensified. Yet duty overshadowed desire—a reminder of their sacrifices and political alliances that shaped their lives. The tension between longing and obligation added complexity to an already intricate dance.

Ailis adjusted the grand table's centerpieces with meticulous care. She sought perfection for Fiona's sake, but she was preoccupied by a more troubling presence.

"Ye seem to be waging a silent battle with those flowers, Ailis," Lachlan McClain remarked, his approach stealthy. She didn't need to glance at him to recognize his disarming smile.

"These blooms are proving quite unruly." Ailis finally met his gaze with a playful spark in her green eyes. "Perhaps they require a firmer hand."

Lachlan offered assistance, stepping closer with a mock frown. "Do ye want me to have a talk with them?"

"Only if ye swear not to charm them into further rebellion," Ailis countered, the corner of her mouth lifting slightly. She knew the power of his charm, and she was certain the man could charm the portraits of her ancestors from the walls.

Their laughter mingled, providing a fleeting escape from the evening's expectations. For a moment, shared mirth secluded them from the world's prying eyes.

MEANWHILE, FIONA SURVEYED the scene from across the great hall. Her face softened with sisterly concern. She observed as Ailis's smile waned when Lachlan's attention diverted and how she subtly guarded her heart.

If only love were as simple as wielding a sword or commanding a battalion, Fiona thought. Then she could guide her sister to safe haven.

It would be good if they had a mother to seek counsel from regarding matters of the heart. Alas, they had one grandmother, and she was Fiona's alone. Ailis had lost her own grandmother just the previous year.

Perhaps she could offer to share her grandmother with Ailis. She laughed at the idea. Ailis knew her grandmother as well as she herself did.

AILIS SOUGHT REFUGE in a quiet corner. Lachlan appeared beside her.

"Escaping the revelry?" His tone was light, but his eyes held unspoken words.

"Seeking peace," she replied.

"Peace can be elusive." He leaned against the wall. "I find it hides in plain sight."

"I find it is hiding from me tonight."

"It's like a lullaby that quiets the world," he whispered.

"Then why must it hide from me?" she asked. "I could use the quiet!"

"But sometimes words are needed, as silence can be too wide for words to fill."

Ailis hesitated before asking, "What does yer heart seek?"

"Every day and night, loyalty to me clan wars with other inclinations," he admitted.

She nodded. "Such inclinations often lead to ruin."

He stiffened. "Do ye think I am just another rogue?"

"I truly do not know what to think when it comes to ye," she answered, her voice barely audible above the music.

"Good thoughts would be nice." He smiled at her.

She shook her head. "I suppose most of me thoughts of ye are good ones. Not all though."

"Ye wound me! It's as if ye dinnae trust me, and here I am, brother ta yer sister!"

"But not *me* brother." She smiled.

"I would hope not."

AILIS ENTERED HER father's war room, seeking refuge from the noisy gathering. She found Moira, her fiery hair a vibrant contrast to the subdued tapestry on the wall.

"Moira," Ailis began, her voice trembling. "I'm lost in confusion."

"Speak, sister," Moira urged, eyes full of understanding.

"It's Lachlan," Ailis confessed. "He unsettles me. There's a pull, like the moon upon the tides, but me heart resists it."

"The battle between duty and desire." Moira leaned forward. "Does he make yer spirit soar while vexing ye?"

"He does," Ailis admitted softly. "I do not know what his intentions are, and I find meself drawn to him anyway. I wish he would speak to Father and ask to court me."

"If ye want him to court ye, shouldn't ye just ask him?" Moira asked.

"I could not! Men are meant to approach women, not the other way around. How could ye even suggest such a thing?"

Moira shrugged. "I dinna think I will ever marry. I like being me own person and not expected to obey rules given by a man."

"Ye ken Father expects us both to make good marriages?" Ailis asked, wondering what was wrong with her sister. Women were meant to marry and bear children.

"Responsibilities shape us but dinnae define us wholly," Moira advised. "Sometimes we must leap into the unknown, trusting the winds to guide us."

"I suppose that's true." Ailis still couldn't decide if she should avoid Lachlan or seek him out. On one hand, she wanted to be with him desperately, but on the other, she worried spending even more time with him would make her fall more in love, and that would simply make life harder if he didn't have the same feelings. It seemed he did, but nothing was ever quite as it seemed.

After returning, Ailis moved among the revelers in the great hall when Lachlan appeared before her, offering his hand. Wordlessly, she accepted. Then they stepped onto the dance floor.

A traditional Highland dance began. Lachlan led confidently and Ailis followed gracefully.

Each touch was electric—fingers grazing, hands clasping, arms entwining. Their eyes met often, glances charged with unspoken emotion. The dance demanded they part and reunite, mirroring Ailis's inner turmoil.

As they spun, Lachlan's grip tightened slightly. It was a silent promise in the clamor. His warmth ignited an inextinguishable fire within Ailis.

For those moments, nothing else mattered. The world narrowed to their shared breaths and the music that fueled them.

The dance ended, leaving them breathless and flushed, unspoken desires reverberating between them. They bowed to each other, the formality doing nothing to ease the simmering heat beneath their skin.

"Thank ye, Ailis." Lachlan's voice was smooth as a serene loch.

"Lachlan," she replied. "I enjoyed the dance."

"I enjoy everything with ye," he crooned before wandering off.

Ailis watched after him, wishing she knew how to get him to speak with her father about courting her. He may be content to take things slowly, but she was ready for something to happen between them.

"I TRUST YER having a pleasant evening?" Ailis asked mischievously as she glanced up at Ian.

Ian's eyes darkened slightly at the mention of the previous day's events. "Very pleasant, though I must admit the memory of me refusal to carry that deer still haunts me."

As it should. Ailis's chuckle tinkled like wind chimes in a gentle breeze.

Ian's gaze upon her softened. A glimmer of admiration shone in his eyes. "I truly do not know what to think when it comes to ye."

She smiled, her green eyes sparkling with amusement. "Ye dinna have to think of me at all," she teased.

Ian shook his head, a playful glint in his eyes. "I suppose most of me thoughts of ye are clouded by the desire to dance with ye," he admitted, extending his hand toward her.

Ailis hesitated for a brief moment, her eyes flickering toward Lachlan, who watched them with a tight jaw and furrowed brows. His gaze was intense, a mix of concern and something deeper that made her heart flutter uncomfortably. Swallowing the lump in her throat, she turned back to Ian and placed her hand in his.

"As much as I appreciate the offer, Ian, I fear I must decline," she answered politely, trying to ignore the pang of guilt that tugged at her. Would Father be upset if he found out she refused to dance with him?

Ian's smile faltered for a fraction of a second before he masked it with practiced charm. "Ah, lass, ye wound me so. Are ye sure ye cannot spare one dance for an old friend?"

Ailis suppressed a sigh. The term "friend" was a veiled threat coming from Ian. She knew all too well his intentions, and she had no desire to give him any kind of hope. "Forgive me, Ian, but I'm afraid I twisted me ankle during me last dance. It'll need time to heal before I can dance with ye," she lied.

Ian's facade cracked slightly, revealing a flash of disappointment in his eyes before his charming grin returned. "Ah, well, I shall have to content meself with watching ye from afar then."

He bowed slightly before stepping back.

As Ian departed, relief washed over Ailis. She turned her attention back to Lachlan, who was now conversing with some of the other guests. His eyes found hers, holding an intensity that made her heart race.

Ailis knew she was playing a dangerous game, caught between duty and desire. Her feelings for Lachlan were undeniable, a whirlwind of emotions that she struggled to contain.

With a heavy sigh, she excused herself from the hall, needing a moment of solitude.

Walking to the moonlit courtyard, Ailis found refuge from the lively great hall. Leaning against ancient battlements, she gazed at the stars as if seeking their counsel.

"Ye find yerself at a crossroads, lass." Laird Duncan McAfee's voice echoed with authority and tenderness. He approached his daughter carefully.

"Father," she began solemnly, "I feel as though I'm wandering in fog, uncertain of which path to take."

Duncan joined her at the ramparts.

"Does duty not dictate the way?" Ailis asked.

"It often lights the path. But even stars need darkness to shine," he replied.

She hesitated but mentioned Lachlan's name tremblingly.

"A man of honor who'd be a fine mate for another lass," Duncan acknowledged.

"Why not for me?" she asked softly.

"Ye are meant to be the lady of a clan. I'll make a good alliance for ye, and ye'll be happy."

Back in the great hall, Ailis moved through the crowd, focused on finding one person. Finally, she spotted Lachlan, his laughter distinguishable even in the lively atmosphere.

"Excuse me," she whispered as she approached him, determination fueling her courage. "May we speak?"

His stormy blue eyes met hers with attentive curiosity. "Of course, Ailis." They sought out a secluded alcove, leaving the noise behind them.

"Lachlan, I'm torn between duty and the heart," Ailis began gravely. "Ye have captured me thoughts, and I can no longer pretend otherwise."

His eyes softened as he smiled. "Ailis, yer words honor me. We cannot ignore the subtle bond that has been forming between us." He paused for a moment. "Yet, I too am bound by loyalties that aren't easily cast aside for personal desires."

"Then let us not speak of setting aside," Ailis implored, holding his hands firmly. "Instead, let's explore how we might unite our paths and intertwine duty with matters of the heart."

"Yer courage emboldens me," Lachlan admitted, his thumb gently caressing her hand. "If there is a way to honor both our hearts and responsibilities, we shall find it."

Ailis's heart danced as she gazed into Lachlan's eyes, their hands entwined. His touch brought comfort despite her turmoil.

"Ye have awakened something in me, Lachlan McClain," Ailis whispered. "Something I feared to let see the light of day."

"And ye, Ailis, have ensnared me heart with yer grace and courage." He lifted her hand to his lips, pressing a kiss so soft it might have been mistaken for a caress of the Highland breeze itself.

Their moment lingered until reality intruded. The sudden clamor of footsteps approaching pulled them back as Fiona appeared around the corner, breathless and urgent.

"Ailis! Father has been asking for ye."

The words hung heavily in the air. Ailis froze with trepidation, knowing full well the importance of such summons on this night of celebration.

"Go to him," Lachlan urged gently, releasing her hand but holding her gaze.

With a nod, Ailis turned to follow Fiona, casting one last glance at Lachlan before disappearing from view.

As she moved through the crowded hall, anticipation mixed with dread filled her thoughts. She longed to weave her future with Lachlan's, but she knew they faced unimaginable obstacles.

"Remember who ye are," her father's words echoed within her—a reminder that love could not easily bend traditions and allegiances.

When Ailis reached her father, he smiled. "I think ye should spend a little less time with Lachlan. I think ye need to focus yer attention on men who will one day be laird of a clan. Lachlan never will."

"But I want to spend more time with him. Not less," Ailis argued.

"That is because ye have spent too much time with him," Duncan told her. "Ye must spend time with others, and ye will see he is just a man like any other."

Ailis nodded obediently, but her heart screamed at her to ignore her father's wishes. "Aye, Father."

CHAPTER FIVE

AILIS ENTERED THE great hall to speak with Fiona, inhaling the aroma of heather that filled the room. Fiona stood in front of the hearth, rubbing her hands together to warm them. It seemed to Ailis that Fiona was an expert in matters of love, now that she had found the man she loved.

Ailis approached, desperately wanting her sister's counsel. She studied Fiona's face, unsurprised to see her sister so happy. "Ye seem pleased, Fiona."

"Oh, I am. How could I not be with Alisdair in me life? I think he is the man God created for me and me alone."

Ailis smiled. "Are ye up for giving some advice in love?"

Fiona laughed. "I'm not certain I can be of help, but I will try."

"Me thoughts are in turmoil. Lachlan makes me feel things I never thought I could. But he has yet to speak to Father about a possible marriage between us. I'm not certain if I'm being impatient or if he is dragging his feet. Is it possible my feelings for him are one-sided?"

Fiona shook her head. "I wouldna say that. I think he feels the same as ye do, or he wouldna keep seeking your company. Have ye asked him if he plans to speak with Father?"

"That would be the wrong thing for a lass to do," Ailis fretted. "It would be very...forward."

"It would. But it would also put yer mind at ease. Why would ye keep worrying about his feelings when ye could just ask?"

"As ye did with Alisdair?"

"Perhaps ye should do as I say and not as I did?"

Ailis chuckled. "I suppose I could. It just doesna seem like the right thing to do. Ye ken?"

"Then ye could keep wondering forever and hanging by a thread as ye let him toy with yer affections. That seems like a logical thing to do!"

Ailis sighed dramatically. "When I'm near Lachlan, me heart races. Ian makes me a bit queasy, if truth be told." She shook her head. "I fear me choice will seed regret for all me days. How do I choose without courting a lifetime of what-ifs?"

"The true path of the heart is not easy. Ye must explore yer own emotions," she advised softly. "True love isn't just an absence of doubt. It's the courage to follow yer heart wherever it leads." Ailis began, "Ian Sinclair… he speaks words that promise wonders, yet he puts me at ill ease. His smiles dinnae reach his eyes. Thus, I do not trust his intentions."

Fiona frowned. "I dinnae think I could ever trust a Sinclair. It is always wise to be cautious. Charm can often be deceiving and not a true measure of one's character."

"I agree. But I feel like spending time with Ian pleases Father."

"I dinnae think so! He doesnae trust the Sinclairs despite his long friendship with Arran. They have changed recently, and I dinnae think he wants us around them. Ye have a choice about whether or not ye continue to let him court ye."

"I hope yer right. I really dinnae think I can continue. He makes me feel as if I want to vomit when I spend a great deal of time with him." Ailis quickly recounted the story of her walk with Ian and how he'd refused to carry the deer back to the keep.

Fiona laughed. "Sounds like a Sinclair."

"He talks about his great prowess with a sword, and what a good leader he is, but…I dinnae ken any of it is true." Ailis shook her head. "It seems to me that he is a boastful man with nothing to be boastful about."

"Lachlan is a better man than Ian for certain. Ian is not a man ye should be alone with. Ever."

"Lachlan makes certain I am not. Kevin is always following behind us."

"Kevin is a good man," Fiona responded. "I would trust him with me life."

"As would I." Ailis was glad she'd spoken to her sister, though she wasn't sure she'd learned anything. She needed to learn to follow her heart. She knew she did, but it was difficult.

THAT EVENING, AILIS and her sisters, as well as the three McClain men spent the evening in the great hall with a group of young people. Both the McClain soldiers who were there and all of the McAfee young people gathered for dice games.

Ailis was not herself fond of dice games, so she spent the evening observing the young people who were surrounding her. They'd had this type of evening often before the McClains had come, often inviting some of the Sinclair youth. Ailis had a feeling that would not happen again.

She watched the group Lachlan played with and saw that he seemed to be enjoying himself. He laughed with Moira, Brodie, and several others from the clan. As the evening was to introduce the youth of the clan to the soldiers of the McClains, there was an equal number of men and women at each table. When there had been one more lass than lad, she had happily agreed to observe.

"I ken we should take a break here before switching groups," Alisdair called out, the obvious leader of the group.

As people walked to the table to eat the light meal the servants had prepared, Lachlan gravitated to Ailis's side. "Join us for the next games."

She shook her head. "We are not evenly matched. I will not ask another to sit out when tis easy enough for me to do so."

"Another lass can take a turn watching," he protested. "I would like to play with ye. Ye are a good competitor."

She shook her head. "Not at dice games. I've never enjoyed them."

"So that is the true reason ye dinnae play?"

"It is. There is no need for another to miss out."

"I would enjoy the time to get to know ye better."

For a moment, she considered telling him he should talk to her father about courting her, but she couldn't get up the courage to speak so plainly. "There are better ways to get to know me," she said.

He stabbed a small piece of meat with his knife, bringing it to his mouth. He studied her as he chewed. "I suppose that is true. I'll find the right way given time."

"Do ye have nights like this in yer clan?" she asked.

He nodded. "We do. The food tends to be more extravagant, but otherwise, the games are very similar. Do ye ever participate?"

"Aye. When there is no reason for me to sit out, then I play. I simply prefer to find a reason."

He chuckled. "I shall remember that about you." He looked at her for a moment. "What other reasons have ye used?"

She smiled, realizing he understood how she felt. "Other than uneven pairings? I've used someone being ill. I sit and watch over them, even if there's no need." She thought for a moment. "I've claimed sleepiness." Shrugging, she said, "I use whatever comes to mind at the time."

"So ye admit that ye make up reasons at times?"

She nodded emphatically. "Every chance I get."

"I'll be watching ye..."

"Ye do that," she said. If his attention was on her, it wasn't on another lass.

CHAPTER SIX

T HE SUN HAD barely risen when an urgent message reached the McAfee keep. Ailis, breathing in crisp morning air from her open window, noticed a winded young boy speaking earnestly with her father. As she watched their exchange, she could tell by the boy's gestures that someone needed her help.

Ailis donned her cloak and hurried through the stone corridors, her footsteps echoing against the walls. Her heart pounded in time with her strides. There was no time for delay. Over one arm was the bag filled with her herbs and other medicinal tools.

She followed the boy to a small hamlet where concerned villagers circled a man whose leg suffered from a misfortunate fall. As Ailis approached, the onlookers fell silent. She knelt beside the injured man, her hands steady and sure. The steadfast resolve within her eyes mirrored the surrounding landscape.

"Ye be brave," she whispered to the villager as she cleansed and bound his wound. She had dealt with many wounds such as his, and she had no doubt she'd deal with many more. Her mother had been a healer before her death, and her grandmother who had died the previous year had taught Ailis all she knew of healing. With each motion of cloth and knot of a bandage, Ailis could sense the man calming down.

She found that healing people this way did her more good than it did them. She loved to help others, and she was certain that it came through when she engaged in the healing arts. This act surpassed obligation. It was good to be there for others and engage in simple acts of kindness.

As she finished tending to the injury, and the villager's relief grew apparent, Ailis allowed herself a small smile—her duty fulfilled. Yet personal yearning still smoldered quietly within her, ever contrasting her responsibilities. She still had to speak with Lachlan and Ian about her decision from the previous day.

Ailis finished the knot and glanced up, spotting a figure at the clearing's edge. Draped in McAfee tartan, the man stood haloed by the setting sun. Though familiar in attire, he remained a stranger to her.

Drawn by his quiet strength and stillness, Ailis approached him carefully. Her heart pounded with a cautious rhythm.

"Good sir," she began, concealing her curiosity. "I am Ailis McAfee. May I ask yer purpose here? New faces are rare in these parts, and ye're even wearing our family's colors."

As he turned to face her, Ailis sensed the weight of his gaze— a heavy scrutiny that seemed to assess more than her words. The air filled with anticipation, awaiting his response.

The man's smile spread across his face. "A pleasure to meet ye, Ailis," he replied, his voice smooth as aged leather. "I am Cameron, returned from distant lands to visit me grandparents who dwell here."

Ailis stepped closer, curiosity stirring within her. "Yer journey must have been arduous. The Highlands can be unkind to those unfamiliar with our ways."

"Aye they can," Cameron conceded, a light dancing in his eyes. "But no road is too treacherous when it leads to family. And witnessing yer care for our kin has been heartening."

Ailis flushed. "I only take care of me father's people," she murmured. "The bonds of a clan are not easily broken."

Cameron closed the distance between them, the fading light framing his face. "Yer dedication speaks of a kind and courageous heart, Ailis—a rare and admirable thing."

She bore the weight of his gaze, full of earnestness and recognition of quiet strength. "Yer words honor me," Ailis replied steadily. "Though it is me duty to provide aid where I can. I'm now the only healer in the clan, and I go where I'm needed."

"Perhaps," Cameron agreed, his smile lingering like the last rays of sunlight on the horizon. "But ye do so with a grace that transcends obligation."

In that moment, duty and curiosity intertwined within Ailis as she stood before this man who saw her worth beyond merely being a healer.

Cameron briefly stepped away, leaving Ailis in the quiet hamlet. He returned with a handful of wildflowers. Their colors were vivid.

"For ye." He offered the bouquet. "A token for yer kindness and beauty."

Ailis accepted the flowers, her fingers brushing his. Their fragrance intermingled with the earthy air around them as she held them close.

"Thank ye, Cameron," she replied sincerely. "I'll treasure these blooms and their meaning."

As they strolled through the village, twilight enveloped them. Cameron shared stories of his grandparents and clan life, revealing both respect for tradition and aspirations beyond their homeland.

"And what of yer dreams, Ailis?" he asked. "Does yer heart desire more than these hills?"

She hesitated before answering. "There is much to cherish here." She glanced at the distant mountains. "But I'm curious about what lies beyond. However, me duty is to me clan—and I will always fulfill those duties. I think I'd miss the Highlands if I ever went elsewhere."

Cameron nodded. "Our obligations shape us, but shouldn't we heed our desires? Aren't we a blend of duties and dreams?"

The poignant question lingered as Ailis was torn between loyalty and personal fulfillment. In Cameron's presence, she found a kindred spirit who understood this delicate balance.

Ailis walked beside Cameron through the hamlet as she lightly brushed the wildflower petals he had given her. The breeze carried the scent of peat fires and fresh earth. He spoke often of his grandparents and their stories.

"The heather is especially vibrant this season," Cameron remarked, pointing toward the purple fields beyond the settlement. "It reminds me of our people."

"Heather is me favorite flower," Ailis replied, gazing at the serene landscape. Lachlan's allure often sparkled like sunlight on water—exciting and enchanting. Yet here, with Cameron, she found a different kind of allure—one that flowed steady and sure, like an underground stream nurturing the land above in silence.

As they passed by the dwellings, children peeked out from behind wooden doors, their eyes filled with curiosity. Ailis smiled and waved at them, each smile mirrored in Cameron's eyes. His attentiveness caused a flutter within her chest—a sensation both foreign and exhilarating. Why, if Lachlan had devoted this much attention to her, she was certain they'd be wed by now.

"Yer heart is open, Ailis," Cameron murmured, as if he could sense her inner turmoil. "It is a rare gift to hold such compassion for others."

"Is it not a burden?" Ailis pondered aloud. "To care so deeply when the world often demands a sterner hand?"

"Perhaps," he conceded. "But I believe it is also what makes us human—the ability to feel, to heal, to love."

Ailis's pulse quickened. She thought of Lachlan then—his laughter that ignited the air and his touch that promised adventure and passion. But in Cameron's earnestness and tranquility, she discovered a different kind of promise—one of steadfastness and solace.

"Love is a curious thing," Ailis remarked. Her heart wavered like a candle flame caught between two competing breezes. The excitement of Lachlan's charm battled with the serene pull of Cameron's character, and beneath the crescent moon, Ailis bore the weight of her indecision.

"Yer company, me lady, has been the highlight of me visit,"

Cameron said.

Ailis glanced up at him, her eyes reflecting conflicting emotions. The allure of Lachlan or the calming presence of Cameron. Her path forward remained unclear.

"Thank ye," she replied steadily despite her turmoil. "Yer words bring solace."

"Ye have a way with the afflicted," Cameron murmured. "It's as if yer touch alone can mend more than just flesh."

Ailis turned to face him, her green eyes seeking the truth. "To heal is to hold another's life in yer hands and pour into it hope."

Cameron hesitated before tucking a loose strand of her hair behind her ear. "Ye do more than just pour hope, Ailis," he confessed earnestly. "Ye inspire it."

In the quiet, their gazes locked, and they leaned closer, lips meeting in a tender kiss bridging the distance between two souls.

As they parted, Ailis gasped. "None must ken of this," she whispered. "For the sake of peace within our clan, and for me own heart's sake, we must guard this secret." She couldn't believe she'd allowed herself to be kissed by a man she'd met merely hours ago. Her father would be aghast.

Cameron nodded. "It will be as though the wind itself carries away our whispers. I shall not tell a soul."

"Will ye be staying in the Highlands for a while now?" she asked, wanting to see him again.

"Aye. I wasn't planning to stay, but now that I've met ye..."

A tear rolled down Ailis's cheek and she stepped away from Cameron, fortitude hiding her inner turmoil. "Goodnight, Cameron," she whispered.

"Goodnight, Ailis," he replied, his voice carrying a promise of a future filled with both peril and possibility.

With those final words, Ailis turned and walked away, clutching the wildflower bouquet which had wilted a great deal during their time together.

As dusk's soft glow illuminated the Highland landscape, Ailis approached the McAfee keep, clutching the bouquet of wildflowers. Each petal silently witnessed her tender moments with Cameron.

The ancient stones loomed before her, their presence reminding her of the weight of tradition and duty she bore. She paused at the heavy oak door before pushing it open. Inside, generations of McAfees had faced challenges of clanship and loyalty. Ailis sensed the magnitude of her predicament. Her family's expectations enveloped her like the tartan shawl around her delicate frame.

Walking toward her chamber, Ailis's thoughts churned like the rapids of a nearby river. Her encounter with Cameron contrasted sharply with the cool touch of obligation. She knew her role—a unifier within her clan—but couldn't deny the passion and connection she found with Cameron.

Her chamber provided no solace as sunlight streamed through the narrow window. Ailis stood in silence, green eyes reflecting an inner conflict. Lachlan's jests and charm once elicited flutters in her chest, but now they puzzled her amid her newfound feelings for Cameron.

Was she being a silly girl? Falling for the first man who paid her any attention? She wasn't certain. What she was certain of was that she wanted to find out. She wanted more time with Cameron as well as with Lachlan. Her heart would eventually choose one of them, wouldn't it?

Ailis gazed out the window, seeking clarity but finding none. Caught between desires and expectations, she whispered to the breeze, "Where does me duty end, and where does me heart begin?"

CAMERON STRODE THROUGH Sinclair village. He reached his assigned dwelling, shedding the guise of the McAfee clan and draping himself in the Sinclair plaid.

He made his way to the keep, entering through heavy oak

doors into the warm embrace of peat fires. Laird Sinclair observed his arrival with a resonant voice that captured attention.

"I have returned," Cameron announced. His eyes held a spark of something profound, a tale waiting to be told.

"Speak then," urged the laird as his sons gathered to listen.

"Today, I spoke with Ailis McAfee," Cameron informed him, carefully choosing his words. "I offered her flowers as symbols of our budding kinship, and she received them kindly."

Anticipation filled the room until the laird prompted him onward. Cameron inhaled deeply before admitting, "We shared a kiss—a promise of possibility between us."

The men understood this act was not just affection. It mingled personal longing and political alliance. As he concluded recounting his encounter with Ailis, Cameron stood tall, aware that every step held consequences far beyond his heart's desire.

"I see," Arran replied, the slow curl of his lips betraying his satisfaction at the news of his man's endeavor. "The McAfee lasses hold our sons in suspicion, thinking them knaves because of the ill-fated abduction of their sister." His voice echoed with authority, tempered by the knowledge of the delicate task at hand.

"Ye must be vigilant, Cameron. Continue to court Ailis with honor."

Within the chamber, tension coiled like a serpent ready to strike as Ian bore witness to the unfolding scene. His countenance, once the very visage of charm, now darkened like the storm clouds that often brooded over the highland peaks. His glare toward his father and brother was sharp as a dirk's edge, a silent testament to the tempest brewing within him. It was clear that Ian was unhappy that the other man had succeeded where he had failed.

Cameron's gaze lingered upon Ian, noting the rigid set of his jaw and the barely restrained energy of his stance. He surmised that beneath the polished veneer of nobility lurked a man who would not easily yield his ambitions. The truth of it settled heavily upon him. It was a reminder that, in the dance of alliance and power, even the most carefully laid plans could unravel at the hands of a single, determined player.

He was honored to have been chosen for such a task. Though it meant upsetting the laird's son, he would continue to do his very best. He would please the laird, and that was all that really mattered.

✦

CHAPTER SEVEN

Ailis FOUND HERSELF confused. She still had feelings for Lachlan, but she loved the attention that Cameron was showering upon her. Perhaps Cameron was the man she was meant to spend her life with, but she couldn't close her heart to Lachlan.

She and Cameron chuckled together, unaware of Lachlan's watchful gaze from afar.

"Ye've a way with words that could rival any bard," crooned Cameron, his smile infectious and disarming. His admiration came naturally, as did their playful teasing.

Ailis's voice carried playfulness and unease as she responded, brushing against a locket at her neck. "Flattery will get ye everywhere, Cameron."

"Only if it's met with truth," he countered, maintaining eye contact. They connected over lore and the natural world. Being with Cameron was comfortable, and she enjoyed his presence.

Ailis shared ancient tales with Cameron, who listened intently. "Ye have a gift, Ailis. It's no wonder ye leave such an impression on those near," he murmured, his warmth enveloping her.

She was torn between expectations and the spark of dangerous delight from connecting with Cameron. The image of Lachlan's eyes haunted her periphery—stories untold and depths unexplored—while she reveled in Cameron's company.

For seven days, he'd come to see her daily. She enjoyed every moment with him, though she often thought of Lachlan. But Cameron had approached her father for permission to court her while Lachlan hadn't bothered. He was busy helping Alisdair train the army, but he had time to speak with her father. She had no idea why he didn't do it.

In the stillness of the garden beneath the twilight sky, Ailis realized that every moment spent with Cameron made her even more uncertain about what she truly wanted.

Before Cameron wished her goodnight, he asked her, "Have ye ever longed to live a different life where ye could do exactly as ye wanted?"

She sighed. "I love me family, but mayhap some time to do exactly as I wish would be nice. Who wouldnae want such a thing?" As she walked inside, she wondered what she would do if she wasn't needed as a healer, and if her time was hers to do whatever she wished. Spending more time with Lachlan was the first thought to spring to her mind.

LACHLAN ENTERED THE McAfee keep's great hall, seeking his brothers' company. Alisdair and Brodie sensed his confusion.

"Brothers," Lachlan began, "I find meself uncertain of exactly what I should do next."

Alisdair urged him to speak his mind, while Brodie remained silent with an encouraging gaze.

"It's Ailis," Lachlan confessed. "Her presence draws me in, yet I dinnae know how to proceed." He shook his head. "I thought she felt the same for me, but now she spends time with Cameron. She appears truly taken with him."

"Ye wish to court her?" asked Brodie.

"Yes," Lachlan answered. "But her bond with Cameron complicates matters. I seek yer counsel. I ken I should have acted sooner, but I didn't. Now I need to know how to proceed."

"Have ye spoken with her father yet?" Alisdair asked. "That should be yer first step!"

Brodie nodded. "Alisdair is correct. Ye'll never understand how the lass feels if ye dinnae at least try to court her, and the first step is speaking with her father."

As Lachlan strode through the halls of the keep, he was consumed by the weight of his brothers' advice. When he finally found himself face-to-face with Ailis, his heart raced with anticipation.

"Ailis," he called softly.

She turned to him, her eyes reflecting a mixture of emotions—surprise, uncertainty, and a hint of longing. "Lachlan," she replied, her voice warm but guarded.

"I wished to speak with ye," Lachlan began, struggling to find the right words. "About us."

Ailis regarded him with a thoughtful expression, her fingers absentmindedly playing with the edges of her shawl. "What about us, Lachlan?"

He took a deep breath, gathering his courage. "I've come to realize that there's a depth to ye that I've only begun to understand. Yer spirit shines bright, Ailis."

A flicker of emotion crossed her face before she composed herself. "And what of Cameron?"

Lachlan met her gaze squarely. "I know of yer bond with him, but me heart tells me that there is something between *us* worth exploring." He tried to read her face to see what she was thinking as he spoke, but she was too guarded in that moment.

Ailis's eyes softened. "Ye speak true, Lachlan. But I must be honest with ye—me heart is torn. Why would you wait until another was courting me if you had the intention of courting me yerself?" If he hadn't, she wasn't certain why he was even having this conversation with her.

"I thought I had time. I knew we were drawn to one another, and I thought ye would wait for me. I plan to speak with yer father on the morrow."

Silence settled between them as they both grappled with their feelings. Finally, she whispered, "I will consider yer courtship if me father approves of ye."

Lachlan nodded slowly, understanding dawning in his eyes. "Then let us learn how we feel together, Ailis. With honesty and open hearts, we shall find our way. Ye'll give me a chance?"

"First ye must speak with me father. If he willnae let ye court me, then there is no reason for us to spend time together. But if he agrees, then aye, I'll give ye a chance." She paused. "And I will still be spending time with Cameron. I enjoy his company."

IN THE MCAFEE gardens, Ailis and Cameron walked among vibrant blooms.

"Ye have a way with children, Cameron," Ailis remarked, giggling.

"'Tis nothing," he replied with an easy smile. "Children are much like wildlings—give them respect and fun, and they'll follow ye anywhere."

Ailis glanced sideways at him, eyes filled with mirth. "And what of the not-so-small wildlings?"

"Perhaps," he teased. "Though such creatures require a more delicate approach."

Their conversation flowed from childhood tales to future dreams. Despite the growing bond, Ailis's thoughts strayed toward Lachlan—the mysterious highlander occupying her mind.

Ailis cherished the simplicity of this connection while delaying the inevitable decision that loomed on her horizon.

LACHLAN MCCLAIN OBSERVED the grand hall's festivities from a distance with an unusual seriousness. Ailis McAfee whisked through the dance with Cameron, her laughter filling the air, and he longed to be the one she was laughing with.

Throughout the dance, Ailis was keenly aware of Lachlan's presence. Their eyes met briefly before she focused on her partner again. Cameron complimented Ailis's dancing, but she shrugged it off modestly. Their stolen glances were charged with unspoken questions.

"Tell me, Ailis," Cameron inquired as the music played, "does yer heart ever yearn for something it cannot name?"

"Perhaps," she answered softly, sensing Lachlan's gaze upon her. "But the most important thing I can do is take care of me duties, and then hopefully, things will happen the way they're meant to."

"True," Cameron agreed with a tender smile. "One must choose wisely, lest the heart lead us astray."

As the dance ended, couples exchanged bows and curtsies, basking in their shared joy. Ailis, however, was fixated on Lachlan McClain, who strode away from the hall with determination.

"Ye have me heart in a birl, Lachlan McClain," Ailis whispered, her hand in Cameron's as they left the dance floor. "And I fear what might come should ye learn to wield it."

"Did ye say something?"

She smiled. "I was merely mumbling to meself."

To Ailis's surprise, Ian appeared beside her, glaring at Cameron. "May I have this dance, Ailis?"

Ailis stood for a moment, trying to decide the easiest way to tell the man she wouldn't be willing to dance with him. "Nay, I've promised the next dance to Cameron," she finally answered.

Ian focused on Cameron. "Are ye a laird's son then?"

"Nay. Just a man."

"Her father will never let ye marry her."

"We'll see," Cameron muttered, his eyes locking with Ian's.

"We will." Ian stood for a moment before retreating. Ailis let out a sigh of relief when he disappeared into the crowd.

"Thank ye for being me excuse not to dance with the man.

He is not someone I care to spend time with." She stopped herself before adding that Ian sickened her.

Cameron smiled, his whole face lighting up. "I'm happy to provide ye an excuse any time ye need it."

AILIS RODE BESIDE Lachlan through the glens and hills of the Scottish countryside. The hazy sun cast a warm glow, dappling the fields with light and shadow. Lachlan had arranged this excursion so they could have time to truly speak to one another.

"Ye ride well, Ailis," Lachlan called over his shoulder.

"Thank ye," she replied, feeling the weight of their growing connection. Truth be told, she had stronger feelings for Lachlan than she did for Cameron. Much stronger feelings. Yet Cameron seemed safe to her while Lachlan felt just a bit dangerous. She could easily lose her heart to Lachlan. "I'm surprised ye were able to take time from yer duties to ride with me."

"Sometimes we must make time for things that are important to us. And ye are important."

"Have ye spoken with me father?"

"Aye. He doesnae mind if we spend time together."

"Good. Then we shall enjoy that time." Ailis's heart raced a bit at her father's approval. It was what she'd wanted so much…before meeting Cameron anyway.

AILIS STOOD BY Cameron among kilted warriors and cheering clansmen. There was an archery contest, and they watched it closely.

"Och," she cried. "I could best every one of them with me knife."

Cameron chuckled. "I've heard tell of yer knife-throwing. Are ye as good as they say? Do ye think ye can best me?"

Ailis smiled. "Is that a challenge?"

Cameron nodded.

Ailis smiled, nodding, while her thoughts lingered on Lachlan.

Ailis stepped forward with poise. She sent the blade sailing into the target's bullseye with a steady hand. The crowd erupted in applause.

"Ye have a talent that rivals yer wit," Cameron gushed.

"Thank ye," Ailis replied, smiling mischievously. She accepted praise with humility but her inner turmoil continued. Her place among the McAfee clan carried expectations. It was obvious by Cameron's face that he still believed he could best her. It weighed on her shoulders heavily.

Cameron took his turn, and he came close, but he could not hit the center of the target as she had. "I must concede to yer greater skill."

Ailis grinned at him, but she saw a spark of something in his eyes that surprised her. He was truly angry she'd beaten him! That was so unlike Cameron.

He bowed to her quickly. "I must return to care for me grandparents."

"Have a good day," she murmured, watching him go. She couldn't help but wonder if he'd stay away now that he realized she could best him with a knife. She wasn't sure if she wished he would stay away so her decision would be easier, or if she wished he would return.

THE SKIES ABOVE the McAfee lands grew dark, forecasting a storm. Ailis and Cameron wandered through the gardens, their conversation meandering like a gentle stream. The scent of damp earth announced the impending rain.

"Do ye know the story of old when the sky cried for parted lovers?" Cameron asked playfully.

Ailis hummed softly. "Aye, it's as if even the heavens cannae bear the sight of heartache."

Raindrops began to fall as they walked. Suddenly, a downpour engulfed them, driving them to seek shelter beneath an ancient oak tree.

"Here we are at the mercy of the storm." Ailis smiled despite her damp cheeks.

"Mercy, or perhaps fate?" Cameron mused, watching her wipe away water droplets.

Underneath this natural refuge, they spoke of everything and nothing, not emerging until the rain had stopped.

LACHLAN APPROACHED THE grand doors, the carved oak standing imposingly before him. He needed some time in his ancestral home to decide how to capture the heart of Ailis. The brisk Highland air couldn't cool his burning chest as he recalled Ailis's laughter shared with another.

Pausing at the door, Lachlan's mind raced with courtly protocols and clan politics. Each step now was a battle between his heart and his station.

"Father," he called firmly. The laird sat at the far end of the hall, his gaze piercing even from a distance.

As Lachlan moved closer, he sensed generations watching him. "I understand ye've been spending much time in contemplation these days, son. What troubles ye?" the laird rumbled.

"It is not trouble that brings me before ye, Father, but a matter of the heart," Lachlan replied carefully. "I seek yer blessing to court Ailis."

The laird studied his son. "And what of her feelings for ye? Does she return yer affection?"

Masking his uncertainty, Lachlan answered, "Ailis is a woman of depth and complexity. I believe there lies a chance for us if I'm given an opportunity to prove me sincerity."

"Very well," the laird conceded. "Ye have me permission to court her. But remember, Lachlan, our alliances ensure our survival as much as our strength. Ye must choose wisely."

Lachlan nodded, his shoulders relaxing from their tension. As he turned to leave, he grew determined. Now that he had permission from both their fathers, he knew he could win her heart. He just had to decide how to proceed on the long ride back to McAfee lands.

CHAPTER EIGHT

THE FOLLOWING AFTERNOON, Lachlan approached Ailis in the courtyard, the scent of damp earth lingering in the air. Ailis stood near the herb garden.

Lachlan paused before her, his earnestness evident. "Good morrow, Ailis." He watched her harvest a sprig of a plant he didn't recognize. "I want to go on a hunt this morning, and Alisdair said he didn't need me. Would ye honor me with yer company?"

Ailis smiled gently and nodded without hesitation. "Aye, Lachlan," she replied. "I shall gladly join."

Lachlan and Ailis set out into the forest. "Tell me, Ailis." His voice broke the tranquility of the woods. "Have ye e'er hunted alongside Cameron?" He tried not to show his jealousy, but he wasn't sure if he succeeded.

Ailis's brow furrowed in contemplation. "Nay, Lachlan. Cameron and I have nae shared such pursuits. He seemed ill-tempered when I bested him at the art knife-throwing. I didn't think it wise to hunt with him. Men hate it when I outhunt them."

The shadows shifted on their faces as Lachlan responded with a sincere tone. "Any man would find himself humbled by yer prowess, Ailis. But where others may harbor envy, I feel naught but pride for yer skill."

Ailis sighed. "He seemed somehow angered by me skill, which made me sad. He tried to hide it, but I could see it in his eyes." She shook her head. "I will not pretend to be bad at something just to make a man feel better about himself."

Lachlan raised his brow. "Angered by yer triumph? He should celebrate it, not resent it."

Ailis traced her knife handle. "Pride can be a man's companion and doesn't take kindly to bruising."

"True," he replied. "But where Cameron finds envy, I find admiration."

A spark of joy appeared in Ailis's eyes. She smiled. "Ye're kind to say so. I'll strive to prove worthy of that regard."

They continued side by side, nature accompanying them as they navigated the terrain of delicate conversations, each word bringing them closer to understanding duty and desire.

"I spoke with yer granny in the kitchen this morn. She has a mind to make rabbit stew for the evening meal, and I told her we would hunt as many as we could."

Ailis smiled. "Ye know she's truly only Fiona's granny."

He shook his head. "Tis odd to me that the three of ye are so close yet have different mothers."

"Our mothers all died in childbirth, so all we've known is Father. And Granny, of course. Me own grandmother lived in the village, and she taught me the healing arts. Yet I've always been closer to Fiona's granny. She has always been there when I need advice."

Ailis scanned the brambles and undergrowth, alert for any signs of her quarry. Beside her, Lachlan matched her focus as they both drew knives from their belts, the blades reflecting the light.

Two rabbits emerged in a clearing, nibbling at tender shoots of grass. In unison, Ailis and Lachlan threw their knives with precision, striking each rabbit.

Ailis knelt by the fallen creature, whispering words of gratitude for its sacrifice. "Ye've given much, little one," she murmured, "May yer spirit roam free in the fields of the heavens, where there will be carrots in abundance."

Lachlan retrieved his prey with respect, acknowledging the

gravity of taking a life.

It wasn't long before they had ten plump rabbits for Granny's stew.

Ailis and Lachlan gathered the rabbits they had felled, their movements efficient and respectful. Ailis's brown hair framed her face as she spoke soft benedictions over each life taken, while Lachlan's eyes seemed to reflect the solemn sky.

"Ye needn't mirror me ways," Ailis sassed, her voice rising above the rustle of leaves. "A sword or bow would serve ye just as well, should yer heart call for it."

"Nay, lass. Yer way is as fine as any," Lachlan replied. "Today, we hunt as equals, sharing methods."

She smiled at him, thinking how much more gracious he was about her abilities than Cameron. And Ian had laughed at the idea of her being better than any man.

They returned to the keep and presented Granny with the ten rabbits. With a nod of approval, she handed Lachlan a bulging wool sack of provisions. Ailis glanced at him curiously as he accepted it gratefully.

Together, they ventured into the woods again and found a secluded glen where they laid out their meal, transforming simple fare into a feast through the beauty of their surroundings and their company.

As they ate, a subtle shift occurred in their camaraderie, deepened by their shared understanding of sacrifice and providing for those they cherished. Their conversation materialized in Ailis's quiet laughter and Lachlan's attentive gaze.

"Tell me," Lachlan began, breaking a piece of bread, "have ye ever seen the stars reflected in the loch at night? 'Tis a sight to stir the soul."

"Many a night," Ailis replied softly, "I have wondered at their shimmering dance." She found his inquiry, unrelated to duty or alliance, refreshing and curious. In his company, she felt an unexpected ease.

As they conversed, Ailis realized Lachlan's wit was matched

only by his attentiveness. His questions sought understanding, not advantage. She found herself fascinated by Lachlan's conversation and eagerly responded to him.

The meal ended, and silence fell between them, thick with unspoken thoughts. Lachlan regarded her with earnest eyes beneath furrowed brows. "If I may be so bold," he began gravely, "are yer feelings for Cameron akin to love?"

Ailis paused. A wildflower's petals now blurred in her hand. It was a question she had pondered alone before. "Nay," she answered clearly, "Me heart does not quicken at the thought of him."

Lachlan nodded silently, an acknowledgment requiring no further words. In that moment, Ailis understood their bond transcended obligation or strategy—a rare connection beyond political machination. For a moment he considered asking if her heart quickened at the thought of him, but he couldn't do it. Nay, he'd let her figure that out in her own time.

As remnants of their feast lay forgotten, they lingered in the glen. Duty would call them back soon enough, but for now, they relished this sacred pause, a respite within the forest's embrace.

Finally, they rose to head back to the keep and their duties.

"Do ye ever watch the sunset beyond the glen?" Lachlan asked gently.

"Many times," Ailis answered, gazing at the fading light. "Each one is like a farewell until tomorrow."

He took her hands in his, gazing into her eyes. "I'm not ready to return. I want many more hours of yer company." Truly he wanted the rest of her life, but he knew she wasn't ready to hear that yet.

She smiled. "Nor I."

"Ailis, ye possess a rare strength," Lachlan gushed. "Not just with yer physical prowess or respect for nature but in yer very essence."

Honored by his words, she replied, "Ye're remarkable too, Lachlan."

Their lips met in a passionate kiss, sacred and destined. As they parted breathlessly, Ailis's heart raced. Her love for Lachlan surpassed any emotion she'd experienced before.

On their return to the keep, Ailis was enveloped by a new-found shyness. Each glance and caress resonated with undiscovered possibilities.

"Ailis," Lachlan began, breaking their silence. "No matter which path ye choose, I'll be honored to walk it by yer side."

Ailis offered a soft smile, exuding emotions deeper than words. In Lachlan's company, she discovered more than just a confidante or suitor. She found a man who shared her spirit.

As the keep's shadowy outline appeared, Ailis braced herself against the emotional storm brewing within. Though duty demanded their separation, the intoxicating kiss forged a bond unbreakable by obligation. The man who could ignite such passion with a simple touch was undeniably her destined partner.

Ailis and Lachlan walked toward the keep, both regretting their need to leave their private spot in the woods. The cool air carried a faint scent of peat smoke from hearths awaiting their return.

A gentle hush enveloped them, solidifying an unspoken bond between two hearts. Lachlan's presence steadied Ailis's fluttering heart.

In the periphery, Cameron stood, weary from the day's toils. Lachlan's gaze flickered in his direction. Recognition flashed within his eyes, followed by a subtle tightening of his jaw. His silence shielded Ailis and himself from past entanglements.

Ailis remained unaware of Cameron's nearness, drawn solely to Lachlan as he guided her through the castle grounds with quiet assurance.

They passed Cameron, leaving behind old shadows for new promises—a future free from doubt or hesitation.

As Ailis went to see where she was needed, her mind lingered on the time she'd spent with Lachlan. She didn't know how she had been confused about whether to choose Lachlan or Cameron. Lachlan was the one who filled her mind and aroused so much passion within her.

Aye, Lachlan was the only man she wanted to be with for the rest of her days.

✦

CHAPTER NINE

THREE DAYS LATER, Ailis opened a missive, her heart fluttering at the sight of Lachlan's name written on the invitation. It described an afternoon by the loch, enticing her to leave her duties.

She prepared a basket filled with McAfee clan harvests: oatcakes with heather honey, aged cheese, and gleaming apples. She arranged each item with precision.

Her journey to the loch was quiet. She found Lachlan waiting. His plaid blanket lay upon the grass, inviting her closer.

"Ye've outdone yerself, Lachlan." Ailis approached him with a smile full of lightness. "But… I dinnae know if I can eat on a McClain plaid. Shouldn't we be using the McAfee plaid?"

Lachlan chuckled. "I dinnae think yer blood will curdle from the food. I mean, it's good McAfee food, right?"

Ailis giggled as she took her seat beside Lachlan, happy to once again have some time alone with him. She traced patterns in the grass with her fingers, finally breaking the peaceful quiet. "Do ye ever wonder what our lives would be like if we weren't bound by duty?" she asked softly, focused on the ripples of the water.

Lachlan's expression turned thoughtful as he considered her question. "Sometimes," he admitted. "But then I remember that our responsibilities shape who we are. Without them, we might not have found each other."

Ailis nodded, an understanding glint in her eyes. "True," she murmured. "Our paths intertwined for a reason, forged by history and necessity. And, of course, by the marriage of me sister to yer brother."

"Ye know," he began slowly, "sometimes I wonder if we're on the right path. Do ye ever feel like we're chasing a dream that may never come true?"

She gazed out at the water, distant yet determined. "I do sometimes," she admitted softly. "But then I remember why we started this journey in the first place. We may not know where it will lead us, but we cannae give up on our dreams just because they seem out of reach."

He nodded, a small smile playing on his lips. "Ye're right. We've come this far together, and I believe we can overcome whatever challenges come our way."

Their words hung in the air, mingling with the soft sounds of nature surrounding them. In that moment, they found solace in each other's company, knowing that as long as they had each other, they could face whatever the future held.

"I am pleased we haven't had trouble with the clanless men in a while, but I fear they will return," Lachlan whispered. "But I will stay with Clan McAfee until we are certain the danger has passed."

Ailis reached out, her hand finding his. "I am glad," she replied, her tone filled with unwavering support. "I like having ye here, whether there is danger or not."

Lachlan's hand slipped into the woven satchel, retrieving a slender wooden flute. Ailis watched with interest, her eyes reflecting the sky.

"Ye play?" she asked.

"Not often, but I do play," Lachlan replied, lifting the instrument to his lips. "A gift from me father, taught by visiting bards."

As he played, a haunting melody cascaded across the loch, mingling with rustling leaves. The tune spoke of ancient battles, love cherished and lost, and the eternal dance between duty and desire. His fingers danced across the flute with precision.

The last note faded. Ailis beamed at Lachlan with newfound

admiration. "Yer music captured the essence of the Highlands."

Lachlan bowed his head modestly as a family of deer emerged near the water's edge, their sleek coats shining in the sun. They remained still, watching the deer graze with delicate serenity.

"There," Ailis whispered.

"Such majesty," Lachlan murmured. "In their presence, one feels humbled."

Ailis nodded, feeling a kinship beyond words. The sight of the deer stirred within her a longing for a simpler life. "I'm happy we're not hunting today. I hate to kill such beautiful creatures."

The tide of responsibility that ruled her life quickly replaced her yearning. As a McAfee, she inevitably had to make sacrifices for her clan's sake.

"In this moment of peace, we're still bound by our duties," Ailis whispered.

"True," he agreed, eyes filled with unspoken promises. "But let's cherish this brief respite."

They focused on the deer, the loch, and the calm that enveloped them. As shadows stretched and light receded, they lingered at the water's edge—duty-bound yet masters of their own hearts.

Lachlan rose to his feet. "Ailis," he called, "would ye join me for a ride through the glens? The beauty of yer lands is something that must be cherished."

Ailis's heart fluttered at the prospect. She stood and regarded him with her vibrant green eyes, full of life. "I would love to, Lachlan," she responded, her voice filled with anticipation.

Together, they approached their horses and mounted them with ease. Ailis's attire whispered of her status, and tokens from loved ones adorned her dress. They set off, side by side, their horses' hooves thudding rhythmically against the soft earth.

The landscape unfolded before them, a testament to the rugged beauty of the Highlands. Ailis took in the sight of heather-strewn hills beneath a sky painted with fading daylight.

Suddenly, Ailis's horse stumbled upon a hidden stone along the path. Lachlan acted swiftly, reaching out to prevent her fall.

Their eyes met—his blue gaze meeting her green—and an unspoken connection formed between them.

"Steady now," Lachlan murmured, calming Ailis's alarm as he helped her regain balance.

"Thank ye," she whispered, a newfound respect evident in her voice. No one had ever tried so hard to keep her from falling before.

As they continued riding, the fragility of their blossoming affection became clear.

Ailis dismounted, her fingers brushing the coarse mane of her steed as she whispered her thanks. Lachlan joined her on the ground, and together they stood before a hidden waterfall, its melody easing the weight upon Ailis's shoulders.

They settled at the water's edge, mist cooling their skin. In that serene space, duty and obligation seemed distant. Lachlan pointed to a cluster of wildflowers nestled among the foliage. "Those are night's whisper," he pointed out, sharing their symbolism of love's endurance through time.

Ailis turned to Lachlan with a thoughtful expression. "Do ye believe in the legends of our ancestors, Lachlan? The ones that say our spirits are tied to these lands for eternity?"

Lachlan's eyes sparkled with a hint of mischief as he considered her question. "I've always found comfort in the stories. They remind us of the enduring strength of our people."

A gentle breeze stirred the heather around them, carrying with it the distant call of a lone bird soaring overhead. Ailis smiled at the sound, her heart feeling lighter than it had in weeks. "There is a certain magic to this place, isn't there? It's as if time stands still in the whispering winds."

Their horses nickered softly, sensing the quiet intensity between their riders. Lachlan reached out a hand to brush against Ailis's own.

"We are but players in a grander design, Ailis," he murmured with wonder. "Our paths intertwined by fate or by choice, who can truly say?"

Ailis met his gaze, her eyes shining with an unspoken bond forged through shared moments of peace and contemplation. "I like to think we have a say in our destinies, Lachlan. That we can shape our futures with each choice we make."

Lachlan took a deep breath, inhaling the crisp air. "Perhaps ye're right, Ailis," he murmured. "We must hold the power to create our own stories—ones that echo through the ages like the songs of old."

Ailis nodded in agreement, her heart brimming with new-found hope and determination. Together, they stood on the threshold of an uncertain yet promising future, bound by duty yet free to choose their paths.

"I like that. We're creating our own stories," she murmured.

"Perhaps one day, ye shall share yer stories with me," Lachlan crooned.

Ailis stood beside her horse, a breeze teasing her hair. Lachlan, mounted gracefully on his steed, gazed at her with eyes lonelier than the moon.

"Shall we race?" he asked playfully.

Laughing, she replied, "I'll give ye a head start." She climbed onto her saddle with anticipation.

They raced across the McAfee lands, their laughter intertwining as they competed for the lead. Approaching the village, Ailis halted, noticing movement among the heather. Lachlan returned to her side, concern in his gaze.

"What is it?" he asked.

Ailis dismounted and discovered an injured bird with a twisted wing. Touched by its vulnerability, they used twigs and grasses to splint its fragile appendage. As they finished, she reassured the creature, "Ye shall soar once more." It wasn't the first time she'd tried to heal an animal, but she was certain it wouldn't be the last.

"Come," Lachlan spoke. "We must return before nightfall."

Finally, they returned to the village and took the horses back to the stables.

"'Tis a rare sight," Ailis whispered, watching a shooting star. "To witness the night's shy beauty."

"Aye," Lachlan agreed. "But even rarer still is the company I find meself in this evening."

She turned to meet his eyes. "Our kin lay claim to lands and titles, yet here we sit, simply as Ailis and Lachlan. Do ye ever wonder what might be if not for the weight of our names?"

"Every day," he confessed. "I dream of a life unshackled by duty. But dreams, like stars, are often beyond reach."

"Perhaps," she mused. "Yet even the loftiest of stars may guide a sailor home. Our dreams might serve us similarly, should we dare to heed their direction."

As their gazes locked, they shared an embrace. In each other's arms, they found sanctuary from the chaos of their world.

"Until we meet again, Lachlan," Ailis whispered against his shoulder, her lips forming a melancholic smile as they separated. She wished she could spend every waking moment with him, but she knew better.

"Soon, Ailis," he promised, fingers brushing her arm before stepping back. "Nothing will stop me from coming back to ye."

CAMERON, CONCEALED AT the forest's edge, watched Ailis and Lachlan part. Anger flooded him as he observed their tender embrace, realizing that Ailis's affection was for another.

"Curse this fate," he muttered, turning away from the scene. Each step back to Sinclair land felt heavier than before, his mind occupied by fear of Laird Arran's anger.

Upon arriving at Clan Sinclair's great hall, he hesitated before entering. Inside, Laird Arran and his sons Ian and Callum stood like imposing statues.

"Laird," Cameron began softly, "I bring news."

Ian fixed a cold gaze on him. "Speak."

"I've failed in the task ye set before me," Cameron admitted. "Ailis McAfee's heart is not mine to claim. She has found love with Lachlan McClain." He stood tall, waiting for the laird's wrath.

Laird Arran's sharp gaze pierced him. "Ye were to secure an alliance that would fortify our lands."

"We must consider our next move with care," Ian added. "Cameron is obviously not the man we thought he was."

With remorse, Cameron bowed his head. "Me efforts were earnest, but she seems to love only Lachlan."

"Enough," Laird Arran commanded. "We will deliberate further. For now, take yer leave."

Cameron retreated, his footsteps echoing against the stone floor. He was happy to be dismissed. It was better than facing the brunt of the laird's wrath.

CAMERON FACED LAIRD Arran, his past failures burdening him. The room was silent, with only the hearth fire's crackling as company. Arran's presence dominated the space, his eyes reflecting a tactician's mind at work.

"Ye have been too subtle," Arran scolded. "We must change tactics. Ailis McAfee cannot fall to Lachlan McClain."

"Laird, what would ye have me do?" Cameron asked, his inner turmoil masked by a steady voice.

"Interrupt them," Arran commanded emotionlessly. "When they are alone, sow seeds of doubt. Tell her Lachlan has been seen with another woman. Do whatever it takes to keep them apart."

Unease coiled in Cameron's gut at the deception he was tasked with, but loyalty outweighed his conscience. He nodded, accepting the unsavory mission.

"Consider it done," he answered, resolve hiding his internal conflict. Arran gave a curt nod, satisfied with Cameron's agreement.

✦ ❦ ✦

CHAPTER TEN

AILIS AND LACHLAN strayed from the evening's festivities, seeking solace in the castle's outskirts. The moonlit path guided their steps as they walked through the quiet night.

Ailis glanced at Lachlan, his presence comforting yet thrilling her heart like a caged bird yearning for freedom.

"Ye seem deep in thought," Lachlan remarked.

"I'm considering me choices," Ailis admitted. "The heart desires, but duty often commands otherwise."

"Dinnae let duty silence yer heart," Lachlan encouraged, his fingers gently grazing hers.

Their connection was disrupted by Ian Sinclair's arrival, presenting Ailis with wildflowers. "For ye, fair Ailis," he offered with his thick Highland dialect.

"Thank ye, Ian," Ailis responded, concealing her discomfort. As Ian spewed compliments and promises, his bouquet became symbolic of the choice that loomed before her.

Ailis clutched the vibrant petals Ian had gifted her, feeling their weight of expectation. She finally addressed him, "Yer attentions are flattering, but they cannot change what is within me heart. These blooms are lovely, but another has claimed me affection. Seek out someone whose heart is free to return yer feelings." She tried to keep her voice calm and kind, so as not to hurt his feelings. Ian was simply not the man she wanted to spend her life with. She didn't even want to spend five minutes with him.

Ian's expression briefly faltered before masking it with a smile. "Aye, fair Ailis, if that be yer wish."

Ailis turned away from Ian and walked toward the loch with Lachlan. His presence filled her with warmth.

"Come, let us wander yonder," Lachlan suggested, offering his arm, which Ailis accepted, her spirits lifting.

"I'm glad to be done talking to Ian. I've been dreading that task for a long time. I wanted to agree to his courtship because Father likes to keep his enemies close, but I knew from the beginning that I would not marry him." She shuddered delicately.

"Ye did the right thing, telling him there was no chance. I canna bring meself to believe his affection was genuine, but I still think he deserves to know the truth. Of course, that means they'll send someone else to court ye if they can." He shook his head. "I wish we knew what they truly wanted from ye. An alliance, certainly, but why? There are other clans with beautiful daughters to marry. Why are they so focused on the McAfee sisters?"

She shook her head. "I dinna know. I think maybe they want to take advantage of the friendship our fathers have had all this time, but it dinna sound like that friendship will last."

They walked to the edge of the forest, their steps matching the steady rhythm of their hearts. A shared glance conveyed more than words could express.

Soon, they discovered a hidden glen bathed in silver light. Laughter spilled as they stepped into the clearing, echoing through the hills.

"Look at this place," Ailis exclaimed. "It feels like we've stumbled into a fairytale."

"Aye," Lachlan agreed, spinning her playfully. "And ye are the most enchanting vision within it."

In this secluded glen, Ailis momentarily forgot the tension between personal desires and political responsibilities. She cherished every second with Lachlan before reality would call her back.

Their laughter mingled with the rustle of leaves as they

twirled in the moonlit glade, Ailis feeling the weight of her worries momentarily lift. She glanced up at Lachlan, his eyes filled with mischief and genuine affection.

"Lachlan, do ye ever feel like we are but players in a grand story, our fates intertwined by forces beyond our control?" Ailis pondered.

"Aye, lass," Lachlan replied thoughtfully, pulling her closer. "But perhaps we can write our own tale of the twists of destiny."

Ailis smiled at his words, feeling a surge of hope in her heart. "And what would our story entail, Lachlan?"

Lachlan's gaze turned tender as he spoke, "It would be one of love and courage, where we face our doubts and fears together. A tale of two souls bound by an unbreakable bond, defying the odds stacked against them. Our story would be filled with adventures under the shimmering moonlight, laughter that dances in the wind, and moments of quiet understanding that speak louder than any other words."

Ailis listened to him, her heart swelling with emotion. She reached out to gently touch his cheek, feeling the warmth of his skin under her fingertips. "I would like nothing more than to embark on such a journey with ye, Lachlan. To write our story together, one page at a time."

Lachlan's eyes softened at her touch, a soft smile playing on his lips. "Then let us seize this moment, Ailis. Let us embrace the uncertainty of tomorrow and revel in the joy of today. For our story is just beginning, and I cannot wait to see where our hearts will lead us."

As he spoke, a shooting star streaked across the night sky, illuminating their faces. Ailis felt a surge of hope and excitement at Lachlan's words, the shooting star a sign from the heavens above. She gazed into his eyes, feeling a sense of peace and belonging wash over her.

"Lachlan, I have never felt more alive than in this moment with ye," Ailis confessed. She felt shy sharing that truth with him, but it felt right at that moment.

"I feel the same with ye. It's as if we're meant to be together."

He lowered his head and kissed her softly, hoping she would understand that his intentions were good and true.

Their kiss deepened, a silent promise passing between them. Ailis's doubts and fears faded away in that moment, replaced by the certainty of their connection. Lachlan's arms wrapped around her, pulling her closer as if trying to shield her from any lingering doubts.

As they finally parted, Ailis glanced up at Lachlan, her heart brimming with newfound courage. "Ye make me ache for ye, Lachlan."

Lachlan held Ailis's gaze, his eyes reflecting the moon's gentle glow. "And ye fill me every thought, Ailis," he murmured, his voice tinged with a mix of desire and tenderness. Their hearts beat in unison, a silent symphony of emotions that bound them together in that enchanted glen.

A soft breeze whispered through the trees, carrying with it the sweet scent of blooming heather. It was as if the world around Ailis and Lachlan had faded into the background, leaving only them in a cocoon of shared affection. She was grateful for this moment of intimacy, for the chance to explore her emotions freely without the weight of expectations.

Hand in hand, they walked back to the castle under the watchful gaze of the moon. The night seemed brighter, filled with possibilities as they embraced the beginning of their shared story.

AILIS HELD THE reins of her gelding while Cameron rode beside her.

"Ye handle yer mount with grace," Cameron called over the wind.

"Thank ye," she replied, glancing at him. Yet Ailis's thoughts lingered on another.

Ailis and Cameron rode side by side through McAfee land. Ailis was awed by the beauty of the world around her, even as she struggled with feeling inadequate. How could she take care of her duties while also following her heart? Was such a thing even possible?

"Ye appear troubled," Cameron observed, matching her pace. "Mayhap I can offer counsel."

Ailis hesitated. "It is naught but the musings of a lass caught between heart and duty."

"But what if the heart's choice could also fulfill one's duty?"

"Can such a thing truly exist?" she pondered aloud.

"Perhaps." Cameron leaned closer, lowering his voice. "But know this—Lachlan McClain was seen just yestereve, lips pressed to those of another lass."

The news hit her like a cold blade. She withdrew, searching for deceit in Cameron's gaze, only finding earnestness.

"Are ye certain of this?" Ailis asked. It was unbelievable to her that Lachlan would betray her that way.

"Me own eyes bore witness," he confirmed gently.

Tension coiled within her, but she held onto her resolve, refusing to let suspicion cloud her judgment without proof.

"Thank ye for telling me," she replied, her mind searching for ways that Lachlan could have been seen kissing another and still be innocent of betrayal. She cared for the man and had always found him to be honest, and the idea that he wasn't was painful to think about.

"Any man would be blessed to have yer favor, Ailis," Cameron stated earnestly, resting a comforting hand upon hers.

Smiling faintly, she remained focused on the rolling hills before them. They continued their ride through the rugged heart of the Highlands in silence.

LATER, AILIS WALKED alone, her heart burdened by doubt as she approached the spot where she was to meet with Lachlan. The heather brushed against her skirts, a quiet solace in her turmoil.

Upon cresting the final hill, she found Lachlan McClain waiting beside a prepared meal in a secluded glen. The breathtaking vista seemed to invite release from earthly concerns.

"Ye've discovered me secret spot," Lachlan chirped, his smile familiar yet roguish. "I hoped it might offer ye peace."

"Thank ye," Ailis responded, settling beside him despite the tension of unspoken questions.

As they shared their meal, silence laden with anticipation persisted. Ailis finally spoke, her voice trembling. "Lachlan, there are rumors that ye were seen with another lass... sharing a kiss. With what I ken of ye, I have a hard time believing that to be true, but I feel I should ask, and ye should know what is being said."

His expression somber, Lachlan met her gaze. "On me honor, Ailis, those tales are untrue. Me affection lies only with ye." He shook his head. "The person with whom ye spoke lied to ye."

Searching for sincerity in his eyes, she fought against lingering doubts. "Ye must think me foolish."

"Never," he replied fervently. "Ye seek the truth, and I'll prove me faithfulness." His hand bridged the gap between them with a gentle touch.

She wanted to believe his every word, but why would Cameron lie? He appeared to be a good man. But ye never truly knew another's thoughts and motivations. Could he have made those claims out of jealousy? Perhaps he realized she had chosen Lachlan?

"Who filled yer head with such unfounded tales?" Lachlan demanded.

Torn between loyalty and honesty, Ailis finally met his gaze, her green eyes revealing her inner turmoil. "It was Cameron who told me." She watched him carefully, curious to see how he would react to the news of his accuser.

Lachlan's expression darkened. "That man would say anything to drive a wedge between us. He seeks to sow discord where there is none." He shook his head. "I canna believe ye listened to him."

Though she felt betrayed, Ailis couldn't ignore the doubt that had taken root within her.

DAYS LATER, TENSION gripped Ailis as she sat with Cameron in his boat on the loch.

"Ye look fair bonnie against the backdrop of the Highlands," Cameron crooned, trying to capture her gaze. He reached out and touched her hand, hoping it would break the tension.

"Beauty fades," Ailis replied coolly. "What remains when it does?" Now that she was with him, she was having a hard time knowing what the truth was. She'd believed Lachlan when she was with him. But now that she was with Cameron, she was no longer certain.

"Power," he answered without hesitation.

"'Tis a poor thing to build one's life upon," she countered. "Cameron, I have made me choice, and it is not ye." She spoke softly and compassionately. She didn't want to hurt him, though she knew some hurt was inevitable.

His oars stilled as silence engulfed them.

"Ye cannot mean it," he began at last.

"Aye, I do." Her words fell like stones into still waters. He appeared much less hurt than angry, and that confused her a bit. Why would he be angry? It made little sense to her.

"Ye'll regret this," Cameron warned, his charm giving way to cold determination.

"Perhaps," Ailis conceded. "But I would rather live with regret than choose a man who doesn't sway me heart." *Or a man who threatened me when I told him me feelings.*

Ailis stepped onto the shore, leaving an unbridgeable chasm between them. Her decision anchored her to a path of peril and passion.

BENEATH THE STAR-FILLED sky, Ailis McAfee wandered the moonlit heather fields near her family's estate. The Highland chill stirred the leaves and made her wrap her cloak tighter.

As she pondered her feelings for Cameron and Lachlan, footsteps interrupted her thoughts. Lachlan approached, dressed in hunting leathers with a longbow slung over his shoulder.

"Ye look lost in thought," he observed, his voice warm in the night air.

Ailis sighed. "I am confused. Sometimes I wish there was a book telling me what I should do in any situation.

"Ye'll figure it out. Yer a smart lass." He grinned at her for a moment. "Would ye like to join me on a hunt?"

Excited by the prospect of spending time with him, she accepted with a soft smile. "I would enjoy that. Spending time with ye is always something I want to do." Now that she was with him again, she knew he hadn't lied. Cameron had been the liar, and though she hadn't wanted to hurt him, she was glad he was no longer an important person in her life.

At daybreak, they ventured into the Highlands together. When Lachlan spotted a red deer, he motioned for silence before expertly shooting it down. He grinned at Ailis, saying "There's more to me than just a charming smile."

"And ye are better with a bow and arrow than most men. Though, Fiona can still outshoot ye." She grinned. Her heart raced as the thrill of the hunt sharpened her senses. The bond with Lachlan transcended mere attraction—it was a connection forged through shared experiences and continually deepened.

Returning with their hard-earned spoils, Ailis was pleased that they were able to combine spending time with one another and doing something for the good of the clan. Choosing between duty and her heart was difficult. For once, she hadn't had to.

IN THE FOLLOWING days, Cameron persistently sought Ailis's attention. One morning, he approached her with gifts: a woolen shawl resembling the loch's deep blue and a silver brooch.

"The gifts are beautiful, but are ye sure ye wouldn't rather give them to someone else?"

"Nay, these gifts are meant to be worn by the bonniest woman in the Highlands, and that would be ye." He bowed slightly.

"But ye remember that I told ye I have chosen another?" she asked, studying his face.

"I plan to change yer mind. Ye must be cold in the Highland air," he offered, as he placed the shawl on her shoulders. "Nothing but the finest for ye."

Ailis accepted the gifts, feeling the weight of expectation upon her. Cameron's compliments held an unsettling urgency.

"Thank ye, Cameron," Ailis replied cautiously. "But ye are mistaken about me feelings. Once I make a decision, I dinnae change me mind."

Cameron leaned closer, determined. "Give me a chance, Ailis. Me heart is true, and me fondness grows each day."

She shook her head. "Me mind is made up, and I love another."

Ailis retreated to the kitchen where Granny stirred a pot of stew. She confided her confusion about Cameron.

Granny met Ailis's gaze. "A gift given freely is light as a feather. If it carries expectations of winning yer affection, it becomes heavy as a millstone."

"What do I do?" Ailis whispered.

Granny touched Ailis's cheek. "Listen to yer heart—it beats a unique rhythm only ye understand. Charm may dazzle, but building a life together takes more than finery and flattery."

Ailis thanked Granny for her wisdom and went outside, where the sun cast long shadows across the land.

LACHLAN STRODE THROUGH the castle's corridors, hearing the echoes of his boots against the cold floor. He had heard whispers that Ailis was beset by doubts—doubts sown by Cameron's lies. His jaw clenched at the thought.

In the pale moonlight, Lachlan saw Ailis in the courtyard below, pacing back and forth in the quiet garden. Her dark hair was subdued under the moon's gaze.

He descended the stairs, wondering what he could say to breach the walls of mistrust between them. He understood that there had been lies told about him, but he had trouble rationalizing why she didn't believe him and chose to believe Cameron instead.

"Fair evening, Ailis," Lachlan greeted as he emerged into the cool night air, his voice disguising his inner turmoil. No matter how confused she was, it was good to be with her.

She turned, her eyes reflecting the stars above. "Good eve, Lachlan," she replied guardedly.

"May I walk with ye?" he asked formally, watching her for any sign of mistrust.

"Of course," she answered.

"Is that a new shawl?" he asked.

She sighed. "Cameron gave it to me. I told him that I was not interested in pursuing our relationship, but he didn't listen. He gave me this and a brooch. I wish he'd go away."

"Well, I dinnae think much of Cameron, but I must admit that yer beautiful in the shawl. It makes yer eyes even more lovely."

Ailis smiled, blushing a little and hoping it was hidden by the darkness around them. "Thank ye." How could she mistrust a man who was so sweet and kind?

"Ye seem troubled," Lachlan ventured. "Do ye want to talk about it?"

Ailis sighed heavily. "I fear I am caught betwixt me own desires and expectations."

"And where do I stand in this tangle of thorns?" Lachlan asked.

"Ye are… a man of great merit, Lachlan. But I've been told of dalliances," she reiterated. She wanted to trust him with everything inside her, but she couldn't. Not after hearing he was kissing another.

"Tales are naught but falsehoods!" Lachlan cried, shaking his head. "'Tis Cameron's deceitful hand at play. Why would ye lend an ear to his venom over me truth?"

Ailis shook her head, filled with confusion. "I told him I would not choose him. Why would he continue to lie?"

"Let me be clear," Lachlan declared. "Me heart beats for none but ye, Ailis. If ye cannot trust me word, then what hope have we?"

Ailis met his gaze, her green eyes pools of resolve. "I sought counsel from Granny, and she bade me follow me heart. Yet, she warned that charm alone cannot sustain us."

"Yer heart knows the measure of a man, not the honeyed whispers of a rival," Lachlan insisted.

"Perhaps," Ailis conceded, hope igniting within her. "But the path I choose must withstand not just warmth, but chill winds."

"Then let us face those seasons together," Lachlan replied steadily. "I care for ye, Ailis. Ye are not a fleeting whim. I will care for ye until the day I am taken from this earth."

Ailis nodded. "I care for ye too. I just need time to sort this out in me mind."

✦

CHAPTER ELEVEN

Shortly thereafter, Ailis McAfee hurried to the cottage where Doirin, a feverish widow who had just given birth to her first child, struggled for life.

Lachlan had followed her from the keep. He stood vigil outside the cottage door, following Ailis with concerns beyond duty.

Inside the dimly lit cottage, Ailis prepared poultices for the fevered Doirin. The baby, close to the hearth, cried softly as Ailis hummed a generations-old lullaby—a soothing balm for both mother and child.

As soon as the mother was seen to, she picked up the bairn and held him close, making certain he was clean, before trying to hand him to his mother to feed.

Doirin was too feverish to understand what was happening, so Ailis put the babe at her breast.

Ailis stuck her head out the door. "I need cold water from the well. She is burning with her fever, and I must bring it down."

"Ye shouldna be here, lass," Lachlan scolded, warmth in his gruff voice. "I cannae leave ye unprotected." He called to a passing soldier. "I need ye to bring me cold water!"

The man nodded and hurried off to do what he'd been told.

Ailis shook her head. "Ye could have left long enough for ye to get cold water."

"I'm not certain of that. I worry about ye when I'm not there beside ye."

She started to ask him why he hadn't had her followed while

she was with Cameron, but she needed to give her attention to Doirin. She turned and moved back to the bed where the bairn was suckling noisily.

While he nursed, she hurried about the cottage, cleaning what she could. She always felt that a person would get better when they were in clean surroundings. Her grandmother had taught her that a woman would worry if their house was dirty, and it would take their energy from healing.

Finally, the soldier returned with the water. She put half on the stove to boil before taking the now-sleeping babe from his mother and putting him in the cradle by the hearth. There he would keep warm, and sleep while she cared for his mother.

She took the remainder of the water and moved to Doirin, rubbing a cloth with cold water over the woman's face and then her arms. She pulled her nightdress up and washed her legs, which still had blood on them. The midwife had obviously failed to clean this mother properly after she gave birth.

When she'd finished, she went back to the door where Lachlan waited. "Please get word to me family that I will be staying here for some days to come. She needs help, not only to break her fever but with the bairn."

"I will find someone to carry the message," he declared. "I'm not leaving ye here alone."

"Lachlan, yer concern is appreciated but unwarranted," Ailis replied without glancing up. "Doirin and the babe are me patients now, and I will care for them. Nothing bad has ever happened to me while I cared for the sick."

"Those duties can wait," Lachlan insisted. "The safety of a laird's daughter—and a healer at that—is not something I take lightly."

Ailis admired his stubborn loyalty despite its conflict with her independence. Clans' expectations hovered over them like ever-present mist. Nevertheless, she served life within these walls.

"Very well," she conceded with an exhausted smile. "But rest assured, Lachlan, I am far from helpless. Please see to it that me father is told where I am."

Lachlan nodded and settled into his post. He remained vigilant outside while inside Ailis ministered to Doirin. He had soldiers bring fresh meat, and she took him a meal every time she ate herself. It wasn't the most comfortable place to be, but he was thankful for the freedom to watch over her.

At dawn, Ailis tended to the hearth, warming the chilly cottage and preparing a simple broth for Doirin's recovery. On the fourth day, her fever began to subside under Ailis's care.

In the afternoon, Ailis sat by Doirin's side, weaving a tale of a fiery-haired lass conversing with stars, seeking their ancient secrets. Doirin found solace in these stories, craving comfort rather than grandeur.

Ailis knew that comforting Doirin's mind was as important as caring for her and her child. It was something she'd learned from her grandmother as a lass. She must make certain the spirits of the ill were taken care of before they could make a recovery.

Lachlan stood watch outside, prepared to protect the people inside from anything that happened. Ailis couldn't help but be grateful for his sacrifice and the hours and hours he spent guarding her.

While Ailis told her story, he listened to every word, smiling at times. She was a wonderful storyteller, and he loved to listen to her.

Ailis's story traversed enchanted forests and towering peaks, soothing the weary soul before her. In this realm, she melded her healer's touch and bard's tongue.

As evening approached, Ailis concluded her tale about the lass becoming one with the night sky.

AILIS HAD BEEN caring for the widow and her son for more than a week when she approached Doirin with a heavy question. "Ye have been a McAfee for barely a year, and yer roots lie with the Campbells. Would ye choose to stay here or return to the bosom of yer kin?" Ailis knew if she were to lose a husband when she had only been a member of his clan for a short time, she would want to go back to her clan. If the decision was made soon, Ailis could accompany Doirin to her family. It seemed the right thing to do, though she was more than willing to embrace the other woman and keep her with the McAfees forever.

Doirin turned past Ailis to the window, determination in her eyes. "Me heart yearns for home, among those who share me blood. I wish to return to the Campbells." She sighed. "I was happy enough here before me Daniel passed on, but without him here, it's hard to stay with people who I've known for a short time. Me parents would be thrilled to have me returned to them. Though, I understand it's a great deal to ask."

Ailis nodded, her decision made. "Then ye shall have yer heart's desire." She stepped outside and whispered to Lachlan what was needed. "She willnae be ready to travel for at least a few more days, but when she is, we need to see her home to the Campbell clan."

Lachlan nodded. "I'll see to it." He stopped a passing soldier and assigned him to his post and hurried off toward the keep where he could speak with her father about taking some men with them on their journey.

He was back an hour later, alerting her that men would be ready as soon as Doirin was able to travel.

Four days later, Ailis told Lachlan that it was time. Afterward, he ventured forth to gather the men they would need.

Lachlan met Ailis's gaze. "We'll guard ye well on the journey," he assured her.

With preparations underway, Ailis and Doirin watched as warriors readied their mounts. Ailis felt the pull of venturing beyond the familiar but remained steadfast to her duty. She would accompany Doirin to her homeland.

Soon, they were on their way, with Doirin riding double with one of the older McAfee men who was ready to guard her, and the babe rode with Ailis until he needed to be fed.

As the group journeyed across the McAfee boundary and into Sinclair land, Ailis's gaze wandered over the heather-speckled moors under the overcast sky. The crisp air carried a sense of impending change.

Ailis rode near Lachlan, observing his stormy sea-blue eyes as he scanned the horizon with vigilance. His posture conveyed duty and responsibility as their company's protector.

The Sinclairs were allies in name, but they were not trusted by Ailis or her father. Nay, they had proven dangerous. No matter how many times Arran claimed the kidnapping of Fiona had been Malcolm's plan alone, she believed that the laird's family had all been involved.

Ailis kept scanning the land, watching for anyone who could try to fight them.

Upon reaching a gentle rise, Ailis noticed two figures engaged in a heated exchange. Recognizing Cameron and Ian, she gasped at Cameron's appearance in Sinclair land. He even wore a Sinclair plaid! How had he fooled her?

She wasn't sure she could ever trust her judgment again because she had trusted Cameron completely. And now, she knew him to be a liar and a fraud.

She maintained her composed exterior and chose not to confront him there, surrounded by prying eyes.

Ailis offered the arguing Sinclairs a courteous nod as they passed. Lachlan, sensing her inner turmoil, asked if all was well. She held her peace for the moment. There would be a time for questions and confrontations later.

"Aye," Ailis replied, resolve in her voice. "We shall speak later, Lachlan."

Lachlan nodded, and they rode on, leaving the Sinclair lands behind.

Upon reaching Campbell land, Doirin was greeted by soldiers who knew her. Her father embraced the girl and smiled down at his grandson. "She will be safe with us," he called out to the group who had accompanied her. "I thank ye for making sure she came home to us."

As the sun set, the McClain entourage made camp upon their ancestral lands. Ailis secured a tent while glancing toward Lachlan, who directed the men with natural authority.

At twilight, she approached Lachlan. "May I have a word?" Her voice was steady but betrayed her inner struggle. She must apologize for believing Cameron, even for a moment. He had been a liar through and through.

"Of course." He led her to a quiet spot by ancient oaks.

She spoke of what she'd seen on Sinclair land: Cameron wearing their plaid and arguing with Ian. "I did not wish to believe ye... but now, I see I was mistaken."

Unable to meet his gaze, Ailis apologized for her earlier disbelief.

Lachlan's expression softened in the dim firelight as the revelation established a fragile trust between them. "I wish ye could have trusted me without proof, but I am pleased ye trust me now," he replied, his voice gentle. "Admitting when we are wrong takes courage."

"Thank ye for understanding," Ailis replied.

Ailis observed Lachlan pacing before her, and she could sense his growing frustration. "Ye say ye are sorry now." He shook his head. "But it took seeing Cameron with yer own eyes to sway yer heart."

"I have acknowledged me mistake, Lachlan," she replied steadily. "Surely ye see that I am trying to make amends."

"Trust is built upon actions, not just words." He faced her directly.

"What would ye have me do?" she asked.

"Believe in me," Lachlan answered simply, his eyes locked onto hers. "Not because ye must, but because ye choose to."

Ailis realized that her doubts had wounded him more than she had thought. His pride and honor were bound in the trust of those he held dear.

"Yer loyalty has never faltered," Ailis conceded softly. "And I did ye a great disservice by questioning it without cause."

Lachlan's voice transformed into a gentle whisper. "We must focus on the future." He reached toward her, hand outstretched. "Can I count on ye, Ailis? Will ye be able to believe in me now?"

Ailis grasped his hand, reassurance tingling through her. "Always," she answered, thankful he was even asking after she'd wounded his pride.

He nodded slightly. "'Tis time for sleep. Go to yer tent, and I'll sleep outside it to guard ye."

Ailis couldn't believe he was still so concerned with her safety, but she was grateful. And she'd find some way to make it up to him that she'd not trusted him completely.

❦

CHAPTER TWELVE

AT THE MCCLAIN keep, Ailis McAfee observed the members of the McClain clan mingling with the men who had accompanied her. Boyd McClain's grin stood out as he wove his way through the crowd. He was the youngest of the seven McClain brothers, being only fourteen.

In a moment of joviality, Boyd caught Ailis's eye before vanishing from sight. She inquired to a nearby clansman who dismissed her concern, saying Boyd was simply quick on his feet. Uncertain, she hesitantly nodded but couldn't shake the lingering confusion. He had been there one minute and was gone the next.

Later, Caitlin McClain led Ailis into the great hall, filled with the scent of roasting meats and herbs. Seated at a sturdy wooden table, an unfamiliar dish was presented—meat atop something she had never seen before.

"What is this?" Ailis asked.

"Something new from far-off lands," Caitlin replied serenely. "We call it taco meat on potatoes."

Ailis sampled the concoction. Bold flavors danced upon her tongue, offering a brief respite from duty and obligation.

"This is wonderful, Lady McClain," Ailis praised sincerely.

"It's a favorite of all me sons, but Lachlan loves it the most. As soon as yer group arrived, he asked me if we could have it for the evening meal.

"I agree with him. I want this always served if I come for a visit." Ailis didn't ask a lot of questions about the food because she'd already been told that there were several recipes that the McClains didn't share. She could happily eat it often, though, and she would make sure Lachlan knew she wanted to continue to visit his family, if only for this meal.

At twilight, Ailis and Lachlan walked along the loch's edge. The water mirrored the sky, while leaves rustled and night birds called softly. "It's so beautiful here," she whispered. "I want to jump into the loch."

Lachlan laughed. "I would agree, but it's cold this time of year. Besides, I'm not sure how me men would react to the two of us looking like drowned rats after our swim."

"Frozen drowned rats!" She couldn't help but giggle at the idea.

"We swam here every summer," Lachlan recounted. "After a long training session, there's nothing better than jumping into the loch and cooling off."

She smiled, imagining him swimming with his brothers. "Upon our return, we must address Cameron," Ailis reminded her. It wasn't something she wanted to talk about, but they must make plans for what would occur when they were back on McAfee land, and face-to-face with Cameron.

Lachlan's eyes smoldered like winter peat fires. "Leave it to me," he assured her. "Cameron will not go unchallenged."

A weighty silence fell between them before Ailis reached out, their brief touch igniting a warmth within her. He swiftly pulled her into his arms, and they shared a passionate but restrained kiss.

"Me father would not be pleased were he to see us," she whispered.

He chuckled. "He would not. But at least there will be no more talk of ye being courted by Cameron, and he'll have to agree to that."

After parting, they returned to the keep hand in hand. That night, Ailis found solace in a luxurious bed—the softness enveloping her worn form as she reflected on the sacrifices demanded by duty and her obligations to the clan.

As she lay in the bed, she thought about Lachlan, wondering if this had been his bed. She knew he was sharing a room with one of his brothers, and the thought of him sleeping in the room she used filled her dreams that night.

DAWN BROKE AS Ailis and her companions readied for their return journey. Emerging from the keep, they gratefully accepted provisions from the hospitable McClains.

Their departure carried a ritualistic farewell, hinting at alliances and unspoken trust between clans. They traveled through landscapes of moor and mountain, heather-laden paths, and murmuring streams. The rhythmic hoofbeats marked the distance between yesterday's warmth and the uncertainty ahead.

As twilight descended, Ailis's family's home appeared in the dimming light. Before its gates stood Cameron, his anticipation clashing with his stoic posture. Ailis felt his intense gaze before meeting it but refused to acknowledge him. Lachlan had stated he would deal with the man, and she would allow him to do so. She had no desire to ever speak with him again.

Firmly gripping the reins, she focused on the wooden doors offering refuge from travel and intrigue. She passed Cameron, dismissing him, and entered her home.

The wooden door to her chamber closed quietly, and Ailis drew in a breath scented with beeswax and linen. As she traced the tapestries depicting McAfee valor, she heard footsteps. Her sisters entered the room, their faces etched with concern.

"Listen closely," Ailis urged. "Cameron is not who he claims to be. He's of Clan Sinclair, and I fear his intentions are dark."

Her sisters gathered around, absorbing the gravity of her words. In the hearth's flickering glow, the room seemed to grow smaller.

"How do ye know?" Moira asked.

"I saw him in a Sinclair plaid, and he argued with Ian. His charm is but a guise," Ailis continued. "Lachlan has asked me to allow him to deal with Cameron, and I have conceded. I have no desire to ever speak with the man again."

Fiona spoke gently, "Remember, ye've chosen Lachlan McClain, and an alliance formed not just of politics, but of love as well."

Ailis nodded, acknowledging her sister's words. "Together with Lachlan, we shall face whatever storm the Sinclairs may brew. And I like the idea of a marriage with Lachlan, but he has not yet asked for the alliance to be a permanent one."

Fiona grinned. "He will. Ye can see it in his eyes when he looks at ye."

She sat with her sisters for an hour, listening to the news of the clan since she had taken up residence with Doirin. It was good to simply sit with them and understand that they supported her completely.

When her sisters left, the servants carried water into the room. As servants poured water into the tub, Ailis watched the ripples dance upon the surface. Once alone, she shed her travel-weary garments and stepped into the bath. The heat embraced her skin, and she sank beneath the water's caress.

As Ailis washed away the journey's grime, the silence around her absorbed her whispered concerns over Cameron Sinclair's deceit.

After her bath, she ate her meal in solitude, each bite fueling her for the trials ahead.

Ailis was torn between duty and her affection for Lachlan McClain. The conflict intensified as she contemplated Cameron's darker motives, wondering if his charm could have swayed her had she not been captivated by Lachlan.

AILIS ROSE, THE morning sun casting shadows across the stone floor. She dressed in silence, fastening a silver brooch at her throat. A hesitant knock sounded at the door, and she opened it to reveal Cameron Sinclair.

"Good morn, Lady Ailis," he greeted with feigned humility, "I have come to offer me sincerest apologies."

"And what are ye apologizing for, Cameron?" she asked evenly.

"Last eve, I was overzealous in me attentions toward ye," he confessed without meeting her eyes. "It was me own folly. I have not had a chance to see ye in several days, and I imagined ye would walk straight into me arms. But that didn't happen, and I could see I made ye uncomfortable."

"Yer words do not sit well with me," Ailis replied, voice cold. "Ye are a deceiver, and I want naught to do with ye. I told ye I had chosen Lachlan, and that decision stands firmly between us."

Before Cameron could respond, Laird McAfee's voice echoed in the corridor. "Cameron Sinclair, attend me in me study!" The command was sharp.

Ailis watched Cameron bow and retreat toward the laird's chambers. He hadn't seemed to realize they knew who he really was, as they'd used the name Sinclair and not McAfee.

Within the study, Laird McAfee stood behind his desk as Arran Sinclair entered. "Arran Sinclair," Laird McAfee began forcefully, "ye have sought to manipulate me daughter's affection through this man's treacherous guise of courtship. Speak now yer intent."

Laird Duncan McAfee's expression showed the difficult path ahead as he announced the termination of their clans' bond.

"Arran Sinclair," he declared, "the bond uniting our houses is now severed. Yer kin's actions destroyed our alliance's foundation. Keep yer people within yer land. We are no longer allies."

Arran Sinclair scowled, his pride obviously wounded, and left without a word or apology, his cloak billowing as if erasing all remnants of their former friendship.

Ailis, hidden in the shadows, shivered with foreboding. After Arran retreated into the distance, Ailis grappled with the potential consequences of this moment.

With Sinclair gone, her father stared at the landscape he swore to protect. Ailis observed his clenched jaw and tightened grip—symbols of resolve.

Ailis contemplated the balance between love and loyalty and how happiness may be sacrificed for duty. A tear slid down her cheek as she questioned if her choice would ignite enmity between once-united clans.

✦

CHAPTER THIRTEEN

MEANWHILE, ARRAN SINCLAIR glanced up at a soft sound and caught a shadow emerging. The man's voice cut through the stillness.

"Arran Sinclair," the man began, "the Sinclair clan stands alone, betrayed by the McAfees. A marriage between Ailis and Lachlan would seal this betrayal. Something needs to be done immediately."

Arran's gaze sharpened, acknowledging the stark truth. "What do ye propose?" he inquired.

"Kidnap Ailis before she binds herself to Lachlan," the figure suggested ominously.

"My oldest son kidnapped McAfee's daughter. It dinna work out. We need to come up with a better plan."

"There is no better plan and time is running out. Ye will do as I say, or yer clan will be left to fight the McAfees and McClains alone."

In the waning light, Arran deliberated and reluctantly nodded. He had known the McAfee lasses since they were bairns. The idea of kidnapping one was distasteful, but he'd walked along the traitorous path for too long to turn back now.

Soon inside the great hall, Arran convened with his sons, Ian and Callum, by the crackling fire. Both were eager to make an alliance with the McAfees any way they could.

"Ian, Callum," Arran began, a weight in his words. "Ailis must be taken from the McAfees."

Ian met his father's eyes as Callum absorbed the grave task ahead.

"Create chaos," Arran commanded. "Command the 'clanless' men to disrupt the McAfee borders. In that turmoil, seize Ailis. It must be done soon."

"An abduction," Ian mused aloud, calculating outcomes. "With our alliance shattered, we have little to lose. And while she is here, I can force her to marry me. It should be simple enough."

Callum nodded in silent acquiescence, resolve etched on his features.

Arran sighed wearily. "Send only our weakest soldiers to fight. Our numbers dwindle rapidly, and we must have a clan left after ye marry the lass."

AILIS RESPONDED TO an urgent call for aid. Hastily dressing, she readied herself to assist an injured woman thrown from her horse, arm twisted unnaturally. The woman was one of the best in the entire clan with horses. It didn't make sense to Ailis that she'd been injured the way she had, but she would be there to help in any way she could.

As she hurried through the great hall, she told her father where she was going. "I must tend to Kirsty, who has been thrown from her horse and has injured her arm. From the description, it sounds like it's broken, and she needs me."

Duncan frowned. "I would like ye to take a guard. I worry about yer safety."

Overhearing, Lachlan offered his unwavering support. "I will not let anything happen to her."

Duncan smiled and nodded. "See that ye dinnae."

As they navigated the rugged terrain together, Ailis cautioned, "Stay close. I fear there's more to this than is apparent. Kirsty is the best horsewoman in the clan, and she often helps with the training. This injury does not make sense."

They arrived to find Kirsty on the ground with an injury that seemed more than should have happened with a simple fall. Ailis tended to her expertly while Lachlan stood watchful and protective.

Lachlan carried Kirsty back to her cottage, where Ailis skillfully tended to her wound with practiced grace, comforting her with gentle words as Lachlan stood guard with a wary eye on their surroundings.

"Do what ye must. I understand it is broken and needs to be mended properly. I expect pain," Kirsty whispered through gritted teeth.

Ailis smiled softly, offering reassurance as she carefully set the injury. "I apologize for the pain I cause, but ye are right. It must be mended."

After the arm was set, Ailis made supper for the woman's family. It would normally be Kirsty's task, and she shouldn't be jostling the arm too much. "I hope yer family likes stew."

Kirsty nodded. "They will be happy with anything ye take the time to fix for us. I thank ye for all the trouble ye have gone to."

"It is no trouble to help me family. What happened? Ye have a reputation with horses, and it's not one of being thrown."

Kirsty shook her head. "I am not certain. I was riding, making certain the horse was tamed enough for its new owner, and it stumbled over a rock that was not there yesterday. It threw me." She sighed. "Dinna worry. The horse is fine."

Ailis smiled. "Ye are a great deal more important to this clan than any horse."

Kirsty glowered at her feet for a moment. "I feel as if I've done something wrong."

Ailis sat beside the woman on her bed. "Ye did yer job, and there was an injury. How could that be yer fault? I am glad someone came for me so quickly." She carefully patted the other woman's hand. "The stew is ready for supper. If ye need me to cook other meals for yer children, send someone to me. I am always willing to help."

"Me mother is next door. She will cook for us. All will be well."

Ailis nodded. "I'm willing to help if ye need it." She stood and walked to the door, frowning when she saw that Lachlan was no longer standing guard. Where had he gone?

It made no sense that he'd left in the space of an hour when he'd spent days and days waiting as she'd healed Doirin.

There was a great commotion she hadn't noticed until that moment. She called to a child who was standing not far from her. "What has happened?"

"Clanless men are attacking again!" a boy called to her.

Ailis frowned. She had heard of no other clans being attacked by these men, but they seemed to plague the McAfees. "Thank ye!" She was certain Lachlan had gone to help with the battle, and she set out for the keep alone.

When two soldiers in McAfee plaids came up on either side of Ailis, she frowned. She didn't recognize these men, and she knew most of the soldiers. "Is the battle over?" she asked.

Each of the soldiers took one of her arms and changed her direction. With everyone distracted by the battle they knew was taking place, no one noticed when she was forced over the border to Sinclair land.

Ailis's heart pounded as thoughts of her family and Lachlan raced through her mind. Would they know of her plight or believe she vanished like mist over the moors?

As the soldiers quickened their pace, Ailis knew this was another betrayal by the Sinclairs. She turned cold with dread, wondering what the Sinclairs intended. Now they had kidnapped two daughters of the laird of Clan McAfee, and they would be brought to justice. There was no doubt in her mind.

A spark of defiance ignited within her. She would not submit without contest. Though they had caught her by surprise, Ailis was a strong woman, and she would find a way back to the people she loved. And the Sinclairs would pay a price for their treachery.

For now, she was a captive on an uncertain path, her destiny intertwined with men who saw her as nothing more than a means to an end—a jewel in pursuit of power.

"Let us face what comes," Lachlan called, his voice commanding as they braced for battle. While Alisdair led the McAfee men, Lachlan led the McClain men who were still with Clan McAfee.

As foes descended upon them, blades clashed in a frenzied dance of steel and valor.

Grunts and shouts of battle cries filled the air as fighters engaged in fierce combat.

Lachlan led his comrades into the fray with unwavering resolve—each swing of his sword driven by duty and loyalty.

In the chaos of battle, their unity strengthened—a bond forged in blood and sweat that transcended mere alliances.

With unyielding determination, Lachlan fought on despite exhaustion looming over him. He fought not just for victory but for those who depended on him for protection and guidance.

The fight continued for more than an hour, every clash of steel echoing through the moors—a testament to their unbreakable resolve as they faced their enemies head-on.

Finally, the few soldiers of the clanless men who still stood turned and ran, and Lachlan called to let them go. There was no use chasing after them. Soon they would be back for another fight, as that's all they seemed to do.

The clamor of battle subsided, leaving only the echo of steel and the panting of exhausted men. Lachlan moved purposefully through the remnants of the fray, his thoughts on Ailis.

He broke into a run and approached the cottage where he had left her. As he neared the threshold, he knew something was wrong. The door swung lightly in the breeze—an ominous invitation.

"Where is she?" His voice emerged barely above a whisper but heavy with dread.

Kirsty lay sleeping on the bed, but there was nothing else to see. He didn't wake the woman and instead, went to talk to anyone close, hoping they had seen what was happening.

He asked several people if they knew where Ailis had gone, but everyone claimed she had gone toward the keep. He raced there, hoping she'd made it safely, but something in the pit of his stomach told him otherwise.

Back at the keep, she was nowhere to be found. She hadn't been seen since morning.

"Alisdair! Brodie!" he called, his voice piercing the stillness.

Bound by blood and common cause, the brothers arrived hastily. Alisdair's eyes met Lachlan's with shared understanding while Brodie surveyed the scene attentively.

"Spread the word," Lachlan commanded, "Ailis is missing."

Brodie studied Lachlan. "I wonder if the attack was to distract us so they could take her. We've all thought that the attacks were by the Sinclairs."

"I hope not," Lachlan huffed, praying they didn't have Ailis.

The McAfee men, burdened with the aftermath of conflict, dispersed into the evening. They searched the land. Whispers of a sighting—two soldiers escorting a captive toward Sinclair lands—stirred them into action.

The boy who had told the tale was barely able to speak he was so nervous. "I thought it was Lady Ailis, but I couldna tell for certain," he said looking down at his feet as his whispered words reached the large man in front of him.

"Sinclair lands?" Brodie questioned.

"We must go there," declared Lachlan. He looked down at the boy who couldn't have been more than six or seven. "Ye did well. Now we ken where to find her."

The boy nodded, smiling slightly.

Lachlan was more afraid than ever before. Ailis must be all

right. He couldn't imagine what he would do without her in his life.

Feeling the pull of duty, Lachlan understood they would be in enemy lands and must be ready to defend themselves.

"Ready yerselves," he commanded. "We must find Ailis."

The three brothers put their heads together and whispered about plans and strategies. Only the three of them would go into Sinclair lands, as it would be easier to hide the three of them than an army.

IN SINCLAIR KEEP, Arran Sinclair penned a message with ruthless intent. "Deliver this to Duncan McAfee without delay," he ordered his swiftest rider. "Inform him that Ailis's life is at stake if she refuses to marry me son Ian."

As the messenger rode into the night, a somber expression crossed Arran's face. He had no problem with betraying the McAfees, but taking lasses prisoner made him feel as if he was doing evil work. But he knew he must obey the mystery man if he was to be second in command, and he longed for the power that would bring.

"LET US HURRY," Lachlan urged. "We must reach Ailis before dawn. I worry that she will be hurt or killed. She will not give in to their demands. Not Ailis."

They ventured into enemy territory. Approaching Sinclair castle cautiously, they knew Arran Sinclair held an unyielding heart.

"Ye ken we maynae be welcome here," Alisdair muttered at the threshold.

"Then let us hope our words will shield us as well as any

dirk," Brodie added, hand on his sword hilt.

In the great hall, Lachlan didn't waver. The Sinclairs watched the McClain brothers with spear-sharp eyes. No one came to fight with them, but it seemed as if everyone held their breath as they waited to see what the brothers would do.

"We seek an audience with yer laird," Lachlan declared. "We've grave matters to discuss."

"Ye accuse us of treachery?" a Sinclair elder asked coldly.

Lachlan replied calmly, "Accusations are unnecessary. We seek only truth… and Ailis McAfee's safe return."

"Ye come here demanding without proof." Ian shook his head. "I'm offended by the very sight of ye.

"Proof lies in the absence of doubt," Lachlan countered. "And there is none left to shelter behind. 'Twas Sinclair men who took her."

The Sinclairs exchanged glances. Lachlan observed them closely, searching for any sign of Ailis's location.

"Grant us time to confer," Callum finally spoke without emotion. "Return on the morrow, and ye shall have yer answers."

Lachlan bowed, honoring the parley customs while suppressing his impatience. Turning to his brothers, their unspoken vow united them: Ailis must be found, regardless of obstacles or adversaries.

AILIS MCAFEE SAT on the only chair in her tower prison. At the sight of the distant hills, she yearned for her lost freedom. The heavy door creaked open, breaking the silence.

Ian Sinclair appeared in the doorway, demanding attention despite any attempted charm. "Ye must ken how much I desire ye, Ailis," he began, a certain hardness underlining his words. "Will ye no' do me the honor of becoming me wife?"

"I will not, Ian Sinclair," she replied, standing firm. "Not today, nor any other day."

His jaw clenched, irritation crossing his features. "Then here ye shall remain until ye see reason."

"I do see reason. I see that ye have taken me against me will. Me father's men will end ye." Ailis spat decisively at his feet.

HOURS PASSED BEFORE Ian returned with gifts: a bouquet of wildflowers and a meal carefully prepared. He presented them as if they could soften her heart.

"See here, lass, how deep me love for ye runs," he began. "I canna let ye go. An' I'll do what I must to protect yer kin. Dinnae make me cause their suffering."

Ailis looked at the flowers with disdain and stomped on them without a word.

"Ye dinnae know how to love," she declared, standing above the crushed flowers. "I will not be bartered for the safety of me clan."

The tension between them was palpable, a battle of wills with freedom at stake. Despite her heartache for her people, her spirit remained unbroken within the tower that had become her prison.

As the sun cast long shadows across the tower chamber's stone floor, Ailis watched Ian Sinclair's silhouette darken her doorway. His frame was tense with determination, his hair catching the last light as if crowning him with a halo he didn't deserve.

"Sweet Ailis," he began, voice fervent but eyes cold, "I desire nothing more than to have ye as me bride."

He advanced toward her without invitation, the air between them charged with tension. The weight of Ailis's plight was heavier than ever. She could see his knife tucked into a scabbard in his belt. If she could just reach it, she knew she could best him.

"Ye know this, dinnae ye?" His words were more plea than

question as he reached out and cupped her face.

Before she could protest, his lips claimed hers with forceful intent. But Ailis McAfee had a core of steel forged by love for her clan and longing for freedom.

With fierce indignation, she stomped on Ian's foot. His grip faltered as he grunted, their lips still locked.

Then, with untamed spirit, she bit down on his lip. The taste of iron flooded her mouth as blood welled up from the wound. Ian stumbled back, hand flying to his wounded mouth, eyes ablaze with shock and something akin to respect.

"Ye may take me freedom for now, Ian Sinclair," Ailis declared despite her racing heart. "But ye'll never take me will. Me soul belongs to me and the McAfee clan. Remember that."

As Ian touched his lip and saw his bloodied fingers, her words hung in the air—undeniable and powerful. In that tower room where personal desires clashed with political plans, Ailis stood unyielding. Her duty to herself and her people outweighed any forced affection he might offer.

LACHLAN MCCLAIN'S BOOTS sank into the damp earth, his brothers flanking him as they strode through the Sinclair lands. The morning mist clung to the rolling hills, concealing the quiet village near the McAfee border. Urgency pulsed through Lachlan with each step.

"Have ye seen a lass by the name of Ailis? She would have been with two Sinclair soldiers," he asked, scanning each villager for recognition. "She has dark hair and green eyes, and stands about this tall." He held his hand up just above his shoulder.

Alisdair approached with precision. "Aye, we must ken where she has been taken."

Brodie canvassed gently, probing the villagers.

Finally, a widow emerged. Her hollowed eyes met Lachlan's.

"I mayhap ken where the lass be," she whispered, too afraid to speak with them.

Lachlan leaned in. "Tell us, and I will grant any boon within me power."

"Promise me," she implored, "a place 'neath the McAfee name, far from the laird and his sons."

"Upon me life, ye shall have it," Lachlan vowed, his words echoing unyielding bonds of kinship and protection.

In the widow's gaze, hope flickered, and was apparent through the fear.

"And ye will take me to safety before ye attempt to rescue her?" she asked.

Lachlan nodded reluctantly. He didn't want to wait to rescue Ailis, but he had to know where she was before he could help her.

The widow whispered, "She be in the east tower." Her eyes darted nervously. Clutching her children's hands, she followed Lachlan across the hills toward McAfee lands—sanctuary.

Crossing the border, the widow's shoulders lightened as if McAfee air itself promised peace and protection.

Close to the McAfee village, Lachlan addressed two soldiers. "We have vowed to shelter this woman and her children," he declared, gesturing toward the family clinging to hope.

"Aye, we'll find 'em a proper hearth and home," one soldier agreed. They all feared for the lass who had been taken from them and understood immediately how important it was to help this woman.

"Thank ye." The widow bowed her head briefly.

With sanctuary assured, the widow and her offspring were escorted to a cottage on McAfee lands.

In the starless sky, Lachlan, Alisdair, and Brodie crossed the shadowy moor toward the east tower of Sinclair Castle. Lachlan studied the shape of the tower, hoping that his Ailis was all right.

Under the cloak of night, they crept closer to the tower. Silence accompanied them until a sudden clamor revealed their presence to Sinclair guards.

"Stand down, McClains," a guard commanded.

Steel clashed as the brothers fought, but Alisdair soon called for retreat against overwhelming numbers. Frustration filled them as they withdrew, leaving Ailis behind.

FROM A COZY cottage within the safety of McAfee lands, the widow held her children close, praying for those who risked everything. And thanking God they had given her sanctuary.

CHAPTER FOURTEEN

I N THE GREAT hall of Duncan McAfee's keep, four men surrounded an oak table laden with history. Lachlan McClain shattered the silence.

"Laird McAfee, we must act while Ailis remains captive within Sinclair's walls," Lachlan implored, eyes burning with determination. "We need to gather our forces—both McAfee and McClain—and storm their castle."

Duncan, experienced in leadership, met Lachlan's ardor with a measured expression. "Yer courage is admirable, but patience," he advised softly. "An army will hasten her end. I fear the Sinclairs would slay her before we breach their gate."

Alisdair agreed silently, his assessing eyes revealing a strategic mind. Brodie stood apart, contemplative.

"How shall we proceed to rescue Ailis without condemning her?" Lachlan asked, seriousness replacing his usual cheer. "We canna do anything that would put her at risk."

Duncan steepled his fingers, signaling a clever scheme taking shape. "Subtlety. Guile where force would fail." He paused, picturing their path forward. "We'll devise a plan that saves Ailis without bloodshed. Our honor demands it."

IN THE TOWER chamber, Ailis McAfee paced restlessly. She was used to being outdoors daily, and her confinement in the tower was going to make her crazy. She had to get out of there and soon.

The door creaked open. Ian entered, his once charming smile now laced with cruelty. "Me bonny Ailis," he began with a silky voice, "I've come to ask ye again, will ye not consent to be me bride?"

Ailis turned to face him, her green eyes fierce and defiant. "I widnae marry ye if ye were the last man in all of Scotland," she declared.

Unfazed, Ian moved closer, intent clear in his gaze. He pulled her into his arms and kissed her without permission. Ailis resisted, stomping on his foot and biting his lip. "Yer very touch sickens me," she uttered through gritted teeth.

Ian stumbled back, anger mixed with grudging admiration in his eyes. Ailis held her ground, her heart pounding. Ian had met his match with her, and she would happily do something she'd vowed as a healer never to do. She would kill him if given the opportunity. The realization that she would take a life and not feel guilt for it shocked her to her core. How could she be so cruel as to kill a man, and not feel as if she would burn in hell? It made no sense to her.

But she knew if she could get her hands on a knife, she would throw it straight through his black heart without hesitation.

OUTSIDE THE KEEP'S walls, Lachlan and his brothers approached in disguise. Cloaked in Sinclair colors and false locks of hair, they moved toward the tower with unwavering resolve.

Upon entering the bailey, Lachlan scanned for any sign of recognition while moving swiftly. As they neared the stairwell, however, Sinclair guards emerged, glaring suspiciously. Forced to speak with them rather than risk discovery, Lachlan engaged them in conversation while secretly agonizing over the urgency of their mission.

"Apologies, good sirs," Lachlan began calmly. "We seek audience with our chieftain on matters most pressing."

"Ye'll find no passage here," one guard replied, barring the way. "Be off with ye, 'ere trouble finds yer necks."

Lachlan withdrew alongside Alisdair and Brodie, their retreat hiding the frustration that threatened to boil over. They left the keep with tension in their shoulders, aware that a more daring plan was now necessary.

Lachlan's jaw clenched as he beheld the Sinclair guards, their eyes narrow with suspicion. Despite the failed ruse, determination burned within him. He would not leave without assurance of Ailis's well-being.

"Before we depart," Lachlan addressed the guard, "I must insist upon speaking with Lady Ailis. I need to know she remains unharmed before any negotiation can commence between our clans."

The soldiers exchanged wary glances but ultimately could not deny his request. They didn't want a full-out war any more than the McClain men did. "Very well," the lead guard conceded, gesturing for Lachlan to follow. "Ye may speak to her through the door. No more."

Lachlan climbed solemnly. He would give anything to be able to see Ailis and verify that she was all right, but he understood it couldn't happen.

At last, they stood before a heavy wooden door holding Ailis behind its barrier. The guards positioned themselves like sentinels, watching Lachlan closely.

"Ailis," Lachlan called, his voice resonating against the oak. "It is I, Lachlan. I need to know ye are safe and unharmed."

"Lachlan? Yer presence warms me heart. I am well enough, though bored in this dreary tower."

He chuckled softly. Only Ailis would complain of boredom while she was kept prisoner. "I regret that I didna think to bring ye something to do. Perhaps I could return with needlepoint or even something for ye to practice throwing."

"Next time bring me a distraction then," she called back. "I'm tired of being trapped here with nothing to do but pace back and forth. A knife would be lovely because I could practice me aim through the window here. Do ye think ye could bring a knife?"

He chuckled softly. She truly brought joy to his life, even when she was held prisoner. "I feel that bringing ye a knife would be frowned upon by yer captors. Hold fast, Ailis," he replied in a tone carrying a promise. "We shall devise a means to return ye to the warmth of yer home and hearth."

He nodded to the guards and descended the stairs, his mind working on a plan that would reunite Ailis with her kin. And with him. The most important thing in his mind was being able to hold her close once again.

LACHLAN FACED HIS brothers, Alisdair and Brodie, in the courtyard. "We must inform Duncan of our findings. Each moment wasted is another with Ailis still captive."

Brodie nodded. "We must act swiftly." He glanced up toward the tower as if trying to see through the walls.

Inside the McAfee keep, Duncan awaited their news. "Ailis remains unharmed but weary," Lachlan reported. "She complained I should have brought her a distraction for her boredom."

Duncan smiled. "Me daughters are the bravest lasses in all of Scotland!"

Lachlan nodded. "They are. But I do worry that she will try something dangerous if she is not rescued soon." He sighed. "She asked me to bring her a knife so she could work on throwing them more accurately."

"Ailis would ask for a knife. I expect nothing less from her. Patience must be our ally as we devise a cunning plan to restore her," Duncan replied.

"Laird," he began, "We should muster our forces and strike at Sinclair's borders. Our combined might could create confusion to mask our true intent—liberating Ailis while their men are engaged. They have lost a great many soldiers to our swords. They would be afraid of losing more."

Duncan considered the proposal, the weight of responsibility apparent on his face. Finally, he nodded. "Yer courage is commendable, but such an endeavor demands precision. Give us a day or two to marshal resources and devise a scheme that ensures Ailis's return and our honor intact."

Lachlan's shoulders relaxed slightly as he acknowledged the laird's decision—the promise of action pacifying his restless spirit. He stepped back, resolved for the trials ahead. "Should we call upon the McClain allies?" he asked.

Duncan shook his head. "We can handle this ourselves. Their army was never what I would call good, and they have dwindled recently in their attempts to attack us."

ONCE AGAIN, IAN interrupted Ailis's thoughts as he joined her in the tower. "Have ye changed yer mind? Are ye ready to marry me and leave this tower?"

"Have ye changed yer mind? Are ye ready to let me go so more blood is not spilled? Have ye thought of how many men ye've already lost in this endeavor?" she countered.

"Ye are a ridiculous lass, expecting me to give up. Ye realize, all the fighting between our clans would be over if ye just would agree to this marriage."

"Ye realize letting me go is the only way ye will get out of this predicament alive? It won't be yer father the McAfee men go after. Twill be ye. They know ye are the one to take me. They know ye are a truly evil person. They will kill ye. Mayhap, they will even torture ye before." She grinned. "Mayhap they will allow me to be the one to torture ye. Have ye seen me skills with a knife? I've never flayed a man alive, but ye make me think it would be a fun way to alleviate me boredom here."

Ian shook his head. "Yer as stubborn as an old goat!"

She chuckled. "Mayhap I am. But ye are as stupid as one."

She was relieved when he left the tower without another word, closing the door behind him. She smiled. She could best him in words and with a knife. And she would be rescued by the combined forces of the McClains and McAfees. Soon, she had no doubt.

LACHLAN STUDIED THE grand table covered in maps and missives, fingers tracing routes toward the Sinclair stronghold. Wax and wood smoke filled the air, evidence of countless strategic hours spent here.

"Here," he muttered, touching the tower imprisoning Ailis. An involuntary smirk emerged as duty aligned with personal desire—rescuing her meant strategy and heartfelt purpose.

"Brother," Brodie broke the silence, "we cannot delay. Striking at dawn brings surprise."

Lachlan agreed. "Brute force won't suffice. I'll lead. They'll watch for me. They'll know we are there to rescue Ailis if I am not with the army. Well, they'll know if we come that we're setting about rescuing Ailis, but I think there is less chance of being recognized immediately if Brodie is the one to fetch her from the tower."

"I'll take to shadows," Brodie resolved. "Retrieve Ailis unseen."

The decision settled within Lachlan's heart. "Yer talent for invisibility is crucial. I would prefer to rescue her meself, but it just is not possible this time."

"Then it's decided." The brothers stood united in determination.

"I am glad she didn't seem lost. She hasn't lost any hope. That hope shall save us both," Lachlan whispered.

Memorizing every map detail, Lachlan steeled himself for action with thoughts of rescuing Ailis from her cold prison. He would face any devil for her.

"Prepare yerself, brother," he urged, approaching the door. "We ride at first light."

CHAPTER FIFTEEN

LACHLAN AND ALISDAIR faced their assembled armies—the McAfees and McClains. The cool morning air crackled with tension. The silence was heavy with unspoken anticipation.

"Men!" Alisdair's voice boomed across the ranks. "Today, we fight for justice, for family, and for the honor of our clans! Ailis McAfee is held prisoner by our former allies, the Sinclairs! We will fight to the last man to get her back!"

Lachlan's gaze swept over the soldiers before him, his jaw set in unwavering determination. Not a word was spoken as the brothers nodded at each other, a silent agreement passing between them.

They could not trust the army with the entire plan, for fear there were Sinclair sympathizers among them. Instead, they would share the need for battle and let Brodie do the work of liberating Ailis.

Alisdair and Lachlan signaled the advance.

An eerie quiet settled over the battlefield as they neared Sinclair territory. A sparse line of Sinclair soldiers awaited them, a clear sign of deception.

"Is this some kind of jest?" Lachlan's voice cut through the stillness.

"Seems they mistake our resolve for weakness," Alisdair replied with a wry smile. "Let us show them otherwise."

"Or it could be a trap," Lachlan cautioned, his senses alert.

With a fierce battle cry, Alisdair raised his sword high, signaling the charge. The ground shook beneath their feet as their warriors surged forward like a wave crashing upon the unsuspecting Sinclairs.

The clash of steel rang out like thunder as blades met in a symphony of war. The metallic scent of blood filled their nostrils as they fought tooth and nail on the unforgiving battleground.

Cornered but unyielding, the Sinclair soldiers rallied against the onslaught. Swords clashed in a cacophony of violence, each strike fueled by desperation and defiance.

Lachlan and Alisdair fought side by side, their movements synchronized as if guided by an unspoken understanding. They carved a path through their enemies with calculated precision, leaving chaos and destruction in their wake.

Lachlan fought as if his life depended on it, knowing that the life he wanted—with Ailis—did. All he could think about was making sure to cause enough of a distraction that Brodie could rescue her.

As they pushed forward, the imposing silhouette of the fortress loomed ahead—a foreboding challenge that beckoned them closer. Ailis awaited them within those formidable stone walls, her fate hanging in the balance. But Lachlan couldn't dwell on the lass. Nay, he had to fight!

The battle raged on around them, each moment fraught with danger and intensity. The brothers knew that the true test lay ahead on those treacherous steps leading to their final prize—Ailis.

And so, with grim determination etched on their faces, Lachlan and Alisdair charged onward into the heart of the enemy stronghold, ready to face whatever trials lay in wait.

Lachlan's sword clashed against the Sinclair soldier's blade, the steel ringing out like a battle cry in the morning air. With a fierce scowl, he pushed forward, his muscles taut with anticipation. Each strike was calculated, precise, and deadly.

"Ye fight well for a McClain," the enemy taunted, a smirk playing on his lips.

Lachlan met his words with a snarl, his grip tightening on his sword hilt. "And ye talk too much for a man about to face Judgment Day."

Their swords met with a resounding clang, the force of their clash reverberating through the keep. Lachlan's focus was unwavering as he pressed on, driving his opponent back step by step.

The Sinclair soldier grunted under the strain of Lachlan's relentless assault. "Ye'll regret the day ye decided to war with the Sinclairs."

With a swift twist of his wrist, Lachlan disarmed his foe, sending the sword clattering to the floor. "Regret is for those who survive," he shot back, raising his blade for the final blow.

As the defeated soldier crumpled to the ground, Lachlan's attention turned toward the tower where Ailis was held captive. His path was blocked by two formidable opponents, their stance ready and waiting.

"Stand aside if ye value yer lives," Lachlan warned.

"Even if we wanted to betray our laird, the punishment would be death! We would rather die in battle than by the hand of the laird's sons!" one of them replied.

The guards exchanged a knowing look before lunging at him in unison. Lachlan met their attack head-on, his strikes swift and deadly as he sought to break through their defenses.

Meanwhile, Brodie fought valiantly on another front, his breath coming in ragged gasps as he faced off against a group of Sinclair soldiers. Each swing of his sword was met with a fierce counterattack, but he held his ground with determination blazing in his eyes.

AILIS WATCHED OUT the window of the tower, her fists clenched in silent support of her rescuers. The clash of steel filled every corner of the chamber, each strike echoing off the stone walls. The scent of sweat and metal permeated the air as combatants fought tooth and nail for supremacy.

She knew that every blow struck in her name brought them closer to victory, closer to freedom.

Outside, the battle raged on unabated, the cries of men mingling with the clash of swords and shields. The fate of clans hung in the balance as each warrior fought with all their might.

Ailis hated that her father's men were in danger because of her, but she knew they did the right thing, for she would rather die than marry Ian—or any other Sinclair for that matter.

The guards rushed down the stairs to fight, leaving Ailis's prison unprotected. She tried to open the door. Without hesitation, she hurried down the stairs, willing to help fight in any way she could. Although she was a woman, she was the daughter of Duncan McAfee, who was renowned for his fighting abilities. Thus, she'd been taught to fight as a man.

As she reached the bottom of the tower, the distant clamor of battle washed over her. In the middle of the chaos stood Brodie McClain, his eyes locking onto hers. Without a word, she ran to him, taking the knife he offered.

She didn't think twice as she threw it and it hit her target, going straight into the heart of a man from Clan Sinclair. She picked up another knife that had been the property of a fallen soldier, throwing that as well. After she killed another, the enemy slowly backed away.

Brodie guided Ailis across uneven terrain toward the McAfee border. Simultaneously, Lachlan McClain fought fiercely on the battlefield, his gaze catching a glimpse of his brother leading Ailis to safety. Relief surged through him, knowing she was unharmed.

He called upon his men. "Take no prisoners!" The soldiers

pressed forward with renewed determination for a future beyond this battle. Lachlan's sword moved with lethal grace while thoughts of Brodie and Ailis lingered.

Lachlan and Alisdair exchanged a determined glance before ascending the slick steps of Sinclair keep. Their swords sliced through the tense air as they climbed, ready for battle.

At the summit, Ian launched his attack, but Alisdair's swift parry created an opportunity for Lachlan. His precise strike sealed Ian's fate. Together, they hurled his lifeless body out the window to rally their own warriors.

Descending the stairs in victory, Lachlan confronted Laird Arran and a trembling Callum among the defeated.

"Arran, yer resistance has failed. Ye and yer son must yield. Though ye'll be confined within McAfee walls, know that mercy was granted today." The silence was palpable as he spoke.

Both Arran and Callum laid down their arms, choosing to live another day. Lachlan was a bit disappointed. He'd wanted to run them both through, but they would live remembering their cowardice. It was enough.

In the shadow of the towering keep, Lachlan stood, marked by bloodshed. Ailis was safe, and she would remain that way.

FROM HIS HILLTOP vantage, Clyde Stewart observed the fallen keep of Clan Sinclair below. The McAfees and McClains had left destruction in their wake, and Lachlan stood triumphant among the rubble. A formidable foe.

Stewart knew the strategy must change. Aspiring to rule the highlands, he could no longer rely on the weakness of others. Strength and cunning would carry him to victory. His mind weaved new threads of conspiracy and influence.

As daylight retreated, a steely resolve settled upon Stewart's face. Events set in motion today would ripple through time. For now, he disappeared into the gathering dusk—a specter of ambition waiting for the moment to seize what was rightfully his.

✦

CHAPTER SIXTEEN

T RAMPLED SINCLAIR BANNERS lay in the mud, signaling their army's defeat. Lachlan huffed, his worry and relief mingling like the Highland mist. He needed Ailis.

"Alisdair," he called, "Lead our men. Attend to the wounded. I ride for the keep."

Mounting his steed, Lachlan spurred it forward, racing toward the McAfee keep. The gates opened upon his arrival, and he dismounted with urgency.

The great hall hinted at past turmoil, now subdued. There stood Ailis, with her sisters Fiona and Moira fussing over her. Her green eyes met his, dissipating the chaos.

"Ailis," he began, striding toward her, "Forgive me for taking so long to rescue ye. Our first thought was to do it without loss of life, but that wasn't possible." His voice bore leadership's weight and sacrifice.

"I am here and unharmed," Ailis reassured them, though shadows lingered in her tone.

Approaching her side, Lachlan attempted a smile that didn't reach his troubled eyes.

"What of Ian?" she asked.

"Alisdair and I dealt with him," Lachlan answered decisively. "His father and brother are at Clan McAfee's mercy."

Fiona and Moira retreated, leaving Ailis with Lachlan. Seating himself beside her, his presence offered silent protection.

"Ye have a mark upon yer cheek," he noted, fingers brushing

her skin gently. His gaze, reminiscent of winter's chill, focused on the bruise.

Ailis faced him, green eyes displaying warmth as she admitted her clumsiness during the tower's descent. "I slipped on one of the steps and fell against the wall. I'm fine, though."

"None laid hands upon ye?" Lachlan asked, gazing into her eyes and praying no one had hurt her.

"None," she assured him. "Well, Ian did, but I stomped on his foot and bit his lip. I feel as if I defended meself well. I am whole, Lachlan, saved by ye and Clan McAfee." Her profound gratitude shone through her gaze.

Lachlan embraced her tightly, his arms solid as stone. Within his hold, they found solace, reassured by each other's steady heartbeats. He whispered into her hair, their breaths harmonizing like life's relentless rhythm.

IN THE KEEP'S great hall, Ailis sat silently with Lachlan. Duncan's boots echoed as he approached.

"Daughter," he called, "Are ye ready to face Arran and Callum? Ye must mete out justice for their transgressions."

Rising from Lachlan's arms, Ailis locked her green eyes on Duncan. "Father, I shall hear what they have to say." Though her heart quivered, she accepted the responsibility.

Duncan nodded and stepped aside. Ailis entered the chamber where Callum and Arran were held. Shadows clung to the walls as Arran wove a tale of deceit and manipulation.

"I swear it wasn't me own volition," he answered tremulously. "A dark, unseen hand compelled our actions."

"And who was controlling this dark, unseen hand?" Ailis asked.

Arran shook his head. "I have no idea. He always appeared to me in shadows."

Ailis regarded him with a neutral expression. Beside him, Callum remained silent, neither confirming nor denying his father's account.

"Speak, Callum Sinclair," Ailis commanded. "Do ye have anything to add?"

Callum shook his head. "I was never told of the man Father speaks of. We were told we must have an alliance with the McAfees before winter, or our people would starve. So me brothers and I went about attempting to court ye and yer sisters. We followed orders, but we were not part of planning what was to happen. We were told to take ye from McAfee lands, and that's what we did."

Arran glared at his last living son. "Ye could tell them I speak the truth."

Callum sighed. "I know not whether ye speak the truth, Father. I do not know whether ye are speaking the truth now, or if ye did when ye spoke to us before."

Ailis observed the two men, feeling the gravity of her decision.

Ailis's solemn gaze fell upon the two bound men. "And what of yer people, the Sinclairs?" she asked icily. "Without a leader, what becomes of yer clan?"

Arran shifted uneasily, avoiding Ailis's unyielding stare. Callum remained stoic, clearly unconcerned for those who once obeyed his every whim. Their silence conveyed self-preservation rather than stewardship.

"Speak," Ailis demanded. Yet their apathy persisted, revealing their indifference to their kin and lands.

With a sorrowful sigh, Ailis turned and approached the oak door, grabbing the iron handle. She hesitated, torn between the healer's heart and the chieftain's duty.

Twice this day, she had crossed the line and killed men out of necessity. It weighed heavily on her soul. Could she condemn these men? They wreaked havoc but now they were simply pathetic. They did not need to die for her to live.

Ailis McAfee could find no solace in retribution. She stepped through the doorway, burdened by command.

Ailis entered the great hall, steps echoing softly against ancient stones that witnessed countless councils. The air was still as she found them waiting—Duncan, Alisdair, Lachlan, and Brodie.

"Ye have me gratitude." Ailis's voice carried both strength and weariness. Her gaze rested on Brodie. His eyes held quiet understanding. Gracefully, she approached him, kissed his cheek, and whispered, "Yer bravery has not gone unnoticed. I thank ye for the rescue."

Addressing the gathered men, Ailis continued, "The Sinclairs are vanquished. Their kin must now choose—to join our clan or rebuild their own under a virtuous leader." Her proposal hung in the air as she sought her brethren's counsel. "I must think more about what to do with the laird and Callum. They do not deserve to live, but I am not certain I can order them killed and still have a clear conscience."

As murmurs of agreement rose around her, Lachlan stepped forward. "Come, let us walk," he suggested with affection.

They strolled through the keep's gardens to a small clearing where the widow who had helped them stood alone. "Elspeth," Lachlan announced softly. "She gave us yer location when we couldnae find ye," he whispered to Ailis.

Ailis approached the widow whose courage had changed their fate. "Ye have me deepest thanks." She clasped Elspeth's hand. "Please let me know if there is anything we can do to help ye and yer family settle on our lands."

Elspeth nodded with a smile that showed resilience and fortitude. In her eyes, Ailis saw the essence of Clan McAfee—strength, loyalty, and commitment to kin. "I would be forever grateful if ye would allow me to serve in the keep. I am a good cook, and I need work."

Ailis smiled. "Come to the keep in the morning, and I will introduce ye to Granny. She is the head cook, and she will be happy for the help."

Elspeth smiled. "Thank ye."

"Nay, thank ye for yer aid, even when it went against yer laird."

"I did what was right, as I always try to do."

As Lachlan guided Ailis deeper into the woods, ancient trees interlaced above them. Ailis's thoughts were tangled with recent events, but Lachlan's presence eased her slightly.

"Ye ken how I feared for ye," Lachlan spoke, weighted by concern. "When I discovered yer capture, 'twas devastating. I'm so sorry I left ye when I was supposed to be standing guard. I will never forgive meself for that."

Ailis glanced up at Lachlan. His eyes reflected both worry and relief. "I do not blame ye. And I'm fine now. I'm happy to be home where I belong."

"Knowing ye are safe once more... It pleases me beyond measure."

Before she could respond, he stepped closer and cupped her cheek gently. His touch was soothing yet filled with unspoken promises.

Their lips met in a fervent kiss that sought to banish fear and affirm life. They kissed again, each caress an echo of longing endured apart. In the forest's serenity, they found solace in each other's embrace.

Lachlan put everything he had into the kiss, as if he could protect her from the world's cruelties through love alone. She accepted each offering. His arms healed wounds seen and unseen.

In Lachlan's arms, Ailis momentarily forgot her burdens. She was a woman reunited with the man who captured her heart. As the woods stood watch, the future—with its trials and triumphs—lurked just beyond the horizon.

CHAPTER SEVENTEEN

I N A DIMLY lit chamber in the territory of Clan Gordon, Clyde Stewart addressed the circle of lairds he had come to trust. He spoke quietly of the failed alliance with the Sinclairs and Ailis's feelings for Lachlan McClain. "We must reassess and weave new alliances," he declared. "The Sinclair clan has been defeated and we must find another way to keep the McAfees and the McClains from strengthening their alliance. I want us allied with the McAfees."

Laird Gordon nodded. "Me clan is allied with the McAfees. Perhaps it would be good if me son, Lucas, courted Ailis. He is a much better warrior than any McClain and a true gentleman."

The other lairds listened intently, their eyes betraying the strategy forming within. Laird MacKenzie suggested his own son Bearnard, while Laird Cameron offered his son Horas. Laird Sutherland, however, had only daughters to pledge.

Clyde contemplated each offer, calculating the potential gains and setbacks. "Yer loyalty does ye honor. We shall present these fine young warriors as suitors for the McAfee maidens. Ailis may yet be swayed from her ill-advised affection. Laird Sutherland, mayhap ye should send yer daughters to flirt with Lachlan and Brodie McClain."

"Laird Gordon, yer ties with the McAfees are strong. I propose a grand ceilidh to entice the two younger sisters and the McClains who court them. We can make certain they are separated and spend time with the people we want them to spend time with."

Laird Gordon was intrigued. "Aye, that can be arranged."

"Invite the McAfees courteously," Clyde instructed. "Present yer sons—Lucas, Bearnard, and Horas—as suitors for Ailis, distracting her from Lachlan McClain."

The lairds leaned forward, envisioning the courtship they would orchestrate. "I believe ye should host Highland Games. The McAfee lasses were raised as warriors, and they will not be able to reject an invitation like that. Each son will challenge Lachlan McClain with honor and skill," Clyde continued.

The ideas flew through the room, each man suggesting ways to separate the McClains and McAfees. "Perhaps even a rumor that the McClains think they are better than the McAfees would help," Laird Gordon suggested.

As the meeting concluded, the lairds exchanged firm handshakes. Clyde watched them leave, satisfaction hidden behind stoic leadership.

"Let the games begin," he murmured. The Stewarts' fate and the Highlands' future hinged on this grand ceilidh's outcome.

THE GREAT HALL of McAfee hummed with anticipation as Laird Duncan informed his son-in-law and the other McClain men of their summons to the Highland Games in Clan Gordon's territory. "Fiona, Ailis, and Moira will compete—a rare opportunity. They specifically asked for them, and they will be allowed to compete against the men."

Lachlan's eyes met those of Alisdair and Brodie before he spoke. "We'll accompany yer daughters to ensure their safety. I worry this is another plan to force yer daughters into unwanted marriages."

"Aye," Duncan agreed. "I must stay to protect our home and make sure no one tries to rescue our captives. I trust that ye three will be able to keep me daughters out of trouble." His gaze lingered on each of the brothers, making sure they understood the importance of their task.

Lachlan chuckled. "Yer daughters dinnae get themselves into trouble. They are all well-behaved."

SOON THE THREE sisters gathered. The honor of competition was evident, as were its political implications. They had only ever been allowed to compete in the games held on McAfee land. Now they could compete and show their prowess to many more people.

"We will go not only to prove ourselves but to uphold our clan's dignity. I'm certain there will be much talk about our clan destroying the Sinclairs. The truth must be told to help the reputation of the McAfees."

Moira's eyes gleamed with excitement even as Ailis sensed the gravity of what lay ahead. To compete meant vulnerability before potential enemies. Retreat, however, wasn't an option for the McAfees.

"Let's embrace this challenge," Ailis murmured. "Through uncertainty, we carry our ancestors' strength and spirit."

"Are ye certain about the tartan?" Moira asked, pleating the fabric around Ailis's waist.

Ailis glanced at her reflection. "We shall wear it proudly, as is our right."

Fiona added, "Let our colors fly high. Let McAfee be synonymous with honor."

As they donned their clan's hues, each sister bore not only cloth but duty—to showcase their skills and navigate alliances and rivalries. This was the perfect opportunity for them to share their side of the story about the defeat of the Sinclairs. It was time the entire Highlands knew of the treachery they had faced.

"STAY VIGILANT, AILIS," Lachlan cautioned, scanning the horizon beyond fluttering banners.

She stared up at him, noting his tense jaw and stormy eyes. "Is there cause for concern?" She scanned the area and found no immediate dangers, but she didn't know what he was seeing. He was a seasoned warrior, and he knew more about the dangers that lurked than she did.

"This event might well be a ruse," he admitted. He had thought about the circumstances over and over. The Sinclairs' allies should've been fighting with the McAfees. Instead, no one uttered a word, and they were invited to participate in Highland Games. It wasn't what was expected. "Why have the Sinclairs' allies not attacked? The timing of these games is odd to me."

"We cannot cower from shadows," Ailis replied. "We shall face what comes with heads held high. I will be careful, but I will not hide." But she would always carry her knife close. Never would she allow herself to be taken prisoner again.

Lachlan agreed and promised to guard her when possible, with Kevin in his absence. Ailis nodded. She would gladly accept the help, having no desire to be taken prisoner ever again.

THE CLAMOR OF hooves against the path signaled their departure toward Gordon Territory. Ailis, atop her chestnut mare, sensed excitement coursing through both McAfee and McClain ranks. The rhythmic march stirred anticipation within her.

The first day of their journey was full of merriment. They all looked forward to the games and the ceilidh. Songs and stories filled the air. Laughter united them all. Ailis hummed an airy tune that mingled effortlessly with the surrounding cheer.

Under a star-studded night sky, they made camp in the middle of towering pines. Lachlan approached Ailis with feline grace, exchanges limited to shared glances and faint smiles rather than words. His constant presence offered assistance during tasks or meals, hinting at a deeper affection beyond duty.

"On the morn of the third day, we shall reach Gordon territory," Lachlan remarked with a mix of determination and caution.

Ailis nodded, focused on the distant horizon. "I sense tension in the air, Lachlan. Do ye think the Gordons will welcome us as allies or view us with suspicion?"

Lachlan's brow furrowed. "It is hard to say, Ailis. Our presence may unsettle them, especially given the recent unrest among the clans."

Fiona joined their conversation. "We must tread carefully and show respect to keep their trust. Our clan's honor depends on it."

Lachlan invited Ailis for a walk away from the camp, and Fiona smiled and nodded at her sister. Ailis readily accepted as she'd had little alone time with Lachlan since she'd been rescued.

As they walked through the rugged terrain, Ailis and Lachlan found a secluded spot by a babbling brook. The serene sound of the water flowing soothed their souls as they sat down on a patch of soft grass. Ailis glanced up at Lachlan's warm eyes.

"I've missed this, just being able to enjoy yer company without any interruptions," Lachlan began softly and sincerely.

Ailis smiled. "I feel the same way. It's been a whirlwind of events lately, but I'm grateful for this moment with ye."

They sat in comfortable silence for a while, simply basking in each other's presence. Ailis reached out and took Lachlan's hand in hers, relishing the familiar feel of his touch. At that moment, surrounded by nature's beauty and each other's love, they knew that whatever challenges lay ahead, they would face them together.

The sun began to dip below the horizon, casting a warm golden glow over the landscape. With a soft smile playing on her lips, Ailis turned to Lachlan.

"Have I thanked ye yet for rescuing me from that dreadful

tower?" she whispered.

Lachlan's gaze met hers, his blue eyes reflecting the fading light. "Aye, ye have. I'm not certain why ye are thanking me. I should have been with ye to keep ye from getting taken in the first place."

A gentle breeze rustled through the trees, as if nature itself was whispering words of encouragement to the couple. Ailis leaned in closer to Lachlan, resting her head on his shoulder. She wanted nothing more than to spend the rest of her life close to him.

"As long as I draw breath, I will always stand by yer side, Ailis," Lachlan vowed. "I am so sorry that I let ye be taken that way."

Ailis was overwhelmed by the depth of Lachlan's devotion. She turned to gaze into his eyes, perceiving not just the playful companion but a man who would protect her with every fiber of his being.

"I have never blamed ye," she whispered.

He leaned down and kissed her softly.

As THEY CONTINUED their journey the following day, Moira rode up alongside Ailis, her face filled with curiosity. "Do ye think we can win the favor of the Gordons, sister? Our skills are unmatched, but alliances are delicate matters."

Ailis smiled at her sister's enthusiasm. "We will do our best, Moira. Father trusts us to act in a way that benefits the clan."

As they neared Gordon Territory, Ailis was gripped by a mix of excitement and apprehension. The challenge ahead was not just about showcasing their skills but also about navigating the intricate web of alliances and rivalries that defined clan relationships. She hoped no one would question them about the Sinclairs, but she had a feeling it would happen and happen often.

Under the watchful eyes of the three McClain brothers, the three sisters rode on, ready to face whatever lay ahead on this journey of competition and honor.

Gordon Territory finally welcomed them, and they were met by enthusiastic cheers from the people gathered. Laird Gordon's booming voice announced a celebratory feast and dance for that very night. Ailis reciprocated his smile. The dance would give her an opportunity to spend the evening in Lachlan's arms, something she never wanted to stop doing.

THE STONE WALLS of the keep loomed as Lachlan watched his brothers and kinsmen pitch their tents on the surrounding fields. His heart weighed heavy with the burden of parting from Ailis. He did not trust that she would be safe, so he spoke with Kevin. "I need ye to guard Ailis through the night. She is staying in the keep, and we're out here in tents. I worry that something will happen to her and her sisters."

"Ye'll guard her with yer life," Lachlan told Kevin firmly. The young man stood outside Ailis's door, entrusted with a duty Lachlan wished he could bear himself. "No harm will come to Lady Ailis on me watch," Kevin assured him.

Lachlan paced the hallway unhappily, since he couldn't be inside the keep with her. The night air whispered through narrow windows, offering little comfort. He paused, letting the cool breeze touch his face before murmuring into the darkness, "Keep her safe."

He walked back out to the tent he would be sharing with Brodie and shook his head. "I dinnae think we should have let them separate us. As soon as we heard the women would sleep inside, and we would sleep outside, we should have turned and gone straight back. This doesn't feel right."

Brodie shook his head. "I dinnae like it either. Together we will watch over the lasses. Kevin will help, and Alisdair is in the next chamber. Surely we can make it through the few days of the games before we head back."

Lachlan sighed. "Yes, we can. But I dinna like the idea of her being unprotected."

"They are not unprotected," Brodie reminded him. "And we must make certain that the reputation of both the McClains and McAfees remains untarnished."

CHAPTER EIGHTEEN

Ailis and Moira sat at the far end of the grand table, distant from Fiona and Alisdair. The air carried the scents of roasted meats and spiced pies, yet a twinge of unease ran through Ailis. She'd expected to be seated with both sisters and the three McClain brothers, but it was just her and Moira at this end of the table.

When they'd arrived at the great hall for supper that evening, they'd been told where they should sit, and it seemed to Ailis she and Moira were deliberately kept away from Fiona, Alisdair, Lachlan, and Brodie.

Beside her, Moira conversed with Horas, Bearnard, and Lucas. These men wore their clan tartan and addressed Ailis and her sister courteously. Horas had a penetrating gaze, Bearnard an assured poise, and Lucas an easy smile that hinted at untold stories.

"Ye have grace in yer words, Ailis," Lucas remarked, filling her goblet with a rich amber liquid.

"Yer hospitality honors us," Ailis replied, her voice weaving through the feasting hall like a calming breeze. However, she couldn't help but glance toward Lachlan. She had expected to be able to spend the evening with him, but here she sat with strangers instead. She was not happy with the arrangement.

LACHLAN AND BRODIE were seated with twin beauties who shared a jest causing giggles. Under different circumstances, he might have enjoyed their pleasing company. Yet, he wanted to be near Ailis, not across the room from where she sat with three young men. Many hosts set up seating arrangements for new groups, but typically people who arrived together were allowed to sit together for meals.

"Yer laughter is as delightful as the piper's music." Lachlan raised his goblet in a toast to their beauty, but merriment didn't reach his eyes. These women were vacuous and talked of nothing important, and giggled more than they should.

His gaze occasionally found Ailis across the room. Her serene presence contrasted with the lively chatter around her. He wondered what thoughts lay hidden behind her green eyes.

He had an idea why they'd been separated as they had, but he hoped he was wrong. Certainly, no one there was trying to keep the two of them apart. At least he hoped they weren't. But there did seem to be some plotting occurring, and he wanted no part of the plot at all.

AS THE PIPER'S melody waned, the great hall transformed into a lively dance floor. At Horas's gentle tug, Ailis accepted his invitation to dance. Drums and flutes filled the air, guiding dancers into motion. As much as she enjoyed dancing, she had no desire to dance with any of the men they'd been seated with.

Bearnard and Lucas ensured Moira and Ailis danced one song after another. The room became a whirlwind of tartans, twirling skirts, and eager partners lining up for the McAfee sisters. She wanted to tell all the men she didn't care to dance with them, but that would be rude, and she was there to represent her clan.

Ailis moved gracefully, her dark hair catching candlelight as she spun. Despite the joy around her, she couldn't ignore

Lachlan's striking presence across the room. His athletic form moved effortlessly amid the dancers, his dark hair contrasting with his partners' lighter locks.

Ailis's heart yearned for Lachlan while her feet followed a different rhythm. She wanted nothing more than to cross the room so they could dance together, but it seemed that every time she even glanced in his direction, one of the men would move between them and ask her to dance.

As the dance continued, Ailis couldn't shake off the feeling of being held back from where she truly wanted to be. She stole glances in Lachlan's direction whenever she could, hoping to catch his eye.

Moira noticed her sister's distracted demeanor and whispered, "Ye seem troubled, Ailis. Is something amiss?"

Ailis forced a smile and replied softly, "I just... I had hoped to dance with someone else tonight."

Moira followed her gaze and understood immediately. "Ah, Lachlan. Does it seem to ye as if we're being deliberately separated from the McClain men?" she asked.

Ailis blushed and nodded, grateful for her sister's understanding.

Just then, Horas twirled Ailis gracefully and remarked, "Ye have the grace of a swan on the loch, Ailis."

"Thank ye, Horas," Ailis responded politely, though her mind was elsewhere.

Bearnard then stepped in to take Ailis for the next dance. "Mayhap this dance will lift yer spirits, lass," he offered with a charming smile.

Ailis couldn't resist his infectious enthusiasm and found herself smiling genuinely as they danced together. Bearnard was a skilled dancer and led her with confidence around the crowded floor.

Meanwhile, Lucas approached Moira with a mischievous glint in his eyes. "Do ye believe in fate, Moira?" he inquired as they danced in rhythm to the music.

Moira raised an eyebrow in curiosity. "I'm not sure I follow, Lucas. Why do ye ask?"

Lucas gestured toward Ailis and Bearnard discreetly. "Sometimes the stars align in mysterious ways," he mused cryptically.

Moira shot him a puzzled glance but couldn't dwell on it for long as the music urged them to keep pace with the lively tune.

Across the room, Lachlan found himself entangled in conversation with Brodie and two other guests. He stole glances at Ailis whenever he could, yearning to be by her side on the dance floor.

Finally breaking free from the group, Lachlan made his way through the throng of dancers toward where Ailis was dancing with Bearnard. Just as he reached out a hand to claim her as his partner, another figure intercepted him—Horas joined the dance, smoothly taking over from Bearnard without missing a beat.

A mix of frustration and longing flashed across Lachlan's face as he watched Ailis whirl away from him once more. Their hosts seemed determined to keep them apart despite their silent desires to be together.

And so, Ailis and Lachlan found themselves dancing closer yet further away than ever before, their hearts intertwined yet physically separated by unseen forces at play.

Ailis's gaze swept the hall, taking in the festivities that concealed her inner turmoil. Trapped in a dance, she couldn't reach Lachlan. Her smile hid her growing frustration as her role prevented any private conversation with him.

As the night wore on, Ailis observed Lachlan engaged in lively dances, his eyes gleaming with mischief. She yearned to draw him close, but the crowded hall hindered her. When the music died down at the end of the celebration, Horas, Bearnard, and Lucas escorted Ailis and Moira through stone corridors to their chambers.

At their doors, Lucas challenged whether they needed their own guard—Kevin—outside their room.

"It is no slight to the Gordon Clan," Ailis spoke diplomatically, "but with such grand assembly, we find comfort in added precautions." She didn't mention how she and her sister had been kidnapped in recent months. She decided that information wasn't any of his business.

With a nod from Lucas and goodnights exchanged, Ailis entered her chamber. She was relieved when she could finally shut the door. Now it was just her and Moira.

Inside the stone chamber, Ailis turned to Moira. "Did ye feel cornered by Horas, Bearnard, and Lucas tonight?"

Moira plucked at her skirt before responding, "Aye, we had no say in our own evening. And Lucas mentioned something about ye and Bearnard, but it wasn't clear. I truly think they were set upon us to keep us from the McClain men. But why?"

Ailis longed for a moment with Lachlan to discuss her theories about what had happened that evening, but she had a feeling it would do no good. Besides, she couldn't get to him without being interrupted. They'd been at the games for less than a day, and she was ready to return home.

The sisters retired to bed, each pondering what the morrow might bring. Sleep evaded them on the coarse mattress while unfamiliar sounds echoed around.

The dance of alliance and courtship chafed against Ailis's yearning for sincerity and choice. She tossed restlessly throughout the night. Moira eventually succumbed to slumber, leaving Ailis awash in longing and the reality of her predicament.

It was after dawn when Ailis finally drifted off, haunted by whispers of unspoken words and distant bagpipes' melody.

The call of the bagpipes disrupted dawn's silence, waking Ailis from her restless sleep. She left the bed she shared with Moira and dressed in formal attire alongside her sister.

In the great hall, Horas, Bearnard, and Lucas circled Ailis and Moira like competing eagles. The chivalrous courtship hinted at more than simple affection. Ailis met each advance gracefully, though her smile never reached her eyes.

AS THE CLANS all gathered together for the archery contest, anticipation filled the misty highlands. The three suitors boasted their expertise with the bow and sought tokens from the sisters. Ailis hid her amusement as she responded, "I'd wager our Fiona will outshoot every man present." And she knew her words to be true. Fiona could outshoot any man she'd ever seen.

The sisters watched the men compete—an embodiment of grace, wit, and subtle rebellion against their expected roles.

Ailis whispered to Moira that the men seemed to think they could actually win the contest, and they both dissolved into giggles, ready to see the men's faces when a mere lass outshot them all.

Anticipation coiled in Ailis's chest while Fiona stood among the competitors, serene amid restless energy. It seemed the three of them were the only women to be competing, but that didn't bother Ailis. She knew that she was the best at knife-throwing, and Fiona could outshoot any man. And no one could match Moira with a sword. Even a man twice Moira's size couldn't defeat her.

"Begin!" called the master of games.

The men took aim and loosed their arrows, drawing cheers or sympathetic sighs. Horas, Bearnard, and Lucas struck near the heart of the targets. Still, everyone awaited Fiona's turn.

Approaching the mark, Fiona commanded silent respect. She nocked her arrow with practiced ease, bowstring brushing her lips. The air stilled as she drew back, eyes narrowing in concentration.

Her arrow flew swift and true. Once, twice, thrice. Each shot showcased Fiona's prowess. Ailis swelled with pride at her sister's triumph.

"Yer aim is as keen as yer wit," Ailis murmured to herself.

Applause erupted like a waterfall after a storm. Even competing archers commended her skill. A child presented Fiona with a heather-colored silk ribbon—the champion's prize—and she held it up, letting it dance in the breeze.

As the contest ended and feasting began, well-meaning courtships blocked Fiona from reuniting with her sisters for a shared meal, despite their best efforts to find a quiet corner.

The sisters settled at a table on the periphery, their hearts burdened by the absence of cherished company. As they ate and drank, their eldest sibling's silent specter lingered, a reminder of duty and decorum parting kin.

Lucas was angry during supper that night. "How did ye know yer sister would win?"

Moira smiled mischievously, her green eyes sparkling with amusement. "Well, ye see, Fiona's skill with a bow and arrow is no secret in our clan or any of our allies. She's been honing her craft since she could walk, and she's never been bested in a contest yet."

Ailis nodded. "Aye, Fiona has a natural talent that surpasses any man's. She doesn't just aim for the target. She becomes one with the bow, the arrow, and the wind itself. It's a sight to behold."

Lucas's brows furrowed in disbelief. "Surely ye jest! A lass besting seasoned warriors with years of training?"

"I find it hard to believe that a woman could outshoot us, skilled as we are," Bearnard chimed in skeptically.

Horas, the most reserved of the three suitors, shook his head. "She did best all three of us."

They exchanged glances, a mixture of admiration and apprehension evident in their eyes.

Moira leaned forward, her stare challenging as she addressed the men. "Ye see, Fiona's prowess with the bow is not merely about hitting a target. It symbolizes her spirit, her determination, and her unyielding strength She embodies the essence of the Highlands—wild, untamed, and free."

Ailis nodded in agreement, her voice soft but unwavering.

"She fights not just for herself but for our family, for our clan. And when she draws that bowstring back, she doesn't just release an arrow. She declares who she is and what she stands for."

Lucas, Bearnard, and Horas observed the subtle exchange between the McAfee sisters, their initial reservations softening into an unspoken reverence. The realization dawned on them that winning the hearts of Ailis and Moira was intricately tied to understanding and valuing the bond they shared with Fiona—a bond that transcended mere sisterhood.

Moira smiled at Ailis. "Ye see, none of us have the same mother, but instead, we were raised by only a father who was determined to raise three women who could act as one. And we can."

Ailis nodded. "Our love for one another is more than it would be had we all shared one mother. We had to lean on one another because all our mothers passed when we were born."

Moira grinned. "I cannae wait until the knife-throwing on the morrow. That one will be fun."

"Will ye compete, Moira?" Horas asked.

Moira shook her head. "Nay. I'm competent at knife-throwing, but me sister is much better than me. Ailis will be the sister to beat at the knife-throwing."

The men gawped at the woman in front of them, the one they'd danced with all the previous evening. "Ye are trying to say that Ailis can outthrow men with a knife?" Lucas cried.

"Ye'll have to wait and see, won't ye?" Ailis sipped the wine in front of her. The men would see. They would all see.

She shared a glance with Moira, and Moira grinned slightly. They both knew how the contest would go the following day, and they were excited for it. It was time the three lairds' sons who had been annoying them for two days realized they weren't the best in the world at everything.

CHAPTER NINETEEN

THE GRAND HALL was filled with the sound of fiddles and pipes, as dancers swayed beneath flickering torchlight. Ailis McAfee's brunette locks framed her demure smile as she followed her partner's lead—once again a man she had not chosen. Across the room, Lachlan and Brodie exuded restrained frustration, separated from Moira and Ailis by the orchestrated dance.

Each step was measured, each turn deliberate. Her green eyes met Lachlan's occasionally, exchanging a mutual glare and a wordless promise for honest conversation.

As the night progressed, energy dwindled, and the final notes signaled the time to retire. Ailis and Moira ascended the staircase, their laughter echoing softly off the walls.

In their chamber, they released pent-up amusement. Moira choked upon recalling the men's expressions when Fiona had bested them earlier that day. Ailis joined in.

"Did ye see Horas?" Moira gasped. "His face was as red as me hair!"

"And Lucas's jaw," Ailis added. "I thought it might never return to its proper place and reside forever at his knees."

Sitting together on Moira's bed, their amusement subsided into contented smiles. Despite being kept away from their family and friends during the festivities, they found solace in shared triumph over expectations.

"Tomorrow," Ailis whispered with determination, "we'll find a way to speak with Lachlan and Brodie."

"This game tires me," Moira agreed. "We are no one's pawns."

With their vow lingering, they embraced sleep, anticipating another day where duty and desire would continue their tireless dance.

LACHLAN OBSERVED THE moonlit courtyard below, leaning against the castle's stone wall. Brodie stood beside him, their breaths misting in the crisp air. Both sensed something was off regarding Moira and Ailis.

"Something is amiss," Lachlan finally whispered. "We must find a way to speak with them without interference. But how?"

Brodie nodded. "Perhaps during the morning activities, we can 'accidentally' cross paths."

"Accidents do happen." Lachlan smirked.

"Aye, they do," Brodie agreed. "If we partner in the archery contest, it may provide the opportunity."

"On the morrow, we decide our own future."

Unseen in the shadows, Clyde Stewart watched them before joining Horas, Lucas, and Bearnard.

"Ye are doing well," Clyde commanded. "Keep close to the lasses. Come the morrow, steal away from the dances and kiss them. Let all see. We must keep them from the McClains, no matter what it takes."

The suitors exchanged glances but understood Clyde's orders carried weight with their fathers.

"Be seen kissing them?" Horas asked. "They are women who best men at war games."

"Aye. Do this, and our plans will unfold." Clyde realized he should have gone to their fathers. The boys questioned him and thought too highly of themselves. He wished there was time for him to choose boys that would suit the sisters better than these three did.

Clyde started to walk away, but turned and added, "The future of our clans may hinge upon yer actions."

With a final glance at each man, Clyde retreated into the darkness.

BEFORE DAWN, AILIS and Moira left their chamber to seek out the McClain brothers. They found Kevin, the man guarding their door, who guided them through dimly lit corridors.

"We must speak with Lachlan and Brodie," Ailis whispered urgently. Kevin nodded solemnly and led them out of the keep and to the brothers' tent.

As they entered, Lachlan turned to them, while Brodie watched silently from the shadows. "We find ourselves in a dire circumstance," Ailis began, explaining how Horas, Lucas, and Bearnard kept them apart from the brothers and stifled their freedom. "We have no desire to be in their presence, let alone have them be the only people we are allowed to speak with."

Lachlan's eyes sharpened like icy shards upon realizing the situation, and Brodie clenched his jaw. "We knew something was amiss." Lachlan shook his head.

Moira added fiercely, "We wish to leave."

Ailis met Lachlan's gaze with determination. "We have been pawns for too long."

Ailis observed as Lachlan and Brodie deliberated in the cool morning air. Their patience contrasted with the unrest in her heart.

"They seem to be carrying on where the Sinclairs left off," Lachlan murmured. "Every action orchestrated by unseen hands."

"Aye, but who is doing it?" Brodie replied. "We must uncover the truth." His eyes met Ailis's.

"I haven't spoken to Alisdair since our arrival," Lachlan confessed, gazing into the distance. "We're pawns on a chessboard, but pawns become queens when they reach their opponent's side of the board. That is what we must do. We must persevere until we become the most powerful pieces on the board."

Moira's hand brushed against Ailis's—a wordless vow between sisters to face whatever game was afoot together. "I suppose that means that we must stay longer to determine what plans they have for us, and what they plan to do in the end."

Lachlan nodded. "I think it best. And we must speak with Alisdair and Fiona. I worry that they are being kept from us, even as we're kept from them."

Moira sighed dramatically. "I do not want to spend another second in the company of those men. They think we should be incapable of being good at shooting and knife-throwing because we are women."

Ailis wanted to mention that a penis didn't seem to be necessary for knife-throwing, but she knew better. It would embarrass all four of them. Perhaps it was something she should say to the would-be suitors who plagued them.

The great hall enveloped them as they entered for breakfast, united in their resistance against invisible constraints. Ailis planned to sit with Lachlan and Brodie, but she worried that something would happen to keep her from doing so.

Yet, moments after sitting at the long table, Horas, Lucas, and Bearnard wedged themselves between them like hawks to prey.

"Good morrow," Lucas greeted with feigned cordiality. "I'm looking forward to the knife-throwing this morning. Ye're to enter as well, Ailis?"

"Good morrow," Ailis replied politely but distant, attempting to see past the human barricade separating her from Lachlan. "I am. And I will win."

The clatter of plates and the aroma of porridge filled the air while unsaid words and weighted glances thickened the atmosphere. Duty warred with desire within Ailis as battle lines were drawn precisely, leaving no room for retreat.

Lucas laughed softly. "Ye only say that because ye've never seen me throw a knife."

Ailis clenched her jaw, tension in her face betraying the storm brewing within. The false air of friendliness suffocated the breakfast table. She turned to Horas who avoided eye contact as he served himself porridge. "And ye've never seen me throw."

"Why do ye insist on following us and keeping us from speaking to Lachlan and Brodie?" Ailis's green eyes blazed. Perhaps the men would be willing to share who held the strings as their puppet master.

Horas finally met her gaze. "Ye mistake our intent, Ailis. We only seek good company." Unease flickered across his face.

"Good company that leaves no room for choice or freedom," she retorted. Their silence spoke louder than words. Ailis could tell that Horas was uncomfortable with the lie. Perhaps he was the one to focus on with her questions.

Later, at the knife-throwing competition, Ailis stepped forward, her heart pounding like war drums of old. She focused on the wooden target ahead, blocking out the crowd's murmurs. She'd been practicing this sport for her entire life, and she was confident she would do well.

With practiced grace, she drew back her arm and released. The dagger spun through the air before embedding itself into the target's center. Whispers of admiration rippled through the onlookers.

Ailis savored a moment of triumph but was weighed down by expectations and political schemes. As she retrieved her knife, she vowed to wield fate with precision and resolve, honoring both her desires and duties.

Lachlan calmly watched Ailis claim victory with a deadly and accurate throw. When his turn came, he confidently hurled his blade, landing it just shy of center. While he earned second place, Lachlan's joy came from witnessing Ailis's skill.

As he approached her, Laird Gordon intercepted him. "Lachlan," he began gravely, "yer skills are commendable. Yer father must be very proud of ye."

"Thank ye, Laird," Lachlan replied respectfully, although his attention remained on Ailis. "He's made sure all of his sons are proficient in fighting skills."

Later, as they observed the bustling grounds, Lachlan voiced his concern to Brodie. "Brother, we must speak with Moira and Ailis without unwanted company. There must be a way."

Brodie agreed. "Aye, let's offer them an escape. Perhaps arrange a meeting away in the glen to unveil the truth. We may not be able to get to them, but we can write a note to meet us and give it to Kevin to give to them. This is ridiculous."

"Let us be cautious," Brodie warned. "We tread upon delicate ground."

Lachlan smiled wryly. "True enough. But we are McClains. Challenges dinnae daunt us." And with that, they began planning their next move.

IN THE GREAT hall, Ailis sat beside Moira at the supper table, venison and freshly baked bread tantalizing their senses. The flickering candlelight showcased Lucas's annoyance as he confronted the sisters.

"Tell me," Lucas began sharply, "do ye truly believe any man would take to wife a lass who can best him in feats of strength and skill?" His eyes challenged Ailis's composure.

Ailis met his gaze, a smile disguising the tension between them. She shared a glance with Moira, whose eyes gleamed with mischief.

"Lucas," Ailis replied, measured words hiding the turmoil within, "a true marriage is a partnership of equals. If a man's pride is so fragile that it cannot withstand the talents of his lady, then perhaps it is not a match forged by destiny." She shook her head.

"I worry for whomever ye take to wife, Lucas. Is she allowed to have any skills of which ye dinnae approve?"

Next to her, Moira laughed. "Indeed," she added, "we seek not to diminish our suitors, but to rise alongside them. Strength recognizes strength. Do ye not see us as strong, capable women?"

Lucas, Horas, and Bearnard exchanged incredulous glances, taken aback by the sisters' response. Their confidence wavered as Ailis and Moira's unwavering resolve challenged their perception of women's roles. The flickering torches cast dancing shadows across the hall, mirroring the shifting dynamics at play.

Horas cleared his throat, attempting to regain his composure. "Ye jest, lasses," he scoffed, his voice betraying a hint of uncertainty. "Men seek women who need protection and guidance, not those who can outshine them in every endeavor."

Ailis raised an eyebrow at his words, a playful glint in her emerald eyes. "Oh, Horas, are ye suggesting that a woman's worth lies solely in her need for protection? Are we to be delicate flowers, wilting under the weight of a man's expectations?"

Moira's laughter rang out like silver bells in the night air. "We shall not diminish ourselves to fit into the box ye have crafted for us, sirs," she declared. "We are McAfee women, strong and capable in our own right. If that intimidates ye, then perhaps ye are not worthy of our company."

The voices around them fell silent, the crackling of the hearth the only sound permeating the tension that hung thick in the air. Ailis stood gracefully, her every movement exuding quiet defiance.

"We are not seeking protection, sirs," Ailis insisted, addressing Horas, Lucas, and Bearnard. "We seek respect, partnership, and understanding. If those qualities elude ye, then we bid ye good morrow."

With a graceful nod to Moira by her side, Ailis turned on her heel and led the way out of the great hall, her head held high and her spirit unbroken. The echo of their laughter followed them out, a melody of independence and strength that resonated through the stone walls of the castle. The flickering torches cast long shadows that danced along the corridor, a silent testament to the fire within the McAfee sisters.

HORAS, LUCAS, AND Bearnard watched in stunned silence as Ailis and Moira departed. The aroma of the feast still hung around them, mingling with the tension that now gripped the hall.

"We cannot let them slip through our fingers," Horas finally spoke, his voice tinged with desperation. "They are slipping away from us. I feel that we need to be more understanding of their chosen pursuits, and not let them know we think they are never going to be able to find men. Me father wants me to marry one of them."

Lucas nodded slowly, furrowing his brows. "Aye, they are not like any other women we have encountered. Their spirit is as untamed as the winds." He sighed. "Unfortunately, me father wants me to marry one of them as well. Me father will not get his way in this."

Bearnard's gaze followed the retreating forms of Ailis and Moira, a flicker of admiration in his eyes. "Perhaps we have underestimated them," he mused.

Their laughter, like a cascade of silver bells, lingered in the air.

Horas squared his shoulders, his expression a mask of determination. "We must show them that our intentions are sincere, that our desire to protect stems from a place of love. We should have been working on our acting skills, not our warrior skills."

Lucas nodded, his rugged features softened by a hint of vulnerability. "Aye, we have erred in underestimating the depth of their spirit. It is not weakness they seek but understanding and equality."

Bearnard's gaze lingered on the doorway through which Ailis

and Moira had vanished, his thoughts a whirlwind of contemplation. "We must prove ourselves worthy of their trust and respect. Actions shall speak louder than words."

"Ye are right," Horas replied. "I just have one question."

"What's that?" Lucas asked.

"What will we do if one of them actually agrees to marry one of us? Will we be able to handle them?"

Lucas laughed. "They are mere women! They will follow our orders as all women do."

"Have ye met them?" Bearnard asked.

⁕

CHAPTER TWENTY

THE OAK DOOR closed behind Moira and Ailis as Kevin approached with a parchment. "From the gentlemen," he murmured, handing it to Ailis.

"Meet us in the glen an hour after supper," Ailis read aloud. Moira leaned closer, scanning the words.

"We should be discreet about this," Moira bubbled, a mischievous spark in her eyes.

"We'll come back here and disguise ourselves after we've eaten supper with the three banes of our existence," Ailis added.

A few hours later, the women escaped the annoying men, claiming they were too tired to keep dancing. When they reached their room, they discussed how to disguise themselves.

Finally, Ailis retrieved two scarves from a wooden chest, draping one over her own hair and handing the other to Moira. They adjusted the fabric to obscure their identities, hoping they would not be recognized on their way to the secret meeting.

"Ready?" Ailis asked as they checked each other's disguises.

"Something is missing," Moira observed. She opened the chest and found two long shawls that would hide the pattern of their plaids and make it easy to go about without recognition. They put the shawls over their shoulders, and with their heads down, left the chamber.

"Ready as ever," Moira replied.

Moira was excited to have some time with Lachlan finally. These few days had passed like a month. It wasn't enough to be able to see him across the room. She wanted to be able to talk to him and touch him.

It was completely dark outside as Ailis and Moira arrived at the shadowy glen. They spotted Lachlan and Brodie approaching with determined expressions.

"Good eve to ye," Brodie whispered. "We have urgent matters to discuss."

Lachlan's gaze locked on Ailis. "Someone is trying to force us apart. We need to find who incites their relentless pursuit and courtship. There must be someone who is telling them exactly what to do, and I mean to find out who it is." He shook his head. "Someone is telling those three suitors they must spend time with ye and make ye fall in love with them."

Ailis giggled. "They are not the kind of man we would even like, let alone love. They told us that men would never love a woman who could best them at fighting."

Lachlan chuckled as well. "I can see they are not endearing themselves to ye." At first, he'd been a little intimidated by Ailis and her knife skills, but now he was simply proud of how good she was at protecting herself.

"Ye are right about that. But time runs short," she replied. "With only two more days of games and feasts, our chance to uncover these secrets nears its end. Do ye think ye can find out what is happening?"

"We must be vigilant and swift," Moira continued. "Within tomorrow's merriment may lie the answers we seek."

"Be wary," Lachlan cautioned. "These games bear political weight. Alliances and enmities form beneath festive masks." He shook his head. "I wish yer father had come, and he could deal with the lairds, as someone who has experience with men of power."

"With courage, we'll navigate between duty and desire," Ailis declared.

Ailis's heart raced with apprehension and excitement. They had returned to the castle along the shadowy path when Moira, ever independent, disappeared through the entrance while Kevin awaited her.

Lachlan McClain held Ailis's arm gently but firmly, urging her to stay. As they stood in Moira's absence, his eyes mirrored unspoken thoughts.

"Stay," he requested softly.

Ailis remained as Lachlan pulled her close and kissed her passionately. Time seemed to pause, allowing the intimacy of their connection to sink in. "I cannae believe how long it's been since ye've touched me. It had to be months. And they've left me ridiculous substitutes who dinnae understand me at all."

"I miss ye," he confessed quietly, reminding her of their separation.

Her heart filled with warmth at his words. "I feel the same, Lachlan. I hate that we are not given a choice in whom we may spend time with," she admitted. "What would happen if we refused to sit where we are told?"

He shook his head. "I dinnae think it would go well for us. There are definitely more people against our being together here than are for it."

She sighed. "We need to find some way to communicate every day, as well as talk to Fiona and Alisdair. Even with their room right beside ours, it feels as if I haven't seen Fiona in a very long time!"

"I'll think on it," he whispered. With another quick kiss, he guided her toward the door. "Goodnight, Ailis."

As Ailis walked through the castle corridors, Kevin spoke to her about Lachlan's feelings for her. "Lachlan truly cares for ye, like a steadfast oak tree," he had insisted as they parted ways.

"Thank ye, Kevin," she replied steadily. "I appreciate yer observation." She wanted to ask what he'd told Kevin about her, but she knew it would be silly to have the conversation with Kevin instead of Lachlan.

Ailis lay in her chamber, heart racing from Lachlan's fervent kiss. The memory of his touch filled her dreams with longing and whispered vows. In sleep, she imagined a world where love was not a pawn in power games.

THE CALL OF the bagpipes woke Ailis the following morning. She dressed and she and Moira descended the stairs together for breakfast in the great hall. Lucas, Horas, and Bearnard were already there, their presence an unwelcome burden. Ailis counted in her head, as she wondered how long it would take one of them to say something stupid. She reached ten when Lucas spoke.

"Which of ye shall grace the field this day?" Lucas inquired mockingly.

"Neither," Moira replied sternly. "On the morrow, 'twill be I who competes in swords."

Laughter erupted from the men. However, it died as they realized the sisters were serious.

"Ye speak in earnest?" Bearnard asked, eyebrows furrowed. "A lass cannae compete against men with swords. Ye'll be slaughtered!"

"Aye, we are very serious," Ailis affirmed with quiet strength. "We are daughters of the McAfee clan, versed in more than what men like ye would call women's work."

AILIS WATCHED THE caber tumble through the air, Brodie's strength belying its weight. Moira's voice rang out in support of him, Ailis adding her own cheer as he succeeded.

"Marvelously done!" Ailis exclaimed, feeling pride well up inside her. It was as if all three of the brothers had joined their family when Alisdair had married Fiona, though Lachlan did not feel like a brother to her.

As dusk fell, Ailis entered the great hall dressed elegantly for the dance. "Ailis," Lucas inquired smoothly while they danced, "why do ye seek the company of the McClain brothers so fervently?"

Horas added his thoughts on alliances. "Ye already have an alliance with the McClains. Wouldn't it be smart to make an alliance with another clan? It would most certainly help the McAfees."

Ailis replied, "We are not going to pursue men to fulfill a need for alliances. We are not those women. We are comfortable with the McClain men, and they treat us with respect."

Bearnard, booming with conviction, passionately stressed the significance of forming alliances in times of turmoil.

Ailis, her mind consumed with thoughts of peace and politics, took a moment before finally speaking from her heart. "We will not be used as political pawns. We are women who understand our own minds and hearts, and we shall follow them. And we need no advice from the three of ye." She didn't say what she wanted to say and tell them all to go away. A tinge of pride tickled her for that. She grew a little prouder when she realized she hadn't kicked any of the three. That was truly something that she would tell her grandchildren someday. She had not kicked the lairds' sons who drove her crazy.

AILIS AND MOIRA made their way to their chambers. "I believe those men live a thousand years in the past." Moira shook her head.

"At least two thousand," Ailis replied. "They make me want to scream. What is so wrong about three strong women?"

Rounding a corner, they encountered Fiona and Alisdair. Drawn together in the hallway, Ailis murmured, "Someone is keeping us from spending time with Lachlan and Brodie. There are suitors following us about."

Fiona's eyes narrowed as she assessed the possibilities. "Lachlan and Brodie are working to find who is dictating their moves. The truth is, the suitors dinnae like us any more than we like them," she added, frustrated yet resolute.

Moira mused, "Who could benefit from such manipulations?"

Alisdair regarded them for a moment, weighing their words, his determined eyes addressing the sisters. "I'll find a way to speak with me brothers. Together, we'll expose this unseen force."

Ailis warned that time was running short, her fingers betraying her calm by trembling slightly. "We only have one more day of games. If we are to discover who is doing this, we must work quickly."

"Let us waste no more time worrying," Alisdair replied before disappearing into the shadows to speak with his brothers.

The chamber door closed, enclosing Ailis and Moira in their temporary bedchamber. Ailis sighed wearily.

"Are ye not troubled by this cloak of secrecy?" Ailis quietly asked.

"Troubled? Nay, sister," Moira replied, unpinning her hair. "For on the morrow, I shall wield a sword with such fervor that no one may dare approach me with devious intent. I plan to best every man here."

"I love yer confidence, sister," Ailis chirped, loosening her own braids. "The men will surely get to the bottom of this."

"'Tis not courage alone that steels me," Moira continued with a mischievous smile. "Brodie has been aiding me in secret. He has honed me skills with a blade so that when I compete, I shall do so as a warrior of the McAfee."

Ailis paused, considering her sister's words. "I'm happy that he has spent time teaching ye more," she acknowledged. "But we must tread with care."

"Let them try to defeat us," Moira declared resolutely. "We are McAfees. We do not bend to whispers in the dark."

"Aye, we do not," Ailis concurred softly. She rose to draw the curtains shut against the night's chill before settling into bed.

Beside her, Moira nestled down.

"Goodnight, dear sister," Moira whispered.

"Goodnight, Moira," Ailis murmured. Her thoughts lingered on Brodie's quiet strength and the impending competition. She had every confidence that her sister would win. She had been one of the best before the extra practice. Now she would outshine all the men.

And in that space between wakefulness and sleep, she sensed Lachlan's kiss. Hopefully, soon, they would be able to spend more time together.

◆━━━◆━━ ✦ ━━◆━━━◆

CHAPTER TWENTY-ONE

THE FOLLOWING MORNING, right after they'd broken their fast, the sword competition began. Everyone gathered to witness the duels, their breaths misting in the crisp air. Contestants faced off within the makeshift arena, each duel displaying skill and valor.

By noon, only two warriors remained undefeated: Brodie McClain, his eyes calm as the distant sea, and Moira McAfee, her red hair like a fiery banner. Ailis stood at the edge of the crowd, pride swelling within her as she watched her sister.

The three suitors—Bearnard, Lucas, and Horas—clustered near Ailis in disbelief. They had boasted of their prowess leading up to the tournament but were bested one by one. None had anticipated Moira's blade slicing through all the men's defenses with such grace.

Ailis couldn't suppress a smile when Moira defeated Lucas. She savored it not for his defeat but for the glint of admiration that flickered in his eyes as he yielded to her sister's superior skill.

The murmurs of the crowd hushed as the final match approached, anticipation heavy in the air. Ailis hummed softly, a tune meant for Moira alone. For now, she cast aside thoughts of duty and alliances, allowing herself to enjoy her sister's impending triumph. Though she knew if anyone could defeat Moira, it was Brodie.

The clash of steel echoed through the air. Ailis focused on her sister Moira and Brodie as they engaged in a dangerous dance of swords, each strike met with a skillful parry.

Ailis observed the intense concentration on Brodie's face as he locked eyes with Moira. His movements were elegant and strong, contrasting Moira's fiery determination. The crowd held its breath, anticipating the result of their battle.

A sudden change in rhythm left Brodie vulnerable—Moira's sword narrowly missed him. He dodged with impressive grace but stumbled onto the damp ground, defeated by Moira's poised blade.

"Yield," she commanded.

"I yield," he responded, smiling despite his loss.

Moira offered a hand, assisting Brodie to his feet as an unmistakable gesture of respect between them. After Moira accepted her victory ribbon, Laird Gordon stepped forward, commanding attention.

"Let it be known," he announced solemnly, "that all winners shall extend their stay for another seven days of celebration." Excitement and curiosity spread through the crowd like wildfire. "We will honor these triumphs with feasts and merriment."

As Ailis considered the implications of this extension, she couldn't help but feel the anticipation. The coming week would bring challenges and revelations. She must prepare to face them with the same courage demonstrated today on the field of honor.

They would have more time to discover who the conspirators were, but they would also have the same difficulties they'd had since arrival. Perhaps they could meet at the same time every night to spend time together. She would discuss it with Moira and see what her sister thought.

Ailis exchanged a glance with her sister, Moira, emotions warring inside her. Was this additional time a blessing or an obstacle to their longing for home?

Their shared gaze was a wordless conversation only they could understand. Ailis was proud of Moira's prowess but also fearful of the unknown that lay ahead.

As evening fell, the great hall filled with torchlight and tantalizing scents of roasted meats and spiced pies. Ailis took her place at the table, observing the assembly. Unfortunately, all three of the men who had been pestering them all week were there with them.

Lucas brooded despite the festivities. His eyes rarely left the trencher before him, occasionally darting toward Moira as if reliving his humiliation. The rigid set of his jaw and clenched fists betrayed his inner turmoil.

The other men who had not faced off against Moira teased him, but he refused to engage, instead eating his meal methodically and pretending he was alone.

His silence would have made the meal uncomfortable, but it didn't bother Ailis and Moira at all. It was nice to not have the men talking about how they would never find husbands because of their warrior ways.

"Are ye sure Moira didn't look different as ye lay on the ground after she defeated ye?" Bearnard asked, grinning at him.

Finally, Ailis had enough of the teasing. "Ye were defeated as well, remember. And not by the person who won the entire competition. Did ye forget?"

Bearnard frowned, annoyed that she'd brought up his own defeat.

"That's true," Horas replied. "Ye were bested too!"

"As were ye," Moira pointed out. "Everyone who entered was. Mayhap ye will quit teasing yer friend about losing to a lass when ye remember that ye lost as easily as he did." Moira didn't brag about her win, but instead pointed out the facts of the men's loss.

"Perhaps kindness would help all of ye get along better," Ailis murmured. "There can only be one winner in a contest, and though ye all thought it would be ye, it was Moira. And a McClain was right behind her. And ye say the McClains are not men we should marry."

Lucas smiled a bit, obviously happy to see his friends bested as well.

As soon as the meal was over, Ailis and Moira excused themselves from the festivities and retreated into the night. Once away from prying eyes, they hurried to the secluded glen where Lachlan and Brodie awaited them. Ailis sighed with relief when the men came into view. It was so good to be with people she respected and away from the men who had been their constant companions whether they wanted them there or not.

Fiona and Alisdair joined them in the glen, their gazes filled with urgency. "Something is amiss," Alisdair fretted. "The fathers of Bearnard, Lucas, and Horas—they are a part of the conspiracy against us. I have no idea what they are plotting, though. That's yet to be found out."

Brodie nodded. "And we must not forget the father of the twins. He must be in league with the others."

Ailis listened intently, her eyes aflame with determination. The truth lay hidden behind noble facades. They must discover what the plot and plans were because they seemed to center around the McAfees.

"Then we stand united," Fiona declared, standing resolute. "We've been invited to stay longer, and as much as none of us want to, this is the perfect opportunity to discover what is truly happening around us."

"We must have watchful eyes and guarded hearts," Ailis stated, her stare cutting through the shadows. She knew the powerful lairds held secrets that could disrupt their clans' fragile peace. Precision was vital.

Recognizing Moira's mischievous glance, Ailis smirked. "Did ye see Lucas's face when ye disarmed him?"

Moira chuckled, "Aye, I fear I've wounded his pride more than if I'd drawn blood." Her grin shone like a beacon in the darkness. She shook her head. "We told them I would best them, but they were incapable of believing such a thing. Now they have no choice."

Fiona laughed as well. "It is always fun to see how men react when they see our skills for the first time. Especially the men who are certain they could never lose… especially to a lass."

"The son of our host, bested by a lass," Ailis scoffed, shaking her head. "I almost feel sorry for him, but… I've listened to him brag about his prowess with a sword since the day we arrived. It was good to see him defeated."

As their laughter mingled with the night, Ailis repeated the men's words—how their combat skills would supposedly repel love. Her fellow warriors, all too familiar with such dismissive remarks, smiled knowingly.

Alisdair shook his head, laughing again. "Little do they ken. When a woman is particularly good at something, her confidence is attractive. I would not wish Fiona to be less skilled with a bow and arrow. I enjoy watching her, and it gives me someone to compete with."

They grew serious and dispersed for their individual tasks. Fiona reminded them to be vigilant as she scanned the darkness. Ailis and Moira sought to uncover the truth about loyalties from Bearnard, Lucas, and Horas—a delicate dance of questioning. But they were determined to find the whole truth and not be victims in their plot any longer.

Alisdair promised to discuss the Sinclairs' predicament with the lairds, gauging reactions for clues. Lachlan and Brodie agreed to travel deeper into the shadows in search of lurking conspiracies. They even seemed to be excited to do it. Ailis knew it was an important matter, but the men seemed to like the mystery of it all.

As Ailis and Moira returned to their bedchamber, they giggled again about the way the lairds' sons had treated them, knowing they would be less confident going forward. Confidence was attractive, but too much confidence was the opposite. And those three men truly had too much confidence.

CHAPTER TWENTY-TWO

A S THEY MUNCHED on their breakfast the next day, Bearnard, Lucas, and Horas eagerly suggested a horseback ride to Ailis and Moira. Ailis hesitated, her mind screaming to decline, but eventually gave in with a heavy heart.

"Aye, a ride sounds pleasant," Ailis fibbed.

Ailis McAfee trailed her sister Moira, unease settling in her stomach, as they approached Bearnard, Lucas, and Horas, who were waiting with their horses. Despite her hesitation, the chance to gather information compelled her to join the three men she was beginning to loathe.

They rode in silence, finally reaching the loch's edge, where they dismounted and settled on a grassy bank for a meal. Moira grinned. "Thank ye for thinking to feed us while we are out. Tis much easier to eat what ye brought than hunt for our own meals."

"Tell us," Ailis asked calmly, "of yer fathers. And of the alliances that yer clan has."

"Me father is Laird Gordon," Lucas boasted. "All of our families are united as allies." He gestured to his friends there with them. "The Gordons are one of the most important clans in the Highlands."

Horas added, "Me sire, Laird Cameron has been allied with the Gordons since I was a small boy. The three of us have been friends since we were young lads."

"And mine own father, Laird MacKenzie is part of the same

alliance," Bearnard chimed in. "We all work toward the same goals."

"None speak of other ties?" Moira pressed lightly. "The Gordons are allied with the McAfees. Isn't that true?"

"Aye, but only the McAfees." Lucas tossed and turned as if he was trapped by his words.

The men exchanged glances before denying any other alliances. Ailis nodded politely while masking her inner turmoil. She knew that the men weren't telling the full truth, but she was certain they would learn all about the other clans. She simply hoped it happened before they left Clan Gordon.

As the afternoon sun filtered through the forest, Lucas lured Ailis away from the others. "Might I have a private word, Ailis?" He sounded inviting, but she knew there was something he wasn't telling her, something that could put her in great danger.

"Of course," she agreed, concealing her unease. The hidden knife against her thigh gave her courage to follow him further into the woods. She knew she could best him with a knife, and he had no sword on his hip. If he had a concealed knife, she was not afraid. Not of Lucas or any other man.

Once surrounded by foliage, Lucas turned to her, his eyes glinting as he leaned in for an unexpected kiss. He moved quickly, and his lips managed to touch hers before Ailis sprang into action.

Ailis pushed back, indignation coursing through her. Swiftly, she stomped on his foot and bit his lip. "Ye have nae right nor leave to lay claim to me affection, Lucas. I decide who kisses me, and ye would not be one I would allow. Never touch me again!"

"Ye'll rue this slight when I gain power in the highlands. Ye will beg for such favor," Lucas snarled.

Unyielding, Ailis retorted, "I shall never long for a man who cannot ken the meaning of consent. Ye are a disgusting man, and I hope I never have to lay eyes upon ye again!" She watched his fury give way to humiliation before he stormed off toward the loch.

Upon their return, Moira's discerning gaze met Ailis's—a

silent question passing between them. Ailis knew Moira had heard Lucas's enraged shouts carried by the wind.

"Is all well?" Moira asked with concern and keen observation.

Ailis smiled. "Aye, all is well. It seems some men must learn the hard way that a woman's touch is hers to give freely or refuse to give."

There was tension surrounding the five of them for the rest of their excursion. Ailis announced she was returning to the castle to ready herself for supper. Moira immediately mounted her horse to return with her sister, not wanting to be left alone with any of the men, and certainly not with all three of them.

As they returned to the keep, Ailis dismounted gracefully, her eyes meeting Moira's already unbuckling her scabbard. The men had followed, saying they needed to be kept safe, but the sisters had ignored them for the ride back.

"Ye're eager for another bout," Ailis observed, a hint of amusement in her voice.

"Not as eager as Lucas is to taste defeat." Moira grinned fiercely.

Lucas had challenged Moira to fight with him again. He seemed to think he would fare better this time.

Ailis laughed. She was oddly detached, preoccupied with alliances and secrets that bound their lives together. She knew Moira would win, and she was certain Lucas did too. Why would he challenge her and allow himself to be beaten by the same woman twice? The man made no sense to her.

This time was much quicker for Lucas. Moira had taken his measure in their first combat, and now it only took her a few minutes to knock Lucas onto his backside. After the fight, the sisters linked arms and returned to the bedchamber they shared. Neither felt the need to talk to the men after their afternoon.

Ailis told Moira exactly what had happened in the forest with Lucas, and Moira shook her head. "I should have plunged me sword through his heart, not allowed him to merely feel disgraced."

Ailis laughed softly. "Nay, sister. I'm a healer. I do not kill indiscriminately, and I dinna want others killing in me name."

NEARBY, BRODIE AND Lachlan dined with Laird Sutherland's daughters, their laughter filling the air. The two sisters seemed a bit addled to Lachlan, and they enjoyed laughing at their own jests, which were not funny to others. He truly wished he could be with anyone more than these two. They exhausted him.

"Do ye follow us under yer father's orders?" he asked, his charming tone masking the gravity of his question.

The twin he was speaking with nodded with a distant gaze. "We must follow ye. Our doing so concerns all of the Highlands. It's our way of keeping the Highlands safe."

While they probed for more information, the sisters' vacant expressions revealed their ignorance of any deeper motives. Clearly, their father was using their beauty to hide his intentions. If only they had minds to match their beauty, they might be attractive, but alas, they were clearly lacking in intellect.

Lachlan longed for Ailis, who had a mind and didn't gawk at him vacuously. She could carry on real conversations about more than simply women's matters. How could a man marry a woman he couldn't converse with?

ONCE IN THEIR room, Moira lamented, "I wish we could choose our own companions. Those three are not to me liking."

"I feel the same, but if we dinnae spend time with them, we won't be able to get them to tell us about their alliances." Ailis shook her head. "I ken they are difficult to be around, but we must continue on as we have been."

Moira sighed. "Ye are right, but I find the idea of even another minute in their company to be intolerable."

"And yet, we must tolerate them. At least we have each other. Imagine if they'd separated the two of us."

All through supper, Ailis tried to get the men to tell them more of their alliance, but they seemed reluctant to tell the sisters anything. "Why would ye not tell us of yer clans' alliances? Are ye planning an attack on the McAfees or something?" she finally asked.

Bearnard shook his head. "Nay. Me father wants me to marry one of ye, so we can *strengthen* our alliance."

Ailis noted that he didn't mention his own feelings. Only his father's. She wasn't surprised though. She knew they'd been hiding something from her and Moira all along.

As the merriment ended that evening, Ailis and her sisters met with Lachlan, Brodie, and Alisdair and Fiona in the same glen as before.

"Lucas tried to steal a kiss today," Ailis told Lachlan, whose eyes sharpened at the news. "I reminded him that a McAfee woman's lips are her own."

"Should I challenge him?" Lachlan offered, half-joking but protective.

Laughing lightly, Ailis replied, "No need. I left him with a lasting reminder." Her smile hinted at strength. "He knows me feelings very well now."

Lachlan smiled. "I'm certain ye did. I hope he has a scar."

"I didn't bite quite that hard," Ailis countered with a grin.

Alisdair cleared his throat, commanding their attention. "I met with the lairds today. They were impassive when I mentioned the Sinclairs' treachery. It was very odd. None spoke for or against them, and they seemed to know what happened all along."

"Didnae they condemn the Sinclairs' refuge with our kin?" Fiona asked worriedly.

"Not a word," Alisdair answered. "It's as if they expected it or didn't care. The Sinclairs shelter with us, yet the lairds remain unmoved. Perhaps they dinnae realize that the Sinclairs will become McAfees and fight with us."

Ailis considered this revelation, her mind racing with potential plots intertwining the clans.

In the silence that followed, they understood that tomorrow would bring more than games and laughter. It held another step in their dance of duty and deceit, another chance to untangle mysteries threatening their clans' fragile peace.

"Consider this," Ailis began steadily despite her inner turmoil. "If the lairds showed indifference at the mention of me abduction, they must have already known about it." Her eyes sought confirmation from the others.

Fiona nodded. "Aye, they knew. I wouldn't be surprised if one of them ordered yer abduction," she agreed. "Their silence speaks louder than outcry ever could. We're entwined in a web woven by all present clans. Could ye tell who was leading the others?"

Alisdair shook his head. "Nay. I dinnae believe the leader was in the room. I'm not certain, but I suspect they didn't know what to say without him."

The others murmured agreement, resolve etched on their faces as it fortified their keep walls. Now—unravelling alliances and betrayals would require even greater observation.

Dispelling the somber mood, Fiona straightened and addressed the group with intrigue in her tone. "Tomorrow is a game day," she announced, adventure gleaming in her eyes. "We'll be divided into teams, and we must accomplish some sort of task with the teams. I know naught more, but it sounds interesting. Our teams are chosen for us, so we shall all play our parts and see if we can get more information."

"Another chance for insight," Ailis murmured. The game,

under the guise of entertainment, would be an opportunity to discern true loyalties and intentions—a chance to pierce pleasantries and uncover the hidden truths behind the motives of the lairds.

Alisdair cleared his throat. "One laird did not join me with the others," he began, voice tinged with gravity. Ailis observed him closely, noting the furrow between his brows deepening.

"His name is unknown, but his presence certain," Alisdair continued, scanning faces before him for counsel. "He may be orchestrating this web we're entangled in. I believe he must be the mind behind whatever they are planning."

A chill crept down Ailis's spine as she glanced at Moira, who shared her concern. The idea of an unseen hand guiding clan fates was unnerving and intriguing.

The meeting ended, and Lachlan stepped closer to Ailis. He leaned forward, kissing her gently.

"Goodnight, Ailis," he whispered.

"Goodnight, Lachlan," she replied, hiding her apprehension. Their paths then carried them away from one another and into the night.

As Ailis and Moira walked to their chamber, they talked about the day. "I wish we were returning to our home" Ailis confessed.

"Me too," Moira sighed. "But tomorrow brings another chance to unravel this mess we seem to be caught up in. I dinnae think we'll be safe until we know exactly what is happening."

Ailis agreed, though tomorrow's game loomed over her like a storm cloud. They would be hunting for the truth hidden behind smiles and veiled alliances.

Their chamber door creaked open—the sanctuary of privacy. As they prepared for slumber, they whispered dreams of returning home.

"Home," Ailis whispered, sinking into her pillow. As she tried to sleep, she clung to hope that tomorrow would bring them closer to where their hearts belonged.

CHAPTER TWENTY-THREE

I N THE GREAT hall the following morning, Ailis sat beside her sister Moira, dreading the game they would play, though she didn't ken what it was. It was the fact she knew she'd be playing with the three suitors, and she was more than a little sick of them. She wanted to drive her knife through Lucas's hand. She didn't think he needed to be killed just yet, but maiming seemed like a good thing where he was concerned.

The aroma of fresh bread filled the air. The laird spoke from the head of the table, his voice echoing throughout the large room.

"Today's quest is one of strategy and cooperation," he announced. "Gather items of significance, present them before the feast, and the successful team shall dine with me in honor."

Ailis and Moira were assigned to Lucas, Horas, and Bearnard as a team. Eager to prove himself, Bearnard tried reading their list of items but struggled with the words. Ailis gently took it and read aloud with Moira. If it was a race, she knew they needed to get the details out quickly, and Bearnard was the only one of the men who was able to read. Thankfully, she and Moira were taught to read as small lasses.

"A tuft of heather from the moors," Ailis began.

"Antlers shed by a stag," continued Moira.

"An unusually shaped stick, an arrow taken from another's quiver," listed Ailis.

"Berries plucked from bramble, forest leaves," chimed Moira.

"Wool strands shorn from a sheep," Ailis added.

"An adornment for hair—perhaps a bow," suggested Moira softly.

"Plaid not woven by kin, water drawn from the loch," Ailis continued.

"A pitchfork from the fields, and a fish from the streams," Moira finished. The diverse list ignited determination in her. The McAfee sisters had always won everything they set out to win, and this challenge would be no different. Ailis felt the weight of expectation mixing with excitement for the hunt.

As Ailis and Moira watched the men bicker over the possible antler locations, they shared a determined nod. They ventured out to gather items on their list.

Moira deftly plucked at a slender, twisted stick adorned with vibrant berries. "Behold!" she exclaimed, scanning the forest floor for more unique finds.

As they ventured deeper into the woods, their excitement grew as they spotted various colorful leaves and plants to add to their collection. "Imagine how well we'd do if the men could figure out how to help us instead of arguing," Moira mused.

Ailis laughed as she moved toward a farmer's wife to ask for a tartan in exchange for the brooch she wore.

"Can we trade for that shawl? It would be lovely on ye," Ailis asked a nearby farmer, holding up the brooch in exchange.

Across the stream, Moira eagerly haggled with a cheeky, giggling girl for a bright hairbow to add to their collection.

The two of them also managed to convince a surprised farmer to lend them his metal pitchfork in exchange for Moira's shawl. As they walked away from the farmer, Moira said, "I dinnae mind being cold for a short while. I do mind losing."

After an hour of exploration and successful trades, they returned to the keep with an impressive bounty of treasures.

After what felt like ages of listening to Lucas, Horas, and Bearnard argue back and forth upon their return, Moira sighed with impatience. She motioned for Ailis to follow as they slipped away into the dense woods, their footsteps rustling through the fallen leaves.

Among the twisted branches and tangled roots, they uncovered a set of magnificent antlers, gleaming in the dappled light. With a triumphant smile, they emerged from the forest and proudly presented their find before any of the other teams could catch up.

As the evening meal was being prepared, Moira couldn't help but feel a sense of satisfaction as she sat next to the very men who had doubted her earlier.

Ailis leaned over to whisper in her ear, "If I had been solely focused on the reward, I would have been much less eager to win."

The warm glow of success filled Moira's chest as she realized that sometimes, winning was its own kind of reward. With a knowing glance between them, both sisters prepared to endure an evening filled with the men's prideful boasts. They would never let on that the women had won the contest for them while they argued. It wasn't in their nature.

SEATED AT THE supper table, Ailis exchanged a weary glance with Moira amidst the men's boisterous claims of triumph. The sisters partook in the meal, its flavors soured by the injustice of unacknowledged efforts. Their contributions were ignored as the men kept bragging of their win.

As the great hall thrummed with music and dancing, Moira approached Lucas with a jest upon her lips and challenge in her eyes. "Lucas, is it any wonder I bested ye with swords? Seems to me all yer clan is adept at is throwing ceilidhs."

Lucas stiffened with offense. "Moira, ye mistake our hospitality for idleness at yer peril," he retorted.

But Moira merely shrugged and turned away, discarding his

umbrage with ease.

Ailis observed, caught between amusement and empathy. In her sister's defiance, she recognized a rebellion against expectations. Yet bound by duty and obligation, she remained a spectator, feeling more annoyed by the moment.

As Laird Gordon's voice rose above the fading music, he announced, "On the morrow, we shall partake in learning a new dance."

The words weighed heavily on Ailis. She exchanged a glance with Moira before they slipped away to their bedchamber. A new dance meant dancing with the same three idiots they'd been forced to dance with since their arrival.

In the sanctuary of their room, Ailis sat at the edge of the bed while Moira paced, the firelight casting shadows upon her face.

"Can ye believe those men?" Moira asked indignantly. "Taking credit for our efforts as if we were naught but ornaments."

"They see only what they wish to see," Ailis murmured. "Our contributions are whispers in a storm to them. There's no way we would have won if we hadn't taken matters into our own hands."

"Promise me, Ailis," Moira pleaded suddenly, standing before her sister. "Promise me ye'll never let me wed someone like Lucas. I'd sooner take vows with an Englishman."

"We may be bound by duty," Ailis agreed, "but our hearts must not be shackled to lazy men such as those."

As night enveloped the castle, the sisters found solace in their shared win. They knew the work they'd done to win the contest, and it didn't matter if others knew. They had won yet again.

AILIS AND MOIRA skipped the morning meal the following morning and left the castle's festivities for the primal rhythm of the hunt. They had felt as if they were only doing frivolous things since the games had ended, and they needed a day to do something productive.

Retrieving their bows from their trunk, they entered the forest, sharing a silent language beneath the sheltering boughs. They could hunt the food they needed for the day and not return to the keep until nightfall.

Hours passed before two noble stags fell to their arrows. They carried the stags to the kitchen, where the cook exclaimed, "Ye were to spend the day learning a new dance!"

"We needed to do something that wasn't frivolous," Ailis declared. She and her sisters had long been working in any way they could find. These people seemed to play before they worked, which didn't sit right with either her or Moira.

THE EVENING WAS filled with swirling tartans and laughter in the great hall, but Ailis and Moira conversed at the edge of it all. Lachlan and Brodie joined them, their easy conversation revealing their shared interests.

Laird Gordon's sharp voice interrupted their reprieve, reminding them of their place within Highland society. "Ye must mingle with those ye do nae know," he commanded, obviously wanting them to stay away from the McClain men.

Ailis and Moira rose, parting ways with Lachlan and Brodie. Ailis wanted nothing more than to spend time outdoors or hide away, but she knew better. She must at least pretend to be trying to be part of the celebration.

As the evening's festivities swelled around Ailis, she yearned for the quiet respite of her chamber. She glanced at Moira, who shared her feelings.

"Let us retire," Ailis suggested. "We've already spent more time here than I would like."

"An excellent notion," Moira agreed wearily.

Their departure was blocked by Bearnard and his companions, Lucas and Horas, all flushed from ale and arrogance.

"Ye're leaving the celebration so soon?" Bearnard asked.

"We've had our fill of frivolity," Moira replied coolly.

"Is our presence not to yer liking then?" Lucas challenged. "Ye weren't here to learn the new dance."

Moira's voice sharpened. "Yer eagerness to take credit for a victory not earned has left us longing for companionship from men who actually know how to work hard."

Ailis added, "Yer quarrels over antlers while we secured our win speaks volumes."

Silence hung heavy before Moira and Ailis maneuvered past the trio. "Mayhap on the morrow ye can reflect on the virtues of humility," Moira suggested over her shoulder.

Then Moira whispered, "Never let me marry someone like them."

"I will not. I assume ye will return the favor?" Ailis asked as they reached their chamber door, anticipating peace and freedom from expectations within.

CHAPTER TWENTY-FOUR

THE GRAND STONE walls of the great hall reverberated with Laird Gordon's booming voice. "This afternoon, we shall partake in a lively game of rum-soaked apple bobbing!"

Ailis and her sister Moira exchanged icy glances, their disdain for such a childish activity clearly evident. Ailis had never enjoyed bobbing for apples, and she knew she wouldn't like the same activity with rum added. With their postures, it was clear that they were both harboring rebellious thoughts behind their composed exteriors.

As they finished their noon meal, the sisters secretly plotted to escape the confines of the keep as soon as possible. Creeping through the quiet corridors, their steps muffled by lush carpets, Ailis and Moira cautiously made their way toward the exit.

But just as they were about to slip out undetected, Laird Gordon appeared before them, blocking their escape with his imposing presence.

"Good morrow," he heaved. "Ye McAfee women are intent on causing trouble at our ceilidh. Where are ye going?"

"We—" Ailis began, wondering how to explain where she and Moira were going.

"Ye cannot leave us now," Laird Gordon scolded. "Ye are integral to today's celebrations."

Ailis stared at the laird in disbelief. "How can two young women be integral to bobbing apples in rum? That makes no sense."

Laird Gordon smiled. "Because ye are. Now return to the great hall."

Their hearts sank at the orders. Having had their hopes of escape crushed, they conceded to the laird.

"We do but wish for quiet before the celebration commences," Ailis forced through gritted teeth. "It's been a loud few days." She didn't add that she and Moira had spent the previous day hunting instead of learning the dance. Shame burned in her chest as she was sure the man already knew of their absence and would use it against them later.

"Ah, but ye shall find serenity in the joy this brings," Laird Gordon commanded affectionately.

Reluctance heavy on their shoulders, Ailis and Moira turned back into the keep. The apple bobbing awaited them—a day filled with dutiful performances expected of them. Whether they were inclined to join or not, they could not bring shame on their clan by refusing.

In the lively great hall, Ailis gazed upon Lachlan, who stood beside a large wooden tub filled with apples in rum. He leaned over the tub, dark hair falling forward as he prepared for the ridiculous game Laird Gordon had planned.

"Watch closely," Lachlan called, eyes gleaming with mischief. "I shall demonstrate the noble art of apple conquest!"

With hands clasped behind his back, Lachlan dipped his head into the barrel. Cheers erupted as he failed to secure an apple, emerging damp and undaunted. He raised both arms above his head in victory.

Ailis chuckled at his efforts. "Mayhap the apples are bewitched, repelling ye like true scoundrels." She loved that he hadn't gotten an apple. The man seemed to be good at everything, and she was thrilled to see that didn't hold true here.

"Or they fear Clan McClain!" Lachlan retorted, shaking droplets from his hair.

Ailis and Moira laughed heartily at his comment before they were interrupted by Bearnard, Lucas, and Horas—their self-appointed suitors—approaching in fine attire and wearing eager expressions.

"Come now, Ailis," Bearnard rumbled. "Yer turn awaits."

Lucas nodded eagerly. "Aye, it'll be grand to see ye best the apples."

Horas loomed a pace behind—an unspoken reminder of duty and tradition.

"Stand aside," Ailis commanded gently. "I am content to observe." She had no desire to stick her face into the barrel. She had never enjoyed bobbing for apples, and when ye added the rum into the activity, she knew she would hate it.

"Observation is the refuge of the timid," Bearnard countered, gesturing toward the tub theatrically.

"Aye, perhaps another day—" Ailis began before being ushered toward the challenge by Lucas and Horas. Now that she was in front of the tub, she worried that if she backed away, she would be seen as a coward.

"Ye needn't fear the rum, nor the apples," Lucas assured her. His eyes seemed to dare her to try the activity, and as much as she despised the man, it was hard for her to back down from a dare.

"Besides, 'tis but in good fun," Horas added, his smile not quite reaching his watchful eyes.

Ailis found herself before the tub and cast a longing glance at Moira. "Very well," Ailis conceded reluctantly. "Let us proceed with this… merriment."

After successfully bobbing an apple, all eyes turned expectantly toward Moira. The youngest McAfee braced herself for battle, defiance flickering in her eyes.

"Moira, 'tis yer turn to partake in the revelry," Bearnard beckoned.

"I think not," Moira retorted sharply. "Such games are better suited for those who find amusement in the spectacle. I'm not one of those." She turned her attention to her sister. "Yer hair is wet and escaping yer braid."

Lucas and Horas closed in on either side of Moira, nudging her firmly toward the tub. With a resigned sigh, she stepped forward. Though she had no desire to participate, if she must, she would do well at it. It was in her nature to always win.

As Moira leaned over the tub, Ailis watched closely, sensing something was amiss. It was then that she realized the men were using the game to lower their defenses with drink.

"Moira," Ailis whispered urgently when her sister resurfaced with an apple. "They seek to cloud our judgment with spirits. We need to keep our senses about us."

Moira's eyes narrowed in understanding. "Fear not, Ailis. They'll find the McAfee sisters are not so easily swayed by a barrel of apples and a splash of rum."

Together, they stood in the middle of the crowd, duty demanding their participation but their shared will seeing them through unscathed. An idea came to Ailis and she leaned toward Moira. "Let's go fix our hair. When we return, we'll try to get more information from the men. Perhaps, they will be addled with drink, as they are trying to force us to be."

Moira and Ailis exchanged glances. Ailis gestured toward the tapestried archway beyond the great hall. As they neared, they were blocked by a guard.

"Back to the festivities," he commanded coldly. "Laird Gordon insists all guests partake until he declares the contest over."

"We would like to repair our hair after our turn was taken. Is that allowed?" Ailis asked.

The guard shook his head. "Nay. Go back."

Ailis sighed and guided her sister back into the crowd for cover. "We'll blend in and find reprieve there," she whispered.

They navigated through the sea of bodies and found Lachlan and Brodie. "Good morrow, Lachlan, Brodie," Ailis greeted. "Our suitors' intentions are very clear—they seek to addle our senses with drink."

Lachlan's eyes narrowed. "Fear not, for ye and Moira shall remain under our watchful eye." Brodie nodded silently.

"Yer aid is most appreciated," Ailis replied. "Ye would think they would know we understand they are trying to ply us with drink."

"We'll stand together," Lachlan declared. "There is no need for ye to give into their schemes."

"We are hoping they will soon be addled from drink, and then we can ask them questions they may finally answer."

"That's a good plan," Lachlan replied with a smile. Then he glared at the raucous scene with disdain. "Patience can serve as a shield in times of folly."

Ailis nodded skeptically, watching another man lunge face-first into a barrel to retrieve an apple with his teeth. "I cannae believe the laird insists we participate in such an absurd task," she mused.

"Truly a spectacle without dignity," Moira chimed in, her lips curling into a wry smile while tugging discreetly at her sleeve.

Lachlan chuckled, eyes crinkling with amusement. "One might argue it reveals more about the people around us than intended."

"However revealing it may be," Ailis replied, "it serves no purpose for those who seek respect and partnership. We'll do what we can to make the most of it though."

Their quiet camaraderie was interrupted by the approach of the three suitors: Bearnard, Lucas, and Horas, each flushed and unsteady. They clumsily inserted themselves between the sisters and the McClains.

"Ah, there ye are!" Bearnard slurred, leaning closer to Ailis. "Ye hinnae had yer turn yet. Come, let us see how ye fair!"

"I have had me turn. I am finished," Ailis replied, doing her best to be polite with the men.

"Aye," Horas added, seeming not to have heard Ailis. "It is a grand tradition that is not to be missed by fair maidens."

"Tradition or not," Ailis began, "I lack enthusiasm for such an activity and since I have taken me turn, I dinnae plan to do so again." Her stance remained resolute as she braced for further protestations.

Moira stood silent, eyes darting to Lachlan and Brodie for support. It was clear that the sisters' afternoon would unfold under the watchful presence of their persistent admirers.

Ailis sensed eyes upon her, their gazes heavy with expectation and tradition. She stood still as Lucas positioned himself by her side, blocking Lachlan's path.

"Lucas," Lachlan cut in, "why do ye stand so close to Ailis? Am I not permitted to be at her side?"

Ailis watched as Lucas faced Lachlan. His features were slackened by drink, but his eyes remained sharp—a window to the sober mind beneath.

"'Tis the plan, Lachlan," Lucas slurred. "We must all follow the plan laid out for us." His tone suggested a path deviation was forbidden.

Lachlan's smile vanished as tension enveloped the group. He clenched his jaw in defiance.

"Who made the plan?" Ailis asked softly, hoping Lucas would say more in his inebriated state.

Horas stepped forward, silencing Lucas. "Enough about plans. We have indulged ye enough for one day."

Ailis caught Moira's eye, sharing a moment of silent understanding. Lachlan glanced at Ailis with concern while Brodie observed the scene quietly.

"We shall retire to prepare for supper," announced Laird Gordon, his voice echoing through the hall. Ailis and Moira exchanged looks of relief. They were going to finally be allowed to be away from the men for a few minutes.

Ailis steadied herself, taking Moira's arm. Together, they moved toward the castle doors, flanked by Lachlan and Brodie. The weight of unspoken questions and unseen plots was heavy with each step.

Once outside, a guard blocked their path. "Please, the hour grows late, and preparations for supper must commence."

Feeling Lachlan's supportive touch, Ailis offered him a faint smile. Moira replied with her usual hint of mischief, "We wouldn't dream of defying tradition."

The guard nodded respectfully and let them pass into the castle. As they climbed the stairs to their bedchamber, the sisters discussed how they would pry as much information as possible from the men that night.

✦

CHAPTER TWENTY-FIVE

AILIS MCAFEE WOVE through the crowd, Moira at her side. Ailis had hoped the evening would grant a reprieve from watchful eyes, but she worried that would not be the case.

"We're like deer being hunted," Moira whispered, her green eyes reflecting torchlight. Ailis nodded.

"Our freedom is an illusion here. We need to find answers so we can leave this place." Ailis couldn't wait to get home.

As they turned toward the throng, rough hands seized them. Ailis found herself caught by Bearnard. His rum-laden breath forced her head aside.

"Why do ye keep asking me to dance when it's apparent ye dinnae have feelings for me?" Ailis asked.

Bearnard's flushed face creased into sobriety as he tightened his grip. "I must perform all me duties, and this is one of me duties. Me father has commanded it."

His gaze held hers, revealing a struggle between rebellion and obligation. She understood that bitter taste of duty mixed with personal desires.

"Why has yer father commanded it? Isn't it odd he would try to force ye to spend time with a certain lass?"

He shook his head. "I do not question. I merely follow orders."

"Let us dance then," she conceded, placing her hand upon his. The hollow echo of their movements barely hinted at the joy the dance intended to evoke. Neither of them wanted to dance with the other, but they both knew their obligations.

Moira reluctantly clasped Horas's hand as they twirled across the floor. The music now seemed a dirge for cherished freedom. As Horas faltered under excess drink, Moira used him to seek out the truth.

"Horas," she asked, "who made the plan for ye and the others to dance with us?"

"Plan?" Horas murmured, struggling to focus on Moira's face. "Ah, me father's rule. We follow, as sons do."

"But who came up with the scheme?" Moira pressed, curiosity sharpening her tone.

"Scheme? I cannot say," Horas replied, confused.

Moira sighed, disappointed with his response. Duty obscured even the simplest insights.

Ailis found herself once again dancing with Lucas, who she loathed even more than Bearnard and Horas. His movements were calculated like a chess piece's advance.

"Lucas," Ailis asked, smiling sweetly, "the plan is working the way it was intended?" He seemed to be the most drunk of the three, so she held high hopes for the insight he could share with her. Surely, he'd tell her what she needed to know, and they could be gone in the morning before anyone knew what they were about.

"Aye," he replied, gaze studying hers intently. "The dance proceeds without fault."

"And who will rejoice at our adherence to this grand design?" she asked, carefully making her voice sound as innocent as she could. Perhaps she and Moira should have studied the Sutherland twins, knowing they had perfect the art of innocence.

"Me father and the Stewart man," Lucas admitted.

Ailis's heart quickened at this revelation. The Stewart? He must be kin to Queen Mary, and he had some sort of plot? She must learn more. She danced on, her mind weaving through implications while her feet moved in time to the music.

AILIS SCANNED THE sea of twirling tartans and gleaming buckles under candlelight. She attempted to reach Lachlan with the knowledge she'd gained, but she was repeatedly blocked by clansmen.

Feeling the weight of her duty, frustrated by her thwarted attempts, she searched elsewhere and spotted Alisdair conversing quietly with Fiona. Navigating the throng with elegance, Ailis intercepted them. They were much easier to approach than Lachlan and Brodie. She didn't know why the couple wasn't watched as carefully as the rest of them, but it gave her the opening she needed to pass along her information.

"Alisdair," she whispered before leaning closer. "I have learned something of grave import."

As the revelry around them faded, Ailis whispered to Fiona and Alisdair, "One of the Stewart men is behind this plan." Fiona's eyes showed a flicker of concern, but she remained stoic.

"Can ye be certain?" Alisdair asked quietly.

"Lucas confirmed as much," Ailis replied. "But the full plan remains unknown. The men are drunk enough that I believe they will tell me everything before the night is out."

"Return to the dance. Learn more if ye can." Fiona appeared as eager to get home as the rest of them.

Ailis retreated into the procession of dancers, her thoughts racing despite her serene expression.

Under the great hall's chandeliers, Ailis danced with Lucas again, swallowing her distaste to get the information they needed so badly. Overwhelmed by the aroma of rum on his breath, she inquired about his family's plans.

"The Stewarts aim to rule the highlands with me father as second-in-command," he confided. "To fracture McAfee strength, one must marry into their line. And we must keep another daughter from marrying a McClain. The McAfees and McClains are both too strong to fight, and together, it would be much more dangerous. So ye canna marry Lachlan McClain. But pick someone other than me. I dinnae like ye."

Ailis hid her horror and probed gently, "I dinnae like ye either! But are ye sure ye dinnae want to marry Moira?"

"Aye," Lucas replied. "The McAfee lasses bring shame upon the Highland ways. They act like men, and they flaunt their warrior skills. No one wants to marry them, but marry them we must. I hope Bearnard has to marry one. I dinnae like him or his name. He's proud of being named after bears, which are ferocious creatures. We need bears in the Highlands."

Once the celebration ended and guests dispersed, Ailis found Moira and they went up to the bedchamber they shared.

"Moira," Ailis whispered, "the Stewarts aim to entrap our clan by severing our alliance with the McClains through marriage. I've told Alisdair part of it, but I believe I know the whole of it now."

As Moira's eyes filled with determination, they joined the others in the glen under the cover of darkness. They moved swiftly through the keep and the grounds, wanting nothing more than to share what they knew so they could leave the following day. The idea of never having to see the suitors again filled Ailis with such joy she all but ran to tell them all what she knew.

Under the stars, Ailis spoke amid her sisters and the three McClain men. "The Stewarts plot to bring the Highlands under his rule by dividing us. Our united clans are too powerful for them to challenge."

Murmurs spread through the group as Fiona met Ailis's gaze, while Moira's hands clenched, her spirit defiant. "Then we must get stronger." Moira smiled.

"What can we do?" Fiona asked.

"I believe we must rally our allies at the McAfee lands," Ailis answered.

Alisdair nodded. "At dawn, we depart to gather our allied clans before the Stewart's plans take root. I will take the ladies and head straight for McAfee lands. Brothers, ye must ride for the McClain lands and tell Father what we know and what is happening."

Lachlan cast a fleeting glance at Ailis, realizing they would be forced to part yet again. "I will do as ye ask, brother. But I want a moment alone with Ailis."

Ailis regretted that they would have so little time before they must part ways. As Lachlan led her a few paces away from the group, Ailis met his searching gaze.

"Ailis," Lachlan began, his voice low yet filled with earnestness, "I ken this parting pains us both. But I swear on me honor, I shall return swiftly to ye once we have secured McClain support."

Ailis nodded, her heart heavy with the weight of their responsibilities. "I trust in ye, Lachlan. I pray we will be together again soon."

Before she could say more, Lachlan leaned in to press a gentle kiss to her forehead, a silent promise exchanged between them. With a final, lingering look, he turned back to join his brother Brodie as they prepared to depart.

With nods of agreement, they prepared for the morrow's journey. Unwavering in their purpose to defy tyranny, they embraced the upcoming challenge.

BEFORE THE FIRST light of dawn pierced the ink-black sky, Ailis emerged from the shadowed threshold of the stables. The cool, pre-dawn air bit at her cheeks as she approached the gathering of horses and men, their breaths visible in the crisp morning.

They all knew this journey would be extremely important for themselves and for the Highlands. "I never thought when Fiona was taken that the treachery could run this deep." Alisdair shook his head. "We've all been blind."

The stable smelled of hay and horse, the earthy scent grounding Ailis as she strode toward her steed, a sturdy gelding with a coat as dark as the night they were leaving behind. She reached out, brushing the horse's mane and finding comfort in its softness.

Her companions busied themselves with checking girths and adjusting stirrups, the clinking of metal and leather a steady cadence beneath their hushed tones.

"Are we ready then?" she asked quietly.

The men nodded, their expressions set in grim lines that spoke of the gravity of their task. Together, they would return to McAfee land, bearing news that could tilt the precarious balance of power in their favor—or spell disaster if not handled with care.

They would ride together for the first day, and then Lachlan and Brodie would head toward McClain land while Alisdair took the others back to the McAfee keep.

Ailis swung herself into the saddle with a grace born of years spent riding the difficult Highland terrain. She spotted Moira, who mirrored her determination, though the shadows beneath her sister's eyes told of restless nights and troubled thoughts. But there was no room for weariness now. The future of their clan— and the entire Highlands—rested on the swiftness of their return and the alliances they could call upon and forge.

With a nod from Ailis, the group moved out. They rode abreast where the path allowed, the thrum of anticipation mingling with the thrill of quiet rebellion in their veins. As the stables disappeared into the darkness behind them, Ailis felt a twinge of relief. The onerous task of playing the dutiful guests to conniving suitors was over, but a new day brought fresh challenges.

Alisdair led the joined party of McClains and McAfees away from their temporary prison, toward the promise of home and the rallying cry for unity. She knew the road ahead would be difficult, but the McAfees were warrior-born, and their will was as unyielding as the highland stone.

CHAPTER TWENTY-SIX

B ENEATH AN ANCIENT oak tree, Ailis dismounted and surveyed the horizon. The ominous clouds above caused unease.

"We're in for a storm," Alisdair remarked to the group, lingering on Lachlan.

Brodie spotted a cliffside cave and pointed it out as their refuge. Lachlan guided everyone toward the cave with haste as rain began. Once inside, the air was damp and heavy compared to the charged atmosphere outdoors, but at least the entire party was out of the rain.

"We'll weather the storm here. It won't be comfortable, but we'll be dry," Alisdair said.

Ailis smiled to herself as she realized they would need to huddle together for warmth, and that meant she could seek out Lachlan's embrace and no one could say a thing. For the first time in her life, she was happy for a storm.

While they waited, time seemed to crawl as they talked about the revelations discovered on their last night on Gordon land. They'd been rude to leave the way they had, but Lachlan had feared they wouldn't be allowed to leave if anyone had known their plans.

Clyde Stewart's plot to control the highlands weighed on their minds. "I worry about what will become of the Highlands if Stewart has his way." Ailis voiced their concerns. "It won't feel like the same place."

Ailis listened intently to Alisdair talk about what he was thinking about the enemies' scheme. "We must do all we can to stop such treachery," he declared.

Fiona nodded, while Moira grappled with the enormity of their task.

"We must decide which clans we can trust to stand with us, and which ones we dare not explain the problem to," Lachlan said. "I worry that word will get out to the wrong people, and it will get back to the Stewarts. We're already targets, but that would paint a big bullseye on our backs." He shook his head. "But word will get out as we gather our allies. I wish there was a simple answer."

"We must stand united," Ailis whispered.

As the storm subsided the following afternoon, Ailis stepped outside into the sunlight. The world appeared lush, but she knew the ground was wet, and the rest of their trip must be taken more slowly.

"We must be careful as we move on." She surveyed the muddy ground that threatened each step. They resumed their journey cautiously.

DUSK SETTLED ON the Highlands, painting the sky in shades of lavender and rose. Ailis bid farewell to Lachlan, as he headed for McClain land with Brodie, while the rest of them moved on toward McAfee land. She fought to hold back her emotions, knowing tears were an unaffordable luxury.

"Be ever watchful, Lachlan," Ailis whispered, holding him tightly. She took in his scent—pine and earth.

"Ye ken I will, Ailis." His reply was soft but firm, his eyes reflecting an enduring promise. "And we shall join ye in McAfee territory just as quickly as we are able." Disregarding the people watching, Lachlan kissed Ailis softly, holding her close. They were forced to part, and he wanted to remember the feel of her in his arms.

Brodie stood by silently, his gaze heavy with the weight of parting. He offered a reassuring nod before the brothers turned, disappearing down the path that led them back to the McClains.

As night fell, McAfee soldiers emerged from the woods. The captain approached Ailis, concern laced in his voice. "Ailis, why has it taken ye so long to return? Yer father sent us out to search two days past." He was obviously worried.

With a steady voice, Ailis recounted their harrowing journey and the crucial information that united them. "We must get home to gather our allies for the coming battle. They will know we left because we know the plan."

The soldiers apparently understood as a sense of determination flooded through the group.

"Then let us make haste toward home," declared the captain. Four volunteered to carry word to allied clans and disappeared into the night like windborne whispers.

The journey continued under a starlit sky, the soldiers' presence a comforting shield against uncertainties. Home called with its promise of warmth and safety, yet Ailis knew respite would be fleeting.

ALISDAIR'S STEED CARRIED him onto McAfee lands, leaving the wilds behind. With the agility of a warrior, he dismounted and surveyed the familiar battlements.

"Alisdair," Duncan McAfee greeted. "What tidings? We expected ye days ago!"

"Grave news," Alisdair replied, describing whispers of treachery from the Stewart who threatened Scotland's unity. "They would not let us speak to one another and kept Ailis and Moira busy by providing three of the lairds' sons to sit with them at meals and dance with them."

Duncan furrowed his brow. "A Stewart? Our queen must not

know. Queen Mary would be angered by the betrayal of her kin." He appeared disgusted that a member of someone's family could betray them in such a way.

"She still resides in France. She will not ken what is happening here."

"We've sent riders to the MacGregors, McDonalds, McDuff's, and Robertsons for unity and strength," Alisdair explained. "We ask for all to gather on McAfee land."

"Then let it be so," Duncan agreed. "We'll stand against those who seek power."

Alisdair exchanged a heavy glance with Duncan by the hearth. "Tomorrow," Duncan began with fatherly concern, "allies will arrive hungry and weary. Me daughters will lead the hunt at dawn."

AT DAYBREAK, AILIS emerged from the keep accompanied by Fiona and Moira. Sinclair women who had sought refuge among the McAfees approached, offering their help with bows and arrows in hand. Grateful, Ailis devised a plan to divide the group into hunters and fishers.

Ailis moved with purpose as she demonstrated knife-wielding techniques. The Sinclair women watched intently, eager to learn this vital skill. The women had been forbidden to hunt while they were members of Clan Sinclair, and now they were finally learning.

"Ye must respect the blade," Ailis began. "For it is an extension of yer own hand." She held the knife before her, its polished surface gleaming. With a swift motion, she sliced through the air. The Sinclair women mimicked her movements.

She showed them how to properly throw a knife, explaining that they had to be very careful not to hurt their friends in the process.

Nearby, Fiona, her blond hair bound in a practical braid, nocked an arrow to her bow. Observing Fiona's stance, the Sinclair women tried to emulate her poise.

"Draw the bow with purpose," Fiona instructed firmly but encouragingly. "Let the arrow fly true to yer intent." As she released the string, the arrow found its mark. Gasps of admiration rose from the observers. "But remember to be careful to know who is around ye at all times. We cannot lose even one of ye. Yer all family now!"

As Ailis continued her knife-wielding demonstration, one of the Sinclair women, Flora, attempted to mimic the swift slicing motion but accidentally tossed her knife backward over her shoulder.

There was a moment of stunned silence before Ailis cried, "Ah, Flora, I did say respect the blade, not send it on a surprise exploration mission!"

Flora apologized profusely, and Ailis just laughed. "No one was injured, and now ye'll be more careful."

Fiona couldn't help but chuckle as she noticed one of the Sinclair women struggling with the bowstring. With a twinkle in her eye, Fiona teased, "If ye keep wrestling with that string like a wild boar, lassie, we might have to recruit ye for a whole new kind of battle formation—the infamous fumbling archer brigade!"

The group erupted into laughter. Everyone knew the sisters were trying to lighten the mood as they learned new skills with dangerous weapons.

While Fiona and Ailis demonstrated with the weapons, Moira walked among the women, correcting their holds of their weapons as needed. Finally, they were ready, and the group of women set out into the woods.

Once they were in the forest, they broke into three groups, each lead by one of the McAfee sisters. With each step through the towering pines, Ailis felt a deep sense of duty. She understood that today's sacrifices would contribute to tomorrow's safety and prosperity while maintaining a delicate balance between collective needs and individual yearnings.

Ailis nocked an arrow to her bow, imagining a time when love and laughter filled these woods. But now, only the hunt mattered—a task of survival echoing through the Highlands.

Ailis watched her sisters and the Sinclair women move among the trees. The rustle of leaves and snap of twigs underfoot punctuated the calm. Their baskets grew heavier with rabbits and small game, slung across their backs.

At the end of the day, six deer lay before them, showcasing the skill of the McAfee and Sinclair women. Pride swelled within Ailis despite her weariness.

"Granny will be pleased," Fiona remarked softly, exhaustion in her voice. Ailis nodded, envisioning Granny's satisfied expression.

"There will be plenty of meat to serve the other clans who join us," Ailis added.

Fish were brought to Granny and Elspeth, who stood ready to prepare the feast for allies in the days to come. "We'll cook as much as we need, and the rest will be smoked and dried so we will have meals even if we are keep-bound," Granny murmured. She had lived through many battles, and she knew the way to keep everyone fed.

Moira rallied the youngest among them. "Children, to the fields with ye," she called authoritatively. Ailis observed as the children ran off, laughter bubbling from their lips, yet their steps carried importance—they had a role in gathering the harvest. It was good to see their enthusiasm for the task at hand.

Ailis leaned against the stone wall of the keep, allowing herself a brief respite. She understood sacrifices had to be made for her clan. And sleep appeared to be one of those sacrifices.

Her green eyes reflected an uncertain future—a future requiring unity and strength. She had never lived through a siege such as the one they were expecting, but she knew she would help in any way possible. Hunting was something she did well, so she would help with the hunt for as long as needed.

"On the morrow, we will tend to our guests," Ailis announced. "If ye have no job in the clan yet, please report to the keep when ye rise. We will need people to help cook and serve."

During a time of need, the Sinclair women's unexpected assistance amazed Ailis as they worked seamlessly with her kin.

"Look at them," Moira whispered to Ailis in awe. "They work as though our cause were their own."

"Aye," Ailis agreed, watching the Sinclairs effortlessly carry heavy game. "They know they have a home with us, and they are grateful."

Fiona joined them, a nod of approval softening her stern expression. "Their eagerness to aid us speaks volumes of their character."

"Perhaps it's our shared love for these lands or a common enemy that unites us," Ailis mused aloud before turning her attention back to the Sinclairs.

"Let's thank them and ensure they're made comfortable," she suggested to Fiona and Moira.

As the sisters moved among the Sinclairs, expressing gratitude, their bonds strengthened. They hoped this alliance would shield them in uncertain times ahead.

As Ailis went about her task of matching children with farmers, a mischievous thought popped into her head. She couldn't help but chuckle to herself as she imagined what chaos might ensue if the children decided to play a prank on the farmers during the harvest.

"Just imagine," she mused aloud to Fiona and Moira, "if instead of helping with the crops, they started a mini food fight with the vegetables! Ewan might end up with more carrots in his hair than in the basket."

Moira giggled. "If we didn't need the food so badly, I would suggest it to the children."

Despite the serious nature of their work, the image of mischievous children turning the harvest into a vegetable battleground brought a lightness to Ailis's heart. Sometimes, a little laughter during hard work was just what they all needed to break the tension and further strengthen their bonds.

⚜

CHAPTER TWENTY-SEVEN

Ailis stood at the edge of her father's grand courtyard. She greeted incoming allied lairds with practiced grace alongside Fiona and Moira. It had been their task to welcome guests since they were old enough, and she enjoyed meeting all the new people.

"Welcome, Laird Robertson." Ailis extended a hand to the next arrival. She observed the accompanying warriors, noting their strength and weaponry. "We're so glad you joined us."

The courtyard filled with voices and clanking armor as suppertime neared. Ailis's attention shifted to Lachlan leading his family's delegation. She was so happy he was back!

Ailis's heart raced as he dismounted and strode toward her. "Good even, Ailis," Lachlan greeted before drawing her aside from watchful eyes. "There's talk of war," he whispered. "Before we battle, I want ye to be me wife. Will ye marry me?"

Her breath caught, joy surged through her at the thought of standing beside Lachlan as his wife, understanding this union meant more than just love. It was also an alliance for uncertain times.

"Seek me father's blessing," she reminded him, formal yet trembling with hope. "But know this, Lachlan—I would be honored to be yer bride."

Her admission hung between them like a fragile promise. As supper's call echoed through the keep, Ailis awaited the outcome of her father and Lachlan's meeting.

LACHLAN ENTERED THE great hall with a pounding heart. Laird Duncan McAfee stood by the hearth. Lachlan approached, feeling the weight of his request.

"Duncan," Lachlan began, inclining his head. "I have a matter to discuss."

Duncan turned to face him, his eyes searching Lachlan's. "Speak yer piece."

"I wish to speak of Ailis," Lachlan continued. "With yer permission, I ask for her hand in marriage, to further unite our clans."

Silence fell as Duncan regarded him. Then, he nodded slowly. "Ye have me blessing. I can see that the two of ye work well together. And though I wanted me daughters to each make a new alliance, it seems to be smart to strengthen our alliance with the McClains at this time. Ye won't take her away until after the war?"

With gratitude, Lachlan smiled. "Thank ye. And no. I will not take her away until after the war, and until after Alisdair feels comfortable with his new job as laird."

HE REJOINED AILIS and announced that they would be wed that evening. Her face bloomed with joy, and she clasped her hands together.

"Then we mustn't tarry," she trilled. "An hour after supper, we shall stand before the priest and pledge ourselves to each other."

As Ailis sat down beside Lachlan for their only meal as a betrothed couple, she realized that neither of them had ever spoken of love to the other. Certainly, he felt for her if he'd asked her to marry him! But... was it love? She couldn't ask him, as she'd never uttered the words either. *He* should say them first.

As soon as the meal was over, her sisters ushered her away to prepare for the ceremony. Ailis allowed herself to be guided, envisioning her life ahead with Lachlan. And though she'd expected to have more time to prepare for her wedding, she knew this was how things were meant to happen. She could feel it deep within her.

Her sisters readied her in silence. They dressed her hair and clothed her in a purple gown that hinted at elegance and strength, its color as deep as the moor's heather.

Ailis studied her reflection in the mirror that had cost a knight's ransom, not recognizing herself. A linchpin of an alliance and beacon of hope, she thought of Lachlan, the man who had claimed her heart in political turmoil. "Let us not keep him waiting. Tonight, we forge our future." With purpose, she went to the chapel.

The chapel's soft candlelight held anticipation as Ailis entered on her father's arm. Each step toward the altar melded her future with Lachlan, whose gaze met hers. There was a slight smile on his face, showing her that he was as happy as she was this was finally happening. They'd practically courted for a lifetime, but in truth it was only a couple of months.

Father Neil, the new priest who was meant to serve both the Sinclairs and the McAfees nervously began the ceremony, stumbling over words as if they were stones. Laughter rippled through the assembly, a moment of levity shared by Ailis and Lachlan amidst their commitment.

When asked who gave Ailis away, Duncan proclaimed himself proudly, his voice echoing with the future of their clans.

Neil hesitated, squinting at the text. "Do ye, Lachlan, take Ailis to be yer lawfully wedded wife, to protect and to cherish, from this day forward?"

"I do." Lachlan's vow echoed through the chamber.

"And do ye, Ailis, take Lachlan to be yer lawfully wedded husband, to honor and to..." Neil trailed off.

"Cherish," Ailis gently supplied.

"Then by the power somewhat vested in me," Neil declared, laughter following his words, "I now pronounce ye husband and wife."

Ailis thought perhaps Neil needed a little more practice when it came to performing marriages. She suspected they must be the first couple Father Neil had married, but that didn't bother her. Nay, she was married to Lachlan, and that was what truly mattered.

Ailis was joyous in the knowledge that they united their people against impending strife. The celebration that followed was filled with lairds and soldiers who came to support this alliance. The great hall brimmed with boisterous voices as goblets clinked in celebration. Amidst the revelry, an undertow of tension reminded everyone of sacrifices made and battles yet to come.

When the last torch flickered, Ailis leaned into Lachlan's side. They watched firelight play upon their allies' faces, knowing they had achieved a unity born of love and laughter.

THE LAIRDS AND their top soldiers greeted Ailis as she entered the gathering in the war room. Their somber expressions and heavy air indicated the gravity of the situation.

"Tell us what ye ken," Laird Campbell demanded, his gaze imploring Ailis to share her knowledge of the dreaded treachery.

Composed, Ailis began her tale. "Lucas Gordon son of Laird Gordon, while deep in his cups, revealed the Stewart's desire to control and oppress the Highlands. He and two of his friends were assigned to keep Moira and me away from Lachlan and Brodie McClain while we were at the Gordon's Highland Games."

She recounted her own abduction and Fiona's capture by the Stewart's command. Her eyes burned with defiance as she warned about the dire consequences if he remained unchecked. "He means to take over all the Highlands, changing our lives completely. I cannot imagine living here under his rule. He must be stopped!"

A heavy silence filled the room before Lachlan spoke. "War comes. We must prepare and stand united against the Stewart's tyranny."

Amidst heated discussion, strategy proposals, and pledges for support, Lachlan added, "Let us be swift and cunning. We shall form an army that will be larger and better trained than his."

As plans took shape and battle lines formed, Lachlan's thoughts lingered on Ailis, knowing she was now his wife lightened his heart in many ways. For her and their future, he steeled himself for the trials ahead. As the meeting adjourned, war echoed in every footstep, duty binding him beyond spoken vows.

IN THE CANDLELIT room, Ailis held her precious mirror, her reflection displaying a mix of anxiety and hope. Fiona and Moira helped her into her nightgown with delicate fingers. The fabric clung to her form as they murmured affectionately about how stunning she was.

"Lachlan will be speechless," Fiona added softly, emphasizing the importance of the night ahead.

Ailis's heart fluttered with happiness, but she also sensed the looming threat beyond the castle walls. "How can I be the wife he needs and also worry about the battle ahead?"

"Ye'll find it's easier than ye think!" Fiona grasped her sister's hands. "Just remember to enjoy what he does. Give yerself to it fully, and do not let thoughts of the battle enter yer mind!"

The chamber door opened, revealing Lachlan. His once-charming expression now bore the weight of responsibility. Ailis crossed the room and gently grasped his arms, asking what troubled him as her sisters left the room quietly.

"The lairds have decided McAfee lands are crucial in uniting this alliance," Lachlan explained. "We'll train together so that we will all be able to fight together easily."

"Our people are at the forefront of the resistance," Ailis realized. He tenderly touched her jaw. "It's how it was meant to be for whatever reason. We were brought in from the moment Malcolm started trying to get Fiona to marry him."

Lachlan sighed. "I dinnae like the battle being so close to ye and yer sisters."

"I dinnae think our feelings matter overly much," she murmured. "We must do our part to stop the Stewart, and that means gathering soldiers here."

He sighed. He had no desire to put her or anyone else in danger, but he must do his duty to help stop the Stewart's plans. "I just hope that the deaths are few and the injuries are easy to deal with."

"Let it be so," Ailis declared. "For love, family, and the Highlands we cherish."

Ailis understood sacrifice. She would stand with him through both their union and war's trials.

The chamber flickered with candlelight as Ailis moved into Lachlan's arms. She wanted to forget all about the battle to come, but she could see by his face he was still troubled.

Lachlan stood by the hearth, his tall frame silhouetted against the flames, eyes heavy with unspoken concerns.

"Ye look troubled, me love," Ailis murmured, smoothing his furrowed brow. Her touch was light but strong in her support. Lachlan's hand clasped over hers, bringing it to his lips in grateful appreciation.

"Tonight, no troubles shall shadow our union," he vowed, drawing her close. Their world outside receded as she moved into his arms.

His touch ignited a remarkable spark within her. The warmth

of his breath against her neck sent shivers down her spine as he whispered words of endearment into her ear.

She could feel his arousal growing beneath his kilt. Her heart raced faster as he explored every curve of her body through her nightdress. She could feel the bulge against her stomach and knew he wanted more than just this dance.

They nestled together on a fur blanket by the fireplace. Lachlan's lips found hers with a fiery passion that left her breathless. They caressed each other's bodies hungrily, seeking out every inch. Moans echoed in the dimly lit room as they explored one another's skin like it was a forbidden land waiting to be discovered.

Lachlan's strong hands gripped her hips tightly while he kissed down her neck and along her collarbone, causing goosebumps to form on her skin. Her fingers dug into his hair, holding him closer as he suckled on those sensitive spots on her neck and collarbone.

His rough stubble scratching against her soft skin only heightened her desire. The coarseness of his facial hair contrasted delightfully with the silky smoothness of her delicate neck as he trailed hot, open-mouthed kisses down to the swells of her breasts peeking above her bodice. Ailis arched into his touch, her body singing with sensations she never knew existed.

Lachlan's nimble fingers unlaced the front of her gown, baring more of her creamy flesh to his hungry gaze. He took his time, savoring each new expanse of skin revealed, worshiping her beauty with lips and tongue. Ailis shivered and sighed, lost to the magic his masterful mouth worked upon her.

"Me bonnie lass," Lachlan murmured reverently against her collarbone, his warm breath tickling her sensitive skin. "I've dreamt of this moment, of having you in me arms as me wife." His voice was low and husky with desire, sending sparks of yearning through Ailis's core.

She cupped his face, bringing his lips back to hers in a searing kiss. "As have I," she breathed against his mouth. "I am yours, heart, body, and soul, from this day until me last."

Lachlan groaned, the declaration inflaming his passion. He captured her lips again, delving deep, his tongue dancing with hers as he fondled her curves possessively. Ailis matched his fervor, giving herself over to the sweet ache building between her thighs.

Their remaining clothes fell away and Lachlan lowered her gently onto the fur blanket. She opened herself to him, welcoming the weight of his muscular frame as he settled between her parted thighs. Locking eyes, a moment of profound connection passed between them—the gravity of their union, not just of bodies but of hearts and families, stretching out into their future together.

He entered her then in one smooth thrust, their bodies joining as intimately as their lives, two halves uniting into one glorious whole. Ailis gasped at the unfamiliar stretching sensation, but there was no pain, only a feeling of incredible fullness and rightness.

They moved together slowly at first, rocking in a timeless rhythm as ancient as the Highlands around them. Lachlan's thrusts were deep and purposeful, stoking the flames climbing higher inside Ailis with each sultry drag of his manhood against her slick, sensitive walls. Their breath mingled in the scant space between their lips. They panted and sighed in unison as pleasure rippled through their joined forms.

Ailis dug into the firm globes of Lachlan's buttocks, urging him harder, faster. The delicious friction sent sparks skittering along her nerves, tightening the coil of rapture winding in her belly.

Lachlan trailed scorching kisses down the column of her throat, latching onto the hammering pulse point as Ailis threw her head back with a blissful cry. He suckled the delicate skin, marking her as his own while his increasingly forceful thrusts pushed them both closer to the pinnacle.

"Lachlan!" Ailis keened, her inner muscles starting to flutter and clench around his surging length. "I… I'm going to…"

"Let go, me heart," Lachlan rasped, grinding against the bundle of nerves at the apex of her womanhood. "I'll catch you, always."

His words sent Ailis careening over the edge. Ecstasy exploded behind her eyelids, wave after wave crashing through her as she convulsed with abandon. Lachlan followed her a moment later. They clung to each other as the tempest of sensation slowly ebbed into their sated afterglow, trading sweet, languid kisses and tender caresses.

Lachlan rolled to the side, gathering Ailis close and tucking her against his chest. She fit perfectly in the curve of his body, two puzzle pieces locking seamlessly together. He stroked her hair, marveling at the silky texture slipping through his fingers.

"I never knew such joy could exist," Ailis murmured dreamily, nuzzling into the warm hollow of Lachlan's throat. "You've unlocked something inside me, something I never want to lose."

Lachlan's arms tightened around her slim frame. "Nor I, me bonnie wee wife. No man has ever been so blessed as I am in this moment."

They lay entwined before the glowing hearth, basking in the warmth of the dying embers and the newness of their physical love. Sleep tugged gently at their sated bodies and they drifted off, secure in each other's embrace.

As dawn's first light crept across the horizon, Ailis stirred, blinking awake slowly. She was momentarily disoriented before the delicious ache in her body and Lachlan's strong arms around her brought the memories of their wedding night rushing back. A secret smile curved her kiss-swollen lips.

Carefully extricating herself from Lachlan's hold, Ailis rose and stretched languidly. She padded barefoot to the window, pushing open the shutters to greet the new day. The first rays of golden sunlight bathed her skin. She closed her eyes, savoring the perfect contentment suffusing her entire being.

— ◆ ❦ ◆ —

CHAPTER TWENTY-EIGHT

AILIS AND THE clan's women gathered at the forest's edge, bows in hand. Lachlan led the men in drills and sparring across the open field, their shouts and clashing swords faded sounds off in the distance.

"Keep yer wits about ye," Ailis reminded her companions, aware of their duty to feed the growing number of people visiting their clan. As they advanced into the woods, she moved gracefully, scanning for game.

A sudden rustle signaled potential prey. Ailis raised her bow, aiming at a thicket where shadows danced. But as she loosed her arrow toward a darting rabbit, fate intervened. The arrow struck not the rabbit but a pheasant mid-flight. Feathers cascaded as it plummeted to the ground.

Despite their important task, the group broke out into laughter. "Seems our hands are guided to what we *truly* need," Ailis bubbled, mischief glinting in her eyes.

"Perhaps 'tis a sign that our endeavors will be fruitful," replied one of the women with a wide smile.

Collecting their unexpected prize, gratitude swelled within Ailis—moments like these fueled her spirit for future challenges.

AILIS SAT ON a stool by the hearth. The door creaked open,

revealing a breathless messenger.

"News from Laird Gordon." He offered her a scroll.

Ailis read the message—terse words about their absence being noted and drunken confessions holding no weight. And a demand they return. Worried, she found Lachlan in the training yard, sword in hand.

"Our absence has been noticed," she informed him. "Laird Gordon says drunken words mean nothing." She shook her head. "I know Lucas was telling the truth while drunk though, and he wasn't before then. Laird Gordon wants us to return."

"I believe Lucas did tell the truth. We're not returning. We were not treated well there. We must be vigilant," Lachlan replied, his eyes like stormy seas.

Ailis nodded. "We'll navigate this situation with care."

As days melded into weeks, clans gathered and alliances formed. Ailis became central to whispered strategies and critical conversations. Their numbers swelled to a formidable force. Power and determination resonated within her.

Despite the burgeoning strength around her, Ailis bore responsibility's heavy mantle. She knew on one level that the whole thing was not her fault, but as she was the one to uncover the plot, she bore some blame.

AILIS ENTERED THE castle kitchen, greeted by the aroma of stewing herbs and root vegetables. Granny stirred a large pot near the hearth.

"Granny, how fair our provisions?" Ailis asked with concern. "Do we need to have more women fishing?"

"We are managing," Granny replied. "But we must seek additional sustenance soon. We want to have meat tucked away for when the siege occurs. It may only last a few hours, but it's more likely to take longer. We'll have to feed all the women and children staying in the keep as well as the soldiers."

"Then we shall hunt and harvest within Sinclair lands," Ailis resolved. "I dinnae know how many of the Sinclairs came here when we offered sanctuary or how many are left, but there should be enough hunting to help us."

The following day, Ailis and Moira led a procession beyond the castle walls. As men dispersed into the woods, women and children worked in the fields. Laughter filled the air, momentarily displacing thoughts of conflict.

A group of dirty children presented oddly shaped roots and stones to Ailis. One beamed as he held up a misshapen rock, exclaiming, "We've found dragon's eggs!"

Moira chuckled beside her sister. "Indeed, but let's hope they dinnae hatch before supper." She winked at Ailis.

"We dinnae want to have to share our meal with the dragons!" Ailis smiled and played along. "Ye've done most wonderfully, me young dragon hunters. But today, let us gather nature's bounty to fill our bellies instead of finding pets who could cook us and eat us."

For a moment she felt badly, asking the children to help with the harvest instead of "treasure hunting," but there were too many to feed for her to dwell on that. The work must be done, and it must be done quickly. There were so many things that must happen before they were ready for battle.

The children nodded enthusiastically and resumed their tasks, leaving Ailis and Moira sharing a knowing glance—a silent acknowledgment of small joys in the worst circumstances.

AS DAWN BROKE over the moors, Ailis stood on the ramparts, her hair whipped by the wind. Below, soldiers from various clans moved in unison, their drills reflecting newfound unity. The sounds of steel and exertion filled the air.

"Father," Ailis called. Her father surveyed the men, his expression weighed down with responsibility. "I've seen these soldiers and observed their ways. Might I stand with them in battle?" She was a formidable warrior after all. Ailis believed she and her sisters could possibly turn the tide of the battle, as no one would expect women.

Her father's face softened as he turned to her. "Nay, me child. Yer duty lies elsewhere." He gave her an understanding look, but she could tell there was no arguing with him.

Later, Ailis sought solace with Lachlan as he sharpened his blade. "Lachlan," she began, frustration clear in her voice, "me father refuses to see me worth beyond domestic duties. Should not I stand with ye all when the time comes? I am ready for the fight!"

Lachlan paused, his eyes meeting hers. "Ailis, I understand yer desire to fight, but I agree with yer father—it's about safety."

"Safety?" Ailis echoed angrily. "Am I to be shielded while others risk their lives? I thought ye would understand. I'm strong enough to help!"

"Understanding does not eliminate danger," Lachlan replied firmly. "Ye are vital to our future. Yer place is here. Ye and the other women must keep hunting and harvesting for as long as ye can."

"Then perhaps I was mistaken about us," Ailis whispered as she turned away, leaving Lachlan conflicted. She could not believe he was taking her father's side over her own. It made absolutely no sense to her.

Their first disagreement as a married couple lingered as Ailis retreated to their quarters. Alone with her thoughts, she gazed at the landscape before her. The Highlands were beautiful, and the idea of losing their unique gifts was unpalatable. She hoped the soldiers who would fight to help the Stewart understood that their entire lives would change if he won. Their beautiful Highlands would never be the same.

AILIS SOUGHT HER sisters out, sharing her grievance with Lachlan. Fiona and Moira listened, features etched with concern.

"Ye cannae be serious," Fiona cried. "To take up arms when yer talents must be used elsewhere? What if someone we love is injured, and ye arena able to help?"

"Indeed," Moira added. "Yer wisdom and care are needed more than ever."

Frustration flickered in Ailis, but she recognized the truth in their words. "Perhaps yer right." Her voice was tinged with melancholy. It would be wasteful not to use her abilities in the battle, but she needed to be healthy to heal others.

At nightfall, Ailis whispered an apology to Lachlan. "I spoke in haste, clouded by pride. I see now that me duty lies in safeguarding our future. There must be someone who can heal the wounded, and that person canna be hurt as well." She sighed. "I just wish I could help with the battle as well. I want to do it all, but it makes no sense."

Lachlan pulled her close, his gaze softening like the twilight sky. "There is naught to forgive. We each have our battles to fight."

Their lips met in a fervent union, their mouths melding together. Their bodies pressed tightly against one another, the heat of their passion igniting and spreading like wildfire. With each touch and caress, a silent language was spoken between them—a language of desire and longing, of love and need. They found solace in each other's arms, seeking comfort and strength despite the uncertainty of tomorrow. Duty and affection intertwined seamlessly, creating a powerful bond that could weather any storm. And in that moment, nothing else mattered except the fire burning within them, consuming everything else in its path.

Ailis's hands slid up Lachlan's broad chest, savoring the feel of his muscular form beneath her palms. She sighed into their kiss, losing herself in his intoxicating taste and scent. The world fell away until there was only Lachlan—his strong arms encircling her, his fingers threading through her hair, his tongue dancing with hers in an ancient rhythm of give and take.

When they finally broke apart breathlessly, Lachlan rested his forehead against hers. "I cannae bear to be at odds with ye," he groaned.

"Nor I with you," Ailis whispered, her eyes shimmering with unshed tears. "Promise me, Lachlan. Promise we'll never let anything come between us again."

"I promise. And speaking of that, there are clothes between us, and that must change quickly."

She giggled, happy to oblige. In this moment, Ailis knew she would forever stand beside Lachlan—their courage reflected in each other's eyes, their purpose intertwined.

As Ailis lay against Lachlan's chest, feeling its steady rise and fall, she traced his jawline with a light touch. "Why do ye object to me joining the battle? Isn't it me right to stand for our clans? And for all the Highlands?" she asked quietly in the darkness.

Lachlan brushed her hair from his chest, sighing wearily. "It's not about rights, Ailis. I fear for ye on the battlefield—it's no place for someone like ye. Ye felt badly for killing two men in battle during yer rescue from the Sinclairs. Imagine how ye'd feel if it had been more than that? We canna risk ye being unable to heal or yer heart being burdened by taking the lives of others." His voice conveyed deep concern as he met her gaze. "I cannae bear the thought of losing ye. Yer presence is me solace during troubled times."

Taking a deep breath, Ailis nestled closer to him and agreed to stay behind, moved by his sincerity. "I will stay in the keep during the battle then. But I want it known if yer injured, I want ye brought to me immediately." The idea of him being hurt or worse…it scared her more than she cared to admit.

"I will tell the men," he assured her.

As sleep approached, Ailis listened to Lachlan's heartbeat. His protective embrace comforted her despite the impending war. In that moment, she was at peace knowing they faced an uncertain future together.

CHAPTER TWENTY-NINE

AILIS OBSERVED THE training soldiers, her green eyes reflecting the turmoil below. The arrival of clans pledging their swords was constant and gave her hope for the future. Lachlan and Alisdair led the training field, while Brodie helped sharpen each warrior's skills with the sword.

A cry interrupted the metallic symphony—a soldier had fallen, clutching his arm in pain. Ailis hurried to aid him, assessing and bandaging the wound expertly. "Ye'll be holding yer sword again soon," she promised as he acknowledged her help with a faint smile.

She continued her rounds, tending to injuries, her hands stained with healing herbs. Swiftly responding to calls for help, she never wavered in her commitment to mend flesh and lift spirits.

AILIS OBSERVED THE clan's women venturing into the dense woods, bows and quivers at the ready. The McAfee lands, once full of laughter, were now filled with people who worked hard. It was good to have the entire clan working as one. They had always worked hard, but there had been time for merriment as well. Now it seemed like there was no time for any idle task.

The forest provided for them, as always, but it was now the

women who brought back the bounty. Ailis paced restlessly within the keep's stone walls, longing to join them but knowing her skills were needed elsewhere.

Injuries abounded as men trained tirelessly with swords from dawn until dusk. Ailis treated wounds and whispered comforting words, yet she missed days spent roaming Highland forests. It was strange how annoyed she'd been by the frivolity of the Gordons while she was there, and now she yearned for just a few moments of fun.

News arrived discreetly: The McKays, tied to the McClains through marriage long ago, secretly served as allies against the Stewarts' alliance, though the Stewarts though the McKays were an ally. Ailis studied their letters carefully—each a flicker of hope during the worry of war.

Despite the valuable intelligence they provided, unease lingered in Ailis's heart. The path they walked was perilous. Sacrifices were made for the greater good. Her hands, once only used for healing, wielded the power to influence future battles.

Ailis's responsibilities constantly weighed upon her. Duty called her to heal the soldiers, but it came at the cost of her tranquility. Each day blurred personal desires and political necessities until she wondered if peace would ever return to her beloved Highlands.

IN THEIR BEDCHAMBER, Ailis found solace in Lachlan's warm embrace. The chaos of the day melted away as he held her, his touch like a balm for her weary body. The walls of the keep, thick and sturdy, seemed to envelop them in a cocoon of safety, shielding them from the outside world.

"Ye are me sanctuary," Ailis breathed against Lachlan's chest, feeling his steady heartbeat beneath her cheek. He pressed a tender kiss to her forehead, bringing her comfort without words.

They filled the quiet with lighthearted chatter, using this precious time together to escape the weight of their responsibilities beyond the keep's walls.

"I wish we could stay like this forever," Lachlan murmured, intertwining his fingers with hers. Wrapped in luxurious fur blankets and surrounded by hushed whispers, they reveled in the tenderness and intimacy that came with being newlyweds, cherishing these moments.

Ailis sighed contentedly, her heart full of love for the man she now called her husband. "As do I. But we both know our duties await us on the morrow." She traced the strong line of his jaw with her fingertip. "For now, let us savor this time, just the two of us, and draw strength from it for the days to come."

Lachlan captured her hand and brought it to his lips, brushing a kiss across her knuckles. "Aye, ye are wise as always, mo ghràdh." His eyes, the color of the lochs on a clear summer day, gazed at her with an intensity that made her breath catch. "I am the luckiest man in all the Highlands to call ye me wife."

"And I the luckiest lass to be yer wife," Ailis whispered, emotion thick in her voice. She reached up to caress his cheek, marveling at the love and devotion shining in his eyes. In Lachlan's arms, she was cherished, protected, and complete.

Their lips met in a tender kiss, a gentle exploration that gradually deepened as passion ignited between them. Lachlan's strong hands roamed her curves, leaving trails of heat in their wake. Ailis tangled her fingers in his dark hair, pulling him closer, craving his touch.

MOIRA AND FIONA led the other women through the forested wilds, returning each evening with game for the tables. Laughter filled the air alongside piper melodies.

Fish from lochs and streams contributed to their feasts, making many Sinclairs join forces with the McAfees for survival. And the McAfees were happy to call more people their allies.

Ailis watched from beside Lachlan, observing faces that revealed hints of looming conflict—laughter edged with tension and somber notes beneath songs of kinship. Yet within the McAfee keep, a fragile sense of normalcy persevered among the embattled people.

"Ye bear the future gracefully," Lachlan murmured, taking Ailis's hand under the oak table.

"It's no small task ahead," she replied. "But we'll face it together." She gazed at him for a long while, wanting to be able to close her eyes and still see his face. She was confident they would win, but in the back of her mind, she was frightened of losing him. But if she could still see his face in her mind, then she would have memories of him.

As metal clashed and men strained in battle, silence enveloped Ailis when an elder woman entered McAfee keep. Her hair flowed like silver streams, her eyes held ancient knowledge, and her hands were marked by years of tending to the wounded and sick. This was Skye, the renowned healer who once aided Ailis's own family.

"Ye're here," Ailis breathed, acknowledging the famed healer. She wasn't sure if she was intimidated by the woman or excited to work with her. "Me grandmother asked for ye on her deathbed, but she died before I had a chance to send someone for ye. She always told me ye were the best healer in the Highlands."

"Yer grandmother's spirit led me here," Skye replied, her voice saturated with earthy tones. "Together, we shall aid those in need."

Under Skye's tutelage, Ailis learned even more about medicinal herbs, pain-relieving pressure points, and healing incantations.

She observed Skye's effortless grace, as each touch provided relief.

One afternoon, a cry interrupted the training field's commotion. Lachlan emerged with a bloodied arm injured from errant steel. His eyes met hers—annoyed with himself for the injury yet embarrassed at the way she hovered over him.

"It's just a scratch," he insisted. The surrounding redness indicated otherwise.

"Skye should tend to it," Ailis urged. Despite wanting to help him herself, she knew Skye had more wisdom in healing, and she longed to become more skilled herself.

Skye approached and began treating the wound using water as clear as a loch and a pine-scented poultice. Ailis absorbed each careful step. She had a feeling she would need every ounce of healing skills she could gain.

"Ye'll recover soon enough," Skye assured him after securing the bandage. "But be more mindful during training."

Lachlan smiled at Ailis. "With such skilled healers around me, how could I not?" His words eased the worry that had tightened around her heart.

"Come now," Ailis urged, her voice light but firm. "We have a duty to heal and protect. Let's prepare for what lies ahead."

They nodded in agreement, understanding the responsibility they carried. As they faced the encroaching night, their devotion to their people, each other, and their homeland remained unyielding.

THE NOVEMBER CHILL had settled upon the McAfee lands with a frosty embrace, seeping into the very bones of the people and the earth alike. Ailis watched as men from various clans, their breaths misting in the cold air, labored side by side to erect the garrison that would shield them from winter's cruel embrace. It was a structure born of necessity, each log and stone placed with the urgency that the encroaching frost demanded.

"Ye work as if the very devil were after ye," Ailis remarked to a group of men securing the roof.

""Tis not the devil, me lady," one of the men called, pausing to wipe his brow, "but Winter herself. She is a most unforgiving mistress."

Ailis offered a nod of acknowledgment, lingering on the sinew and sweat that bound the men in their common purpose. It filled her with a sense of pride and heavy responsibility that her home could be a bastion for so many.

Later, Lachlan found Ailis near the loch's edge. With a tender hand upon her shoulder, he coaxed her away from the fortress.

"Come, me heart," he crooned, his blue eyes reflecting the water's tranquility. "Let us steal a moment for ourselves."

Hand in hand, they strolled around the loch, the water lapping gently at the shore like a whispered conversation between old friends. Their steps were leisurely, allowing the world and its burdens to fade into the background.

Lachlan broke their comfortable silence. "Imagine a time when this land knows naught but peace, where our children may roam freely, unburdened by the clang of swords and the cries of war."

Ailis's heart swelled at the vision he painted, her own wishes mingling with his. She leaned into him, feeling the solid warmth of his arm as it wrapped around her. "Aye, that is a dream worth fighting for," she murmured, her breath forming a cloud in the chill air.

They stopped to watch the sky, now streaked with purples and pinks as day surrendered to night. In that quiet moment, Lachlan turned to her, cradling her face with a gentleness that contradicted his warrior's strength. His lips met hers in a kiss that spoke of promise and hope, a tender seal upon their shared dreams.

"Wherever the future leads us, we'll face it together," he

vowed, his forehead resting against hers.

"And with ye as me guide," Ailis added, her green eyes gleaming with the last light of dusk. "We shall weather any storm."

As they entered the keep, Ailis chilled. The great hall was alive with murmurs and laughter, contrasting the somber mood that had settled upon her. She was a newlywed, and she dearly loved her husband, but the threat of impending battle became closer and closer each day, and her mood was suffering.

"Gather 'round, me dear ones!" Fiona's voice rang out like a bell, drawing the clan members closer to her by the warm hearth. Her eyes sparkled with an unfamiliar light, and their curiosity was piqued. "As ye all know, the McAfee blood flows strong in our veins," Fiona began, a proud smile on her face. "And I am thrilled to announce that our family will soon welcome another into our fold. I am with child."

Gasps of surprise and cheers of joy erupted from the kinfolk as they surrounded Fiona, congratulating her and showering her with affection. Ailis couldn't help but feel a twinge of envy as she forced a smile onto her face and joined in the celebrations.

She longed for a child of her own, but it was her sister who carried the next potential laird of Clan McAfee. As much as she loved Fiona, Ailis couldn't help but wonder what it would be like if she were the one expecting a child.

Later, seated beside Lachlan at the feast, Ailis's hand rested lightly on his arm but found no solace now. Her thoughts were tangled with jealousy she dared not confess. She so desperately wanted to be happy for her sister, but she was caught in a sadness that would not seem to leave her.

"Are ye well, me love?" Lachlan questioned with concern. He could tell something was bothering her, and he wanted to help if he could.

"Aye," she lied, gazing at Fiona. "I am merely…overwhelmed by the tidings."

"I think it is wonderful she is expecting. The McAfee line will carry on with this child." Lachlan smiled. "We will be hopeful that our turn will come soon."

"Hope," Ailis echoed flatly later in their conversation. Beneath the table, her fingers curled into a fist. It was hard to keep feeling hope day after day knowing a battle was coming, and she would most certainly lose clan members if not her own husband.

As the night wore on, torches flickered and shadows lengthened. Ailis remained lost in thought, her eyes tracing intricate patterns of tapestries that told tales of valor and sacrifice.

"Are ye certain nothing ails ye?" Lachlan persisted.

"Naught but the weight of duty," she confessed softly. It was an honest answer, if incomplete.

Lachlan nodded, his blue eyes searching hers for the unspoken words. "I know we're all faced with difficulties, but I know that we can get through it if we work together."

Ailis forced a smile, nodding in agreement. Yet as the celebration continued around her, the image of Fiona, aglow with impending motherhood, lingered in her mind—a stark reminder of the life growing inside her sister, and of the unspoken ache within her own heart.

The distant strains of a lute filled the hall, weaving a melody that danced with the flickering firelight. Ailis watched as couples twirled gracefully, their laughter mingling with the music. She excused herself from the table, needing a moment of respite from the revelry.

The irony of the situation wasn't lost on her. She'd been thinking she needed a little frivolity, and here it was being offered, and she chose to move away from the fun the others were having.

Stepping out into the crisp night air, Ailis found herself drawn toward the courtyard. As she wandered deeper into the garden, she spotted a figure emerging from the darkness.

"Lachlan," Ailis greeted, her voice soft yet tinged with turmoil.

He turned to face her, his expression reflecting concern. "Ailis," he replied, closing the distance between them. "I sensed yer unease. What weighs upon yer heart? And dinnae tell me it's naught because I know better."

Ailis hesitated, her emotions roiling within her like a tempest threatening to break free. She met Lachlan's gaze, the moonlight painting his features in shades of silver and shadow. "It is Fiona," she admitted. "Her news…it fills me with a longing to have a bairn of our own. As happy as I am for her, I'm just that much disgusted that it's not us. I know I make little sense, but it's how I feel."

Lachlan's brow furrowed in understanding as he reached for her hand, his touch grounding her. "Ailis," he soothed, "Each path we walk carries its own burdens and blessings. Fiona's joy does not diminish what we share."

Tears welled up in Ailis's eyes and spilled down her cheeks. "I fear I am being selfish," she confessed, her words heavy with the weight of unspoken fears and desires.

Lachlan brushed away her tears with a gentle thumb, his eyes filled with compassion and love. "Nay, Ailis," he murmured, pulling her into a tender embrace. "Yer heart is as generous as it is burdened. Yer feelings are valid, and I am here to share them."

In the solace of Lachlan's arms, Ailis allowed herself to release the emotions she had held back for so long. The moonlight bathed them in its silvery glow, casting a tranquil aura over the whispered confidences that passed between them.

"I know not what the future holds," Ailis confessed. "But in this moment, with ye by me side, I find solace."

"And I will be by yer side for the rest of me days," he vowed, resting his cheek atop her head. "And we'll have a child, just not today. Remember they've been married longer than we have."

She sighed, snuggling close to him. "I do remember. And I know it will happen. It just won't happen soon enough for me." She smiled a little at how silly she was being. If she was expecting as well, she wouldn't be able to be there for her sister as she needed. And Fiona, and the new life within her, needed to be a priority, not something that caused her jealousy.

❧

CHAPTER THIRTY

CLYDE STEWART OBSERVED his most trusted men. The leaders of four loyal clans stood with him. He settled into a chair that resembled a throne, as the air grew thick with anticipation for his counsel.

A knock at the door interrupted the gathering's focus. A messenger from Clan Gordon entered and reported, "Me laird, a Sinclair soldier has information ye'll want to hear."

Clyde gave a nod, allowing the young soldier, Connor Sinclair, to enter and deliver his dire news. He spoke of secret alliances and ominous preparations. "The McAfee clan gathers strength, me laird. Many clans join them. They prepare for war."

Silence filled the chamber as they weighed Connor's words against the consequences. Each man sensed a tightening bond of kinship and loyalty. Eyes met, acknowledging the challenges ahead. Clyde considered the path honor demanded—war loomed on the horizon, and they must meet it with cunning and force.

In the tense atmosphere, Clyde prompted further discussion with a deliberate gesture. The lairds leaned forward expectantly while Connor remained steadfast under scrutiny.

"Ye've seen the clans gather," Clyde asked, "but what of their numbers? Their armaments?" His question lingered like mist over the moors.

Connor spoke, "They train with sword and shield, knives, and the bow and arrow, me laird. Their numbers swell like rivers in spring. It seems more soldiers arrive every day."

"How many does McAfee command?" pressed Laird Cameron.

"More than two score clans, each with scores of able men," Connor replied.

Clyde addressed Connor, "Choose a new banner to follow for yer loyalty has been proven."

"I wish to join the Stewarts," Connor replied, cognizant of where the power in the group was coming from.

"Then it shall be so," Clyde decreed, dismissing Connor. "Wait here for me, and I'll introduce ye to the leader of me army.

Connor frowned. "Ye dinnae lead yer own men?"

Clyde shook his head. "Nay, I plan the battles, and I make the alliances. I leave the fighting to the soldiers." Clyde wasn't sure why anyone would think he would be involved with the dirty job of leading and training men.

As the door closed, Clyde began pacing. "This changes our plans," he stated. "We must move up the timeline of our attack, and it must now be focused on the McAfees."

"We must unite all our allies," agreed Laird MacKenzie.

"Train we must, for battle comes upon swift wings," added Laird Cameron.

Laird Sutherland smiled. "We will beat them. Our numbers are vast, and our men are loyal."

Clyde paced, his face betraying the fact he wasn't listening to the other lairds. "Yet how did the secret get out? How did the McAfee women come to know our intentions?" Clyde mused aloud.

"It was me son, Lucas," confessed Laird Gordon. "He spoke out of turn to Ailis McAfee when he was well into his cups. The three boys tried to get the sisters drunk and managed to become drunk themselves." He shook his head. "The boy understands that he hurt our cause, but it's too late to change things now."

Clyde halted his pacing. "Such breaches cannot be tolerated. We stand upon the precipice, and loose tongues may cast us into the abyss. He must be punished for his disloyalty."

"Forgive the boy," pleaded Laird Gordon. "He is young and doesn't yet understand the game of kings and lairds."

"Let this be the last of such follies," Clyde warned. "For the next may cost more than words can repay. What if they'd been told the day and location of our attack?"

The Stewart's gaze was cold and angry as he stared at the heavy wooden door. "Bring me Lucas," he commanded. The chamber fell silent, lairds standing like ancient oaks.

The door swung open, revealing a young man with a confident stride: Lucas Gordon. He hesitated under the weight of his father's legacy as he approached the table.

"Ye ken the gravity of yer actions?" Clyde's voice came in a steely whisper. His eyes didn't stray from Lucas.

Lucas trembled beneath Clyde's piercing gaze. The gathered lairds encircled him, their faces etched with grim determination and unwavering judgment. The meeting room seemed to close in around Lucas, the once grand tapestries and flickering torches now looming as silent witnesses to his disgrace.

"I-I beg yer forgiveness, Laird Stewart," Lucas stammered. He dared not meet Clyde's eyes, instead fixing his gaze upon the cold stone floor. "I acted rashly, without thought fer the consequences. I see now the folly of me actions."

Clyde remained unmoved, his broad shoulders squared and his jaw set firm. "Ye betrayed the trust of yer clan, Lucas. Ye were disloyal to yer own kin, giving our enemies information that was not theirs to have. Such treachery cannot go unpunished."

"Please, me laird," Lucas quavered. "I was drunk, and I spoke out of turn. I see now the error of me ways, the depths of me betrayal. I beg ye, show mercy upon a foolish man who has strayed from the path of honor."

With trembling hands, Lucas reached out in supplication, his fingers grasping at the air as if searching for a lifeline. In a swift motion, he dropped to his knees, the hard stone floor sending a jolt of pain through his body.

"I implore ye, Laird Stewart, and all the honored lairds gathered here today," Lucas cried, his voice echoing off the ancient walls. "I am a man undone, a wretch who has strayed from the path of righteousness. I have brought shame upon meself and me clan, and I can bear the weight of it no longer."

Tears streamed down Lucas's face, leaving glistening trails upon his ashen cheeks. Lucas's voice broke as he poured out his anguished plea, his words tumbling forth in a desperate torrent. "I am a broken man, me laird, a shell of what I once was. Me actions have torn asunder the very fabric of me honor, leaving naught but tattered remnants in their wake. I come before ye now, humbled and contrite, me pride shattered like a clay pot upon the unyielding stones."

With shaking hands, Lucas reached out and grasped the hem of Clyde's kilt, his fingers clutching the rough wool as if it were his only tether to salvation. "I beg of ye, Laird Stewart, show mercy upon me wretched self. I am but a wayward lamb who has strayed from the flock, lost in the mists of me own folly. Guide me back to the path of righteousness and show mercy to me father and me clan!"

"Speak nae more," Clyde cut him off, standing tall and imposing. "Should ye put even a toe astray henceforth, I swear it'll be me who'll deliver ye to yer maker." The menace in his tone cast a shadow across the room.

All the lairds watched as Lucas bowed his head and thanked Laird Stewart for sparing his life. Laird Gordon's mouth opened as if to protest but no words came out. A nod dismissed Lucas and the men around the table knew the next move would be fraught with peril—each piece determining ruin or victory.

AILIS MCAFEE'S HANDS were steady as she penned a message for the McKays, her heart fluttering like a caged sparrow. She needed to know if the McKays had more information for them about the time and place of the attack.

"Take this to Clan McKay with haste," she urged the messenger.

The messenger departed into the highlands where loyalties shifted like tides. As weeks passed, word reached Ailis that more than thirty clans had pledged their swords—only five opposed them. The balance of power teetered precariously as they prepared for the inevitable conflict.

Ailis returned to her duties, her hands and mind occupied by strategy while weaving together new alliances through a shared purpose.

Though not on the battlefield, her role remained critical. She moved among her kin, soothing aches and pains, her words a veiled rallying cry.

TWO WEEKS HAD passed since they sought information about their adversaries from the McKays.

In the bustling kitchen, Ailis found her role serving her clan by feeding their growing number of allies. "I'm going to fetch more turnips from the root cellar, Skye," she called. Ailis and Skye were helping Granny with the meals and the men had been told to go to the kitchen if there was an injury.

Their laughter and encouragement created a bond within the kitchen.

"Ye have the heart of a lioness and the touch of an angel," Granny told her. Ailis responded with gratitude.

During this busy routine, a dust-covered messenger arrived with news from the McKays. Laird Gordon had rallied his forces, gathering all his allies. "Clan McKay can no longer be our eyes in enemy lands," he declared. "They are joining us to face whatever may come."

Ailis paused briefly, absorbing the gravity of the message

before resuming her work with renewed determination. "Soon there would be even more soldiers to feed."

"Tell them to hurry," Ailis instructed, her heart swelling. "We need every ally as conflict approaches."

As the messenger left, she focused on her duties, the kitchen bustling. Old tales intertwined with survival strategies in her mind. When the McKays arrived, they would find a united McAfee clan ready to face whatever came next.

The discordant voices reached Ailis in the kitchens, contrasting with the methodical sounds of chopping and stirring. Brushing a stray lock behind her ear, her eyes mirrored her concern as the looming gatherings were marred by clashing clans.

"More squabbles?" Skye asked, pausing her dough-kneading.

Ailis nodded. "Alisdair and Lachlan must try to stop rivalry between those who should be brethren."

Outside, Alisdair's authoritative voice demanded unity among quarreling men. Lachlan supported him with stern resolve, offering action only in service to the camp. The rival clansmen were tasked with building a protective wall around the entire village together, channeling their strife toward a shared objective. Ailis understood that they sought to make the men act as friends, as well as strengthening them. It was a punishment that would teach them as well as benefit them as warriors.

"Alisdair and Lachlan make an example of them," Ailis reflected, shaping loaves for baking. "Their conflict becomes unity through sweat and toil. And they will learn to act together as friends, while becoming stronger."

Skye contemplated the situation. "Perhaps their hands will learn what their hearts have yet to comprehend: true strength lies in harmony."

As evening fell on the encampment, construction sounds merged with the night. Former adversaries worked side by side under the McClain brothers' gaze, proving necessity trumped pride.

THE CHAMBER THAT had been turned into an infirmary provided respite from the cacophony of the training grounds. Ailis moved gracefully among the wounded, her gentle hands healing both body and spirit.

Two men were carried in, faces contorted with pain, their shallow breaths and protective postures indicating broken ribs. With delicate precision, Ailis examined them.

"Ye both need rest," she advised. "A few days at least."

Lachlan entered with confidence, his gaze stern. "No, Ailis. They chose to fight like children. Again. Men who fight with one another and hurt themselves get to work while in pain. They will be assigned to help build our new wall."

Tension thickened the air as Ailis faced Lachlan. "Ye cannae expect them to work like this," she argued. "Even God rested on the seventh day."

"They will be an example to all the soldiers. They must all realize we are one army, or they will fight one another on the field of battle, instead of addressing our enemies," Lachlan countered forcefully. "We may lose men to enemy swords or arrows, but we will lose no men to our own."

Ailis rebuked him. "Human flesh is not yer sword. To force them is to ignore their need for healing."

"'Tis discipline that binds us," Lachlan replied, his steadfast gaze betraying a hint of uncertainty.

Their silent standoff reflected opposing perceptions of duty and sacrifice—Ailis seeking to protect from further harm, Lachlan focused on maintaining harsh lessons.

"Mercy has its place, as does severity," Ailis finally conceded, tending to her patients again. "Let's not forget either."

"I will not forget. But these men may be what the others need to see to forget their petty squabbles." Lachlan observed her practiced movements, pondering her words while the weight of their argument lingered. The balance of power within the clans was fragile, resting on their shoulders—even when their hearts disagreed.

their argument lingered. The balance of power within the clans was fragile, resting on their shoulders—even when their hearts disagreed.

CHAPTER THIRTY-ONE

THE MCKAYS CRESTED the hill, their approach thundering with hooves. Time was running out to forge alliances and prepare for conflict, but they were happy to welcome a strong new army to their alliance.

Lachlan stood observing the procession of his grandmother's family. The McKays's arrival signaled the mending of old wounds and rejoining bloodlines after years of separation. Lachlan and his brothers watched cautiously. They knew what had caused their mother to leave the McKays, and they knew they must watch the others to be sure women were treated well, but they knew the strength of the McKays would help them out a great deal.

Training commenced in earnest, valor and strength evident in each sword swing and parry. Lachlan used his offbeat sense of humor to bridge the gap between clans, laughing through the ranks, easing tensions, and reminding all of their kinship.

The McKay laird strode up to Lachlan with a grave expression. "I have news, lad," he began, his voice low and serious. "Only two clans were willing to support us."

Lachlan's jaw tightened, but he maintained composure as he replied, "Thank ye for yer efforts and insight, we will make do with what we have." He clapped the older man on his back. "Remember, we would have no real insight without yer knowledge. We thank ye for it."

As the clans mingled, sharpening blades and honing strategies, anticipation of battle filled the air. Personal desires now lay dormant beneath duty. It was time for leaders to continue to stand strong, warriors to brace against fate, and for united McClains and McAfees with their various allies to face the impending war.

The training had to be split into two groups who trained simultaneously, leaders barking orders and swords clashing in preparation for the upcoming battle. There were now simply too many men to all train in the same place. So Lachlan and Brodie worked with the soldiers who were better with swords, and they left Alisdair and their father to train the men with bows and arrows.

From a distance, Lachlan observed his father and Alisdair's cooperation and discipline, their presence commanding respect among the men. He returned his focus to his own group as Brodie explained the importance of control in sword fighting.

As the sun began to set, the training session came to a close. Lachlan walked to his father, troubled by the overwhelming size of the enemy's army.

"Father," he fretted, "what will we do?"

His father regarded him with calm confidence. "We have our family's legacy and our strategic advantages," he reassured Lachlan.

Nodding in understanding, Lachlan thought about their intertwined roles in the unfolding story ahead of them.

His father squeezed his shoulder and walked toward the encampment, leaving Lachlan alone. He surveyed the empty training grounds.

Lachlan exhaled and headed for the keep and his bedchamber, finding solace in his father's confidence despite the uncertain path ahead.

THE MAKESHIFT INFIRMARY, carefully arranged with four neatly made beds, filled Ailis with pride. The crisp white sheets stretched taut over the wooden frames, creating a sense of order and comfort. She and Skye had worked tirelessly on this space for two weeks, determined to create a place of healing in the midst of war.

Skye bustled about like a whirlwind, her long skirts swirling around her as she checked supplies and tidied up. "Ailis, do ye think we'll need more willow bark?" she asked, concern etched on her face.

Ailis smoothed out the creases in her apron and took a moment to survey their handiwork. The shelves were stocked with jars of herbs and salves, ready for any injury that may come their way. "We have enough for now," she answered softly. "Let's hope we won't have the need to use it all." Her thoughts turned to the brave soldiers who would soon be filling these beds, wounded and in need of healing.

She closed her eyes and sent up a silent prayer, hoping that the battles would not injure too many men. But she knew deep down that they would do everything in their power to heal those who came through their doors. That was why they had created this safe haven amidst the chaos of war—because every life mattered, no matter which side they fought for.

As Ailis opened her eyes, a commotion erupted outside the infirmary. Skye rushed to the door, peering out into the courtyard. "It's the McClain brothers!" she exclaimed. "And it looks like one of them is injured."

Ailis hurried to join her friend, her heart racing as she caught sight of the three men. Lachlan and Brodie supported their eldest brother, Alisdair, between them. His face was pale, and a dark stain spread across his shirt.

Without hesitation, Ailis pushed open the door. "Bring him inside," she commanded despite the fear that gripped her heart. The brothers carried Alisdair into the infirmary, laying him gently on one of the beds.

Ailis immediately set to work, cutting away the bloodied shirt to assess the wound. A deep gash marred Alisdair's side, still seeping crimson. She grabbed a clean cloth and pressed it firmly against the injury, eliciting a groan from the eldest McClain.

"Skye, bring me the yarrow and comfrey salve," Ailis instructed, focusing on her patient. Skye nodded and hurried to the shelves, gathering the needed supplies.

Lachlan and Brodie hovered nearby, their faces etched with worry. "Will he be all right?" Lachlan asked, his usually playful demeanor replaced by genuine concern.

Ailis glanced up briefly, meeting his piercing blue eyes. "I'll do everything I can," she assured him before turning her attention back to Alisdair.

Skye returned with the yarrow and comfrey salve, handing them to Ailis with steady hands. Ailis worked quickly, cleaning the wound and applying the healing herbs with practiced precision. As she wrapped a clean bandage around Alisdair's torso, she could sense the tension in the room, thick and heavy like a wool blanket.

Lachlan paced the length of the infirmary, his boots echoing against the stone floor. "How did this happen?" he demanded. "Who dared to attack me brother?"

Brodie placed a calming hand on Lachlan's shoulder. "It was a mere accident. We must focus on Alisdair's recovery."

Ailis tied off the bandage and stepped back, assessing her work. Alisdair's breathing had evened out, the color slowly returning to his face. She placed a gentle hand on his forehead, relieved to find no sign of fever.

"He needs rest now," she murmured, facing the McClain brothers. "The healing herbs will help, but it will take time for his body to mend."

Lachlan nodded, clenching his jaws. "Thank you, Ailis," he murmured, his eyes never leaving his brother's face. "We owe you a great debt."

Ailis shook her head. "There is no debt. He is family. I only wish to see Alisdair recover." She glanced at Brodie, who stood quietly by the bed, his brow furrowed with concern. "You both should rest as well. It has been a trying day for us all."

Brodie nodded, his piercing blue eyes meeting Ailis's gaze. "Aye, we'll take turns watching over him. Thank you, Ailis, for all you've done." His voice was soft yet sincere, a flicker of gratitude shining in his eyes.

Ailis laughed softly. "Do ye really think Fiona will let him out of her sight? Someone should fetch her while the two of ye return to yer duties. And Alisdair will be fit as a fiddle in a day or two."

Skye hurried from the room to fetch Fiona, obviously understanding the import of the injured man's wife being with him as he recovered.

Despite everything they'd done to ready themselves for the coming battle, worry lingered. Ailis mustered a smile as she approached Lachlan who had just arrived. "How goes the training?"

"The men are ready, as ready as they can be," he answered distantly. "I wish we had another six months to train, but that's just not possible."

"Excuse me a moment," Ailis told Skye before leading Lachlan into the corridor.

Outside, Lachlan's expression turned grave. "Ailis, we need to talk."

She braced herself for the imminent disagreement.

"The danger is closer than we thought," he warned. "I need ye to promise that ye'll hide at the first sign of trouble."

"Lachlan," she pleaded. "Ye know I will if I can. But I cannae just stand by and do nothing. I want to help. Perhaps I can use me knife from the safety of the keep. I can throw through a window!"

Frustrated, he ran a hand through his dark hair. "We need yer healing expertise, Ailis. If something happens to ye, who will tend to the wounded? Who will care for yer sisters?"

"I will be careful," she insisted. "I will hide if it becomes too dangerous. But until then, I need to do what I can. Ye of all people should understand that. Ye wouldn't back off from training the men, even if ye knew it would kill ye."

He seemed to hold conflict between duty and understanding, but Ailis knew he respected her determination.

"I just want ye to be safe," he gently assured her.

She touched his arm briefly. "I know. And I want the same for all of ye." She wished she could walk into his arms and reassure him right there in the hall, but…it didn't feel like the right place or time.

Lachlan straightened. "Remember yer promise."

"I will," she replied.

"Ailis, thank ye—for everything." He strode away while Ailis returned to the infirmary where Skye sat rubbing her temples as she watched over Alisdair, waiting for Fiona to join them.

"Everything all right?" Skye asked.

"As much as it can be," Ailis admitted, sitting beside her. Images of Lachlan and her sisters filled her mind, duty and desire tugging at her relentlessly.

"We're ready," Skye confirmed. "Ye need not worry about what else should be done."

Ailis nodded. "As ready as we can be."

They shared a quiet moment in the infirmary, the calm before the storm.

IN THE DIM castle kitchen, Ailis and Skye carefully tended to strips of meat hanging above the hearth. The air held a smoky, salty scent. Their task—drying the meat for sustenance—had an urgency that weighed on them. If they were unable to leave the keep for fresh meat, this would have to last them. More was brought in daily, and it was all they could do to keep up with the drying and smoking of the meat.

"We must ensure it's dried properly," Skye noted. "If it spoils, we'll have naught to fall back on."

Ailis nodded, her thoughts preoccupied by Lachlan, her sisters, and their uncertain future. As they worked in silence, they could hear hurried footsteps. A winded man entered. "News from the Campbells," he panted, "The army has crossed their lands. They'll be here within a few days."

Skye took the note from him, her face composed even as fear flickered in her eyes. "We'd best finish here. The soldiers will need provisions, as will the women and children who take refuge within the keep."

With renewed urgency, Ailis and Skye prepared rations of dried meat and oat cakes. As they completed the last bundle, Skye reassured Ailis. "They will be grateful. Ye know as well as I do we've done all we can."

Ailis stared at the rations, conflicted with duty and desire. "Should we add blankets? Flagons of ale?"

A distant horn sounded ominously. Skye removed her apron. "The men will assemble. We should go."

Ailis picked up a ration, feeling its weight. "Give me a moment. I'll catch up."

Skye left the kitchen, leaving Ailis to her thoughts. The hearth's shadows flickered on the walls as she clutched the ration.

In the courtyard, warriors gathered with heavy expressions. Ailis found Lachlan among them, engaged in conversation with another captain. As she approached, he turned and noticed her.

"Ailis," he gasped. "Ye should be with yer sisters."

"For ye, and for them," she replied, offering him the ration. "We've made up enough for each soldier to have one. If we had more time, I could make more, but I just dinnae think there will be enough time to do so. We'll do what we can to make more as there is time. We can work on that within the keep, even after the battle starts. And we can throw them to the army out the windows."

Lachlan accepted it gratefully. "Thank ye. Knowing ye are working to do all ye can while staying away from the battle fills me with confidence."

"Be safe," she whispered, placing a kiss on his cheek before turning away. With as close to the time of battle as they were, she would touch him and kiss him every chance there was.

Inside the great hall, Skye awaited her arrival. "Are ye ready?" she asked.

"As ready as we can be," Ailis answered, steeling herself as they entered together.

THE LAIRDS GATHERED in private, devising battle strategies with utmost care. In the great hall, the army leaders discussed their plans, solemn expressions marking their faces.

Ailis observed from a distance, anxiety haunting her thoughts. The McAfee clan had always been more inclined to storytelling and peace than war, but now they faced an unavoidable conflict. And every man woman and child was helping to prepare, but still she was uneasy.

The men who were not soldiers took up digging tools and carved hidden pits into the earth, hoping to break and delay the enemy soldiers' march. They wanted to do all they could to help turn the tide of battle.

Lachlan supervised them, his authoritative voice directing their efforts. He was respected for his skill with a blade and unyielding dedication to the clan.

As he assessed their progress, Lachlan's thoughts strayed to the consequences of war and the families that would be affected. Beyond their lands lay Sinclair territory—a buffer against their foes.

Ailis's concerned gaze lingered in Lachlan's mind, reminding him of her plea for safety. But duty came first. Personal desires had no place in times of war.

The sound of a spade striking rock interrupted Lachlan's thoughts. One of the men cursed, and he assessed the shallow trap. The earth refused to yield easily. They needed much deeper holes for their traps, so the men would be injured. He'd thought of adding spiked poles to the bottom of each trap, but he wanted no more deaths than absolutely necessary. He wasn't certain if he felt that way because Ailis was a healer, and he wished to stay on her good side, or if he truly worried about loss of them. Either way, the traps would be kinder than they could have been.

"Leave it," Lachlan decided. "Move to the next site." Thankfully Alisdair was healed and back to leading with their father at his side.

As his men relocated, his gaze lingered on the horizon, anticipating the approaching enemy. When they arrived, they'd find the traps a minor obstacle. The true challenge would come from steel clashing and unwavering hearts.

With one last glance at the incomplete pit, Lachlan followed, caught between loyalty and fate.

FOOD WAS STOCKPILED for the impending siege. Ailis and Moira fretted over Fiona, who hunted daily despite the approaching army. To protect her sisters, Ailis taught Moira and Fiona infirmary aid. It would be better if she had another task to accomplish, rather than feeling as if her only task was helping with the hunt.

"If nothing else, we'll need ye to wash the fevered men's faces with cold water. But there is always a great deal to do to help in an infirmary, and if there are many wounded, Skye and I won't be able to do it all ourselves."

Fiona nodded. "I understand not wanting me out hunting with an army coming our way, but I will do whatever is needed."

"We both will," Moira added. "We can come here, work in the kitchens, or simply take care of children. We dinnae care, but we need to work. Somehow."

Ailis nodded. "I'll let Granny know she can have ye both when ye're not needed in the infirmary. She will be glad for the extra help with all the people we are feeding." She smiled. "And she will be thrilled to have someone else to help with the smoking and drying of the meat and fish. It's a long, onerous task, and not one that I relish, but perhaps ye'll find it more enjoyable than I do."

CHAPTER THIRTY-TWO

GOLDEN MORNING LIGHT bathed the courtyard where Lachlan approached the newly fortified walls. Masons' hammers rang out. "Will they be ready on time?" he asked.

The head mason nodded. "If we have to work without sleep or food until the enemy arrives, we will do so. It will be done." He wiped sweat from his brow with the back of his hand. "Most of the work is done now that the stones have been moved together and stacked into a wall."

"I appreciate all ye're doing to help the effort. And I thank ye from all of us." Lachlan wanted every man, woman, and child gathered to understand that their role was integral to the effort.

Later, Lachlan addressed the soldiers gathered. "Men, we stand united as brothers to protect our lands and people. Our enemy is the Stewart Clan and their allies. Let's remember not to fight with our allies, and only with the enemy! I dinnae want to have to send more of ye to build walls in the middle of battle. I think we'll need every one of ye!"

Lachlan paused briefly for the laughter to die down. "I suppose the next punishment would be mucking out stables, but I dinnae want to have to lose any of ye!"

His face and demeanor became serious. "But in all seriousness," he continued, "Stand firm, fight with honor and courage. Victory will be ours because we possess an unbreakable bond of family and unity."

After Lachlan's serious call to arms, he paused for a moment before grinning mischievously. "Remember, lads," he chuckled, "if we can handle cleaning up after stubborn livestock, facing the Stewart Clan will be a piece of cake! Just think of them as particularly unruly sheep with swords."

Lachlan raised his sword high. The men responded with a resounding battle cry. In that moment, he was proud. Determination surged within him. Failure was not an option.

AILIS NAVIGATED THE busy courtyard, sunlight glinting off her hair as she searched for Moira. The cacophony of laughter and clattering pots filled the air, echoing the tension of the impending battle.

"Moira!" Ailis called. "We must gather the women and children and tell them they are welcome to come here during the battle. We need to keep everyone who is not part of the army safe."

Moira left a tent, concern flashing in her eyes as she registered Ailis's expression. "What's happened?"

"The battle is near," Ailis answered. "Our people need safety in the keep, and I'm not certain the Sinclair allowed the women and children to stay in the keep during battle. I dinnae think it was that way when our army attacked, so we must let all the women and children know they should seek out safety with us."

Nodding, Moira added, "Let's round them up. They cannae be harmed."

The sisters corralled their people, anxiety gnawing at Ailis as she faced their frightened expressions. She addressed them firmly, "To the keep as soon as we hear the army approaching. It's safest during battle. The walls will protect all of us."

As everyone entered the keep, Ailis suggested to Moira, "We should do more—to support and strengthen our men."

Curiosity sparked in Moira's eyes. "How so? I think we've

prepared in every way we possibly can in such a short time!"

"A banquet," Ailis replied. "A respite before battle to boost morale and unity through shared meals and companionship. We'll have dancing after, but we'll stop it earlier than we normally would, so our soldiers will get plenty of sleep."

Surprised but grinning, Moira agreed. "Ye're right—we need a ceilidh. Let's do this with Fiona. She's better at planning parties than either of us are. Going into the battle, remembering good times with each other will help the men remember what they are fighting for."

When Fiona appeared nearby, Ailis called her over urgently. "Fiona—help plan tomorrow night's banquet for everyone in the keep. We'll have the whole clan and all the soldiers. We celebrate the Highlands and customs, and perhaps the men will be able to remember why we dinnae want things to change."

Fiona's eyes shimmered with anticipation. "We'll create a feast to remember, one that fuels our people for the upcoming battle. And a dance after?"

"Of course," Moira replied. "But we'll need to remember to stop the music and dancing early, so the men are well-rested for the battle ahead."

Ailis surveyed the bustling great hall, filled with soldiers, women, and children gathered for the party. As she navigated the crowd, Ailis greeted each soldier with sincere gratitude. "Thank ye for yer bravery. Skye and I will tend to any injuries during and after the battle."

She moved from table to table. The scent of roasted venison, freshly baked bread, and mulled wine filled her senses as laughter and conversation echoed throughout the hall. "Please make certain not to over imbibe on the wine. Ye'll need all yer senses about ye tomorrow."

Despite the merriment, Ailis remained vigilant. She urgently spoke to each woman, insisting they take refuge in the keep during the battle. "Promise me ye'll keep yerselves and the children safe."

The women nodded, fear and resolve on their faces. Ailis saw their determination to protect their families, and she knew they would listen and join them in the keep. They may not worry much about their own safety, but each woman would lay down her life for her child.

Ailis felt a gentle hand on her arm and turned to spy Lachlan beside her. "May I have this dance?"

She hesitated but agreed, letting Lachlan lead her onto the dance floor. They moved together in time with the music, and for a moment, she forgot their trials, lost in his company. "I have told all the women to bring the children to the keep," she informed him.

Lachlan nodded. "I saw ye talking to the soldiers as well."

"I was simply reminding them that they are all appreciated and invited them to pick up rations in the kitchen before they leave tonight."

But Ailis noticed some Sinclair women talking intimately with soldiers from other clans. Worry pierced her thoughts of them leaving after the battle. However, she knew many of them were widowed, and perhaps they would find happiness with the soldiers. It would be good for them to find love again.

As the dance concluded, Ailis thanked Lachlan softly. Before he could reply, Duncan appeared at her side, concern etched across his face. "Ailis, may I have a word?" he asked gravely.

"Of course, Father. What is it?"

Duncan's voice was low and urgent. "Have ye given any more thought to the punishment for Arran and Callum? They've been here for months now, and I believe it's time they faced the punishment for their actions."

Ailis shook her head. "With the war at hand, I had forgotten about them. I cannae ask they be executed, as I won't have that blood on me hands. And I dinnae think anything less is appropriate, so do as ye will." Truth be told, she'd forgotten all about their Sinclair prisoners, and simply thinking of a punishment for them was too much for her to handle while they were on the eve of battle.

Lachlan stepped forward. "If I may, Duncan, perhaps I could be the one to mete out their punishment?"

Duncan nodded. "Very well, Lachlan. I trust ye will see that justice is served. It was yer wife who was kidnapped, so in a way, it was a slight directed at ye."

Ailis focused on her duty to her people and the clan as the conversation shifted to other matters.

Later in their chambers, Ailis turned to Lachlan, concern evident on her face. "How do ye plan to punish Arran and Callum?" She didn't want to think about how he would punish them, but it seemed important at that moment. She didn't want blood on his hands any more than she wanted it on her own.

"Dinnae worry about it," he told her gently but firmly. "It's not yer burden to bear. Ye are me wife now, and I will take care of the men who took ye prisoner."

"Lachlan, please," she implored, stepping closer. "I dinnae need any more blood on me hands."

"The blood will be on me hands," he assured her. "I will do what must be done for our clans and our future together."

Ailis leaned into his touch, feeling both love and fear for what the dawn might bring. She whispered, "Make love to me, Lachlan."

Lachlan captured her lips in a fervent kiss. Ailis responded, tugging at his clothing, eager for their skin to touch.

Ailis melted into Lachlan's embrace, heat searing through her veins as his lips caressed hers with a passion that stole her breath. His calloused hands slid along the curves of her waist and back, igniting trails of fire through the thin fabric of her gown. A soft moan escaped her throat, spurring him on.

Lachlan's nimble fingers made quick work of the laces at the back of her dress. The garment slipped from her shoulders and pooled at her feet. Ailis shivered, though not from the cool evening air on her bare skin. No, the trembling arose from the smoldering intensity in Lachlan's eyes as his gaze roved over her, drinking in every inch.

Lachlan pulled her flush against him, the heat of his body searing her bare skin. Ailis gasped as she felt the evidence of his arousal pressing insistently against her stomach. Her own desire pooled low in her belly, aching and urgent.

Lachlan's hands roamed her curves reverently, calluses rasping deliciously along soft, sensitive flesh. "I want to worship every inch of you," he breathed against the shell of her ear before nipping at the lobe.

Ailis shuddered and arched into him. "Yes, please," she managed, her own hands tugging impatiently at the fastenings of his shirt. She needed to feel his skin against hers, with no barriers between them.

He aided her efforts, shrugging out of the garment and letting it fall forgotten to the floor. Ailis splayed her fingers over the hard planes of Lachlan's chest, reveling in the feel of firm muscle beneath heated skin. "Mo ghràdh, you are so beautiful," he groaned. Lachlan captured her hands and brought them to his lips, kissing each palm reverently before guiding them to the belt holding his kilt in place.

Ailis's fingers trembled as she unfastened his belt, her eyes never leaving his. The intensity of his gaze sent shivers racing down her spine. When the last tie loosened, Lachlan kicked the garment away impatiently, leaving him bare before her.

Ailis drank in the sight of him, all hard planes and angles. An awed whisper fell from her lips. "Ye're magnificent."

A roguish grin tugged at Lachlan's lips as he gathered Ailis into his arms, his hardness pressing insistently against her belly. "And you, mo chridhe, are a goddess," he murmured, his voice husky with desire. "I plan to spend the rest of my days loving ye."

Ailis shivered at his words, liquid heat pooling between her thighs. Lachlan lowered his head, trailing scorching kisses along the column of her throat as he walked them backward toward the bed. The back of her knees hit the mattress and they tumbled onto the soft furs, a tangle of eager limbs and heated skin.

Lachlan's weight settled over her, delicious and grounding. He captured her mouth in a searing kiss that left her breathless and aching for more.

Ailis buried her fingers in Lachlan's thick, dark hair as she returned his kiss with equal fervor. His tongue delved into her mouth, tangling with hers in a sensual dance that left her dizzy and wanting. She could feel the evidence of his need, hot and heavy against her thigh.

Breaking the kiss, Lachlan began to explore the ivory column of her throat with lips and tongue and teeth, wringing breathy sighs from her kiss-swollen lips. Slowly, torturously, he mapped a path of fire along her collarbone and down to the valley between her breasts.

They came together with heat, both of them worried this would be their last time to make love.

Afterward, they lay entwined, hearts beating together while savoring brief tranquility. With Lachlan by her side, Ailis knew their love would be a guiding light amid uncertainty.

Basking in the afterglow of their lovemaking, Ailis nestled closer to Lachlan, her head resting on his broad chest. The steady rhythm of his heartbeat soothed her racing thoughts. She traced intricate patterns across his skin, committing every scar to memory.

Lachlan tenderly brushed a stray lock of hair from her face, his calloused fingers lingering on her cheek. "Ailis," he murmured, resonating through her very being. "Ye are the light that guides me through the darkest of times. Without ye, I would be lost."

Ailis lifted her head to meet his gaze, her emerald eyes shimmering with unshed tears. "And ye, Lachlan, are the rock upon which I stand. Yer strength gives me courage.

Ailis's heart swelled with the depth of her love for this man, her husband, her everything. "I cannot imagine a life without ye by me side," she whispered, her voice trembling with emotion. "Promise me, Lachlan, that ye will return to me. That ye will fight with all yer strength and cunning to come back to me arms."

Lachlan's eyes, as blue as the lochs on a clear summer day, held her gaze with an intensity that stole her breath. "I swear to ye, mo chridhe, I will move heaven and earth to return to ye. But…" He hesitated, his brow furrowing with the weight of his words. "If the fates are cruel and I fall in battle, ye must promise me that ye will love again. That ye will find happiness."

A single tear escaped Ailis's eye, trailing down her cheek like a glistening pearl. She shook her head vehemently, dark locks cascading around her face. "No, Lachlan. I cannot promise that. Ye are the only man I will ever love, in this life and the next. If ye fall…" Her voice broke, the mere thought of losing him too painful to bear. "If ye fall, I will never forgive ye. I will never love another as I love ye."

Lachlan's hand cupped her face, his thumb gently wiping away the errant tear. "Ailis, mo ghraidh, ye must not let grief consume ye. Ye have too much light, too much love to give to the world. Promise me that ye will find a way to go on, to find joy again, even if it is without me by yer side."

Ailis's heart clenched at the thought of a life without Lachlan. She gazed into his eyes. With a trembling hand, she traced the strong lines of his jaw, memorizing every beloved feature.

"I cannot bear the thought of losing ye," she whispered, her voice thick with emotion. "Ye are the very air I breathe, the beat of me heart. Without ye, I would be but a shell of meself, wandering lost through this life."

Lachlan's arms tightened around her, pulling her flush against his bare chest. She could feel the steady thrum of his heartbeat, a soothing metronome that anchored her in the midst of her turbulent fears.

"Mo ghràdh," he murmured, his breath warm against her ear.

As they fell asleep in one another's arms, Ailis knew he would be all right. He had to be. For she wasn't sure she could go on without him.

CLYDE STEWART STOOD tall and imposing before the sea of gathered warriors, their eager faces illuminated by the light of flickering torches. The men shifted restlessly in anticipation of the coming battle. Stewart's unwavering gaze swept over them, a calculating glint in his eye.

With a voice that carried like thunder, Clyde addressed the assembled throng. "Men of the Stewart clan and all assembled allies, the time has come for us to seize our destiny! For too long, the McAfees and McClains have stood in the way of our rightful dominion over these lands. But no more!"

He paused, allowing his words to sink in. The warriors hung on every syllable, their blood stirring with the promise of glory and conquest.

"Two days hence, we strike at the very heart of our enemies," Clyde continued, his tone laced with grim determination. "We will catch them unawares, reveling in their foolish celebrations. They think themselves safe, but they have grown soft and complacent. They are no match for the might of the Stewarts!"

A roar of approval erupted from the gathered men, their weapons clanging against shields in a cacophony of anticipation. Clyde raised a hand, silencing the crowd. His eyes blazed with the fire of a man possessed by a singular purpose.

"We will show no mercy," he declared menacingly. "Every McAfee and McClain shall fall beneath our blades. Their blood will soak the earth, and their cries will echo through the hills. We will claim what is rightfully ours, and the Stewart clan will rise as the undisputed rulers of these lands!"

The warriors erupted in a frenzy of cheers and war cries, their spirits enflamed by Clyde's words. They brandished their weapons, ready to follow their leader into the jaws of battle.

Stewart's voice boomed across the clearing. "On the morrow, we march into Sinclair lands to take what is rightfully ours."

A rousing cheer rose from the assembled host. Clyde Stewart allowed a grim smile, holding up a hand for silence.

"Each man here has a vital role to play in our triumph. Fight with courage and conviction, and glory shall be yers. Bring me victory, and ye will earn a place of honor in the kingdom we shall forge together!"

The men roared their approval, slamming weapons against shields. Their bloodlust was palpable, stoked by Stewart's words. He nodded in satisfaction, his speech complete.

As the army began dispersing to make camp for the night, Stewart turned and strode to his tent, where servants jumped to attend him. Tomorrow, they would take the Sinclair castle, and he would be one step closer to conquering the Highlands and bending them to his will. His eyes gleamed with ruthless determination, already envisioning his enemies crushed beneath his boot.

LUCAS STOOD SILENT and still, positioned at the very rear of the army. He kept his head down, praying that Stewart's keen gaze would not pick him out among the crowd. To draw the laird's attention was to court death itself.

Lucas's stomach churned as he watched his fellow clansmen hang on Stewart's every word, their faces alight with zealous devotion. Did they not see the cruel ambition that burned in their leader's eyes? The hunger for power that would consume all in its path?

Stewart's words were gilded poison, promising glory and riches, but Lucas knew the truth. Behind the charismatic facade lurked a vicious, uncompromising tyrant who would sacrifice a thousand men to achieve his aims.

The urge to speak out, to warn the others of Stewart's true nature, rose in Lucas's throat. But fear stilled his tongue. To openly defy the laird was to sign his own death warrant. Stewart's spies were everywhere, always watching for the slightest hint of disloyalty.

No, he must bide his time and choose his moment carefully. Revealing Stewart's duplicity would require irrefutable proof and powerful allies. Alone, Lucas stood no chance against the laird's iron grip on the clan.

As the men began making camp, Lucas slipped away into the shadows, his heart heavy with foreboding. Stewart's thirst for conquest would lead them all to ruin, and the Highlands would drown in blood. There had to be a way to stop him, but Lucas feared that such a path would demand a steep and terrible price. In the face of Stewart's implacable ambition, how much would he be willing to sacrifice for the greater good?

Lucas watched from the shadows as Stewart retired to his opulent tent, a dozen servants scurrying to attend to their master's every whim. Even on the eve of battle, the laird insisted on the trappings of luxury, as if to remind all who saw him of his elevated station. And he wouldn't lead. He would simply tell the leaders how he wanted them to proceed. It seemed to Lucas that he wasn't a true Highlander at all. Just a power-hungry man who cared nothing about the people who died for his cause along the way.

The sight filled Lucas with a bitter mix of envy and disgust. How easy it must be, he mused, to send men to their deaths from the comfort of a gilded pavilion. Stewart need never feel the bite of cold steel or hear the screams of the dying. His hands would remain clean while others spilled their blood in his name.

As the camp settled into an uneasy silence, Lucas's thoughts turned to the future. If the Stewart succeeded in his bid for power, the Highlands would become a vast chessboard, with clans and families as mere pawns to be sacrificed at the laird's whim. The ancient traditions and fierce independence of the Highland people would be ground to dust beneath the heel of Stewart's ambition.

"Nae, it cannae come tae pass," Lucas muttered, clenching his fists at his sides. "Stewart's madness must be stopped, ere it consumes us all."

But even as the words left his lips, Lucas was weighed down by his helplessness. He was but one man, a solitary voice of dissent against a tide of unquestioning loyalty. What could he hope to achieve against the might of Stewart and his allies?

For the sake of the Highlands and all who called it home, Lucas would see Stewart's ambitions shattered and the laird's name cursed for generations to come. It was a vow he made to himself, to the stars above, and to the land that had borne him. One way or another, Clyde Stewart's reign would end, and Lucas would be the one to bring him low.

✦ ⸻ ❦ ⸻ ✦

EPILOGUE

AILIS SAT BESIDE Lachlan on the stone bench, the warmth of the sun caressing their faces as their grandchildren played merrily in the garden. With a gentle touch, she traced the faded scar above his brow, a reminder of battles long past.

"I am ever so grateful to have you by me side, me love," Ailis whispered, her green eyes shimmering with affection. "Me life would have been a mere shadow without your presence to brighten it."

Lachlan turned to her, his blue eyes crinkling at the corners as a charming smile spread across his face. "And I am the luckiest man in all the lands to call you me wife, me dearest Ailis. Every day spent with you is a blessing."

Their lips met in a tender kiss, a testament to the enduring love they shared. The innocent groans of their grandchildren broke the moment, eliciting a hearty chuckle from Lachlan.

"Ah, the youth find our affection unsavory, do they?" he remarked with a mischievous grin. "I shall give them a merry chase to occupy their energies!"

With a wink to Ailis, Lachlan sprang from the bench and playfully pursued the giggling children around the garden, their laughter ringing through the air like a joyous melody.

As Ailis watched Lachlan and their grandchildren, a serene smile graced her lips. Her mind drifted through the years, painting a vivid tapestry of the life they had built together. From the moment their paths had intertwined, Lachlan had been her rock, her unwavering support through every trial and triumph.

She thought of the countless adventures they had shared, the battles they had fought, with each other and enemies as well. Lachlan's strength and loyalty had never faltered, even in the face of the most daunting adversities. His love had been a constant beacon, guiding her through the darkest of storms.

Ailis recalled the day they had taken their vows. It didn't matter to her that the wedding had been hurried. The love shining in Lachlan's eyes had taken her breath away, and she had known in that moment that their bond was unbreakable. Through the years, their love had only grown stronger, weathering the tests of time with grace and devotion.

With Lachlan by her side, Ailis had found the courage to face any challenge, to overcome any obstacle. He had been her confidant, her partner in every sense of the word. Together, they had built a family, a legacy of love and laughter that would endure for generations to come.

As the sun began to dip below the horizon, casting a golden glow over the garden, deep contentment washed over Ailis. She knew that no matter what the future held, she and Lachlan would face it together, their love a timeless testament to the power of true partnership.

Lachlan, having successfully worn out the grandchildren with his playful antics, returned to Ailis's side, his eyes shining with adoration. He took her hand in his, pressing a gentle kiss to her knuckles.

"What occupies your thoughts, me love?" he asked soothingly.

Ailis smiled, her heart overflowing with gratitude and love. "I was just thinking about how wonderful our life together has been. With you by me side, I have known true happiness and fulfillment. I am blessed beyond measure to call ye mine."

Lachlan pulled her close, his strong arms enveloping her in a tender embrace. "And I am forever grateful for the love and light ye have brought into me life, Ailis. Our journey has been a beautiful one, and I look forward to every moment yet to come."

About the Author

USA Today bestselling author Kirsten Osbourne knows how to write. Each book is an experience that transplants the reader, indulging them in decadence, intense emotion and sweeping love.

Kirsten was born in Wisconsin, and now lives in Idaho, but she's lived in Minnesota, Texas, and Louisiana along the way.

She writes contemporary and historical romance, venturing into the realm of paranormal romance and women's fiction. She invites you to join her in her world of fantasy, love, and make believe, no matter the location, where there is always a happily ever after at the end.

www.ingramcontent.com/pod-product-compliance
Lightning Source LLC
Chambersburg PA
CBHW072107300726
48975CB00003B/738